I0647753

The Miscreants

A Novel

KATHERINE B. HEATON

ISBN: 0692865586
ISBN 13: 9780692865583
Library of Congress Control Number: 2017904685
Katherine B. Heaton, Redlands, CA

ABSTRACT

This is a novel about a woman from a different era... Claudia Fitzpatrick (Parker, Henderson), the wealthy and stunning 1952 New York debutante of the year...

It chronicles her journey from a young, emotionally neglected, lonely, and sexually abused child, an adult who suffered two failed marriages, years of agonizing and reprehensible misdiagnoses of mental illness and unimaginable domestic abuse, who emerges from the crushing circumstances of her life to become a confident, brilliant, insightful and integrated woman, with a compelling desire to encourage and inspire other women who have lost hope.

"The Miscreants" is absorbing and provocative. In addition to the powerful story line of the main character, the book presents an honest portrayal of domestic abuse that includes realistic scenes and explores the complicated issues facing women who are recipients of this "crime." It also presents frank discussions of suicide, legal and non-legal drug use, alcoholism, homosexuality, depression, divorce and the resulting financial inequities, and an important focus of alternative medicine and correct medical diagnoses. It should be required reading for every clergy person who counsels, for every person in the medical profession, for law enforcement agencies, for college students seeking careers in counseling and/or medicine, for professors of psychology, and for any individual seeking to deepen their understanding of important social issues.

ACKNOWLEDGEMENTS

This book is fiction and the characters contained herein are fictitious.

I thank my dearest friend, Connor, who helped me so much with the mechanics of this book, for the respect, patience and kindness that was extended to me.

And, first and last, I thank my higher power whom I choose to call God, for the insight and wisdom that he chose to give me on a daily basis and for the gifts of humor and compassion that have enriched my life... and for all the persons he placed in my life... those who loved and supported me, those that helped me to grow, and those that brought me closer to realizing his unconditional love.

LIST OF MAJOR CHARACTERS

Claudia Fitzpatrick [Parker, Henderson]

The stunning debutante of the year, struggling to overcome a loveless and untenable childhood, sexual abuse, domestic abuse and years of medical misdiagnoses. Through sheer will, became a victorious, integrated woman.

Elizabeth Fitzpatrick

Claudia's Mother... endured a harsh childhood, evolved into a beautiful, opportunistic woman, self-absorbed, and obsessed with social status.

Edward [James] Fitzpatrick, III

Claudia's Father... wealthy, handsome, charming, shrewd and amoral...harboring a childhood sorrow.

Jamie Fitzpatrick [Edward James Fitzpatrick IV]

Claudia's beloved brother... a life ended too soon, he was a major source of love and stability to his little sister.

Constance Fitzpatrick

Claudia's sister... 20 years older...pretentious, selfish, controlling.

Gerald Parker

Claudia's first husband and Father of her three children...his impoverished childhood produced a man driven by ambition and money...secretive, fearful of his vulnerability.

Joshua Henderson

Claudia's second husband...rich, handsome, charming and abusive...escaped from a somewhat nefarious and austere English childhood when he came to America to live with Uncle Lucas, but could not escape his inner demons.

Margaret Connelly Henderson and Angus William Henderson

Joshua's beautiful, once-wealthy Mother...destined to a life of abuse and mental illness with her alcoholic, abusive husband.

Lucas Connelly [and his wife, Holly]

Joshua Henderson's enormously wealthy American uncle... a world renowned attorney, loved and respected by all who knew him... wise and altruistic...brother of Margaret Connelly.

Kitty Borg [and husband, Norman]

Kitty...a respected, Licensed Psychologist. Norman...a secret hero. The leaders in Claudia's ultimate recovery.

TABLE OF CONTENTS

PROLOGUE

Claudia Marie Fitzpatrick was dying... Two weeks ago, her doctor had compassionately held her hand and had predicted it would be within 6 months... Claudia wasn't surprised... nor was she apprehensive ... she had no fear of death, but prayed that the process would be relatively painless and that it would not be prolonged. Two days ago, she had celebrated her 86th birthday, quietly, and much to her liking. A short hour's drive to the coast... a delightful lunch at her favorite restaurant with her favorite person... her son, who, in his usual spirited manner, kept her amused and interested with his intriguing conversation and engaging stories, a genetic quality that had not escaped her attention.

Claudia had a great deal to accomplish before that appointed time... and today had been a busy day. Now it was twilight... that magical time before the world is enveloped in darkness, when the skies explode with color and then fade to a peaceful, satisfied conclusion. She loved to sit in her chair by the large floor to ceiling windows each evening to watch the colossal expanse of rosy hues... pinks, violets, reds.... splashed across the sky with an abandon she had often tried to effect in her own paintings. Tonight, the sky was ablaze with color interspersed with puffs of storm clouds lined in silver, and when the last of the sun sank into the horizon, flashes of reds and mauves reminded her that no artist could ever capture the light and beauty of this moment. Perched on a small Victorian desk next to her cream colored recliner chair, a CD player provided accompaniment... a recording of Jussie Bjoerling singing a tender aria from Puccini's opera, La Boheme... "che galida manina..." ["how cold your little hand is..."] and she knew as the colors became more diffused, Bjorling would sing the exhilarating "Nessum Dorma" from Turandot, ["Nobody shall sleep"] an opera he had never performed, but the aria was her favorite as it evoked rare, pleasurable memories of her father. When she was but five years old, Edward James Fitzpatrick III, had taken her to hear Bjorling in concert at Carnegie Hall, telling her to remember, *always*, that she saw, in person, the most talented of all operatic tenors... and then, shortly before James Fitzpatrick died, he sent her this CD, at that time a newly released collection of operatic favorites.... Tosti's "L'alba separa dolla luce l'hombre," ["The dawn divides the darkness from light..."] and from Massenet's Manon, the powerful "Ah, fuyez. douce image..." ["Ah, flee, sweet image..."] She knew it was his way of saying, *I am sorry.* Now, as Bjorling's silvery tones filled the air, her whole being thrilled to the extravaganza.

The light began to fade, the sky now bathed in tender shades of mauves with a touch of orange, receding into the oncoming blue of the higher sky. In this dwindling light Claudia was in silhouette... the deep creases in her aging skin softened, and one could imagine a face that was once quite beautiful. Her original flaxen blond hair was now a soft white, worn in a simple, early Sassoon style. Claudia had never had a permanent wave... in her early years, her hair had been naturally curly, and she had stood for hours while her Mother had impatiently curled the strands around those long, beautifully manicured fingers so that each individual curl was approximately 5 inches long... the Shirley Temple influence, no doubt.

Claudia's once slim, lithe body was now quite ample, which she detested, but comforted herself by remembering her grandmother's similar build, a woman she loved and revered, and as she aged and began to look like the other seven obese women in her combined fraternal and maternal families, became convinced that it was next to impossible to overcome genetics. God knows she had tried from the age of 35 by dramatically altering her lifestyle, adhering to a strict, vitamin enriched diet, whole grains and fiber, avoiding all sugars, watching her fat intake, scarcely touching red meat and yet had succumbed to the Western diseases.

Tears welled. She was not feeling sorry for herself, nor was she sad. If she were asked she would probably say, "I think I am so overwhelmed with the beauty of this moment.... so at peace with nature.... so captivated by the creativity of God.... well, there are no words to describe it.... I only wish I had someone to share these moments with!"

The truth was that loneliness had been an unwelcome companion to Claudia most of her life.... it was no different now... but through the years she had learned from experience the many different faces of loneliness.... a childhood filled with parental rejection and emotional abandonment ... the trauma and loneliness after a loved and trusted family member violated her... the grief and desperate loneliness she experienced after the death of her beloved brother... the loneliness she so often felt with many women who pretended to be involved in "sisterhood" but who were caught up in backbiting, cruel judgmental attitudes, jealousies and fabrications that had led to her basic mistrust of women in general... husbands that were unfaithful and abusive... the shame and loneliness accompanying the abuse was merciless... during the long hours of night, did one ever recover from the memories of the miscreant behaviors of others?

This had been a difficult day for Claudia ... the stinging chest pains were becoming more frequent, the headaches more painful, the stomach pains relentless and the fatigue incapacitating. Walking was challenging due to the unremitting pain of diabetic neuropathy and peripheral artery disease. The insulin she injected three times a day contributed to the obesity and she often thought about giving up the whole adherence to responsibility, but her value system prevailed. Tonight, probably due to the chronic pain and exhaustion, she wondered how much longer she would have to wait until she could enjoy the peace and love she knew awaited her.

Claudia flipped on the Tiffany lamp next to her chair. Now, legally blind, she disliked the darkness that had settled in for the next 12 hours. The light cast a soft glow in this room she loved so much and she ritualistically congratulated herself for the professional decorating job she had achieved. A year ago, her son had purchased this cozy condo for her to live in. At the time, it was in shambles, but with her artistic eye, she had been able to see the possibilities and had gone about refurbishing and redecorating every square inch. The result had been astounding, even to her! Claudia was an interesting person with highly diverse talents and abilities and the room reflected her eclectic and charming style. The furniture, coastal and contemporary in design, softened by pastel colors... the lavender, blue and mauve hues of the sky and mountains. A large white stone fireplace was a focal point in the room, and the custom made white marble mantle showcased several unique pieces collected from her travels to Europe and Asia... a candelabra from Lausanne, a unique perfume bottle found in a hidden back alley on the left bank in Paris, and a small, limited edition Matisse she had stumbled upon in London. Most treasured, the Beleek tea service found in County Clare, Ireland that now sat on an intricately carved ebony Asian style side table. One wall of shelves was lined with books, vases of flowers and small, lovely sculptures and memorabilia. The other walls displayed Claudia's original art, with a few rare finds from memorable places. Her needs had become simple and her decorating style mirrored this simplicity of spirit. She had nothing that overwhelmed, and everything that was harmonious.

Claudia was satisfied with what she had accomplished today, finishing the process of shredding 18 file drawers of papers and files. Through the years, boxes of personal and business records had accumulated, and it was now time for review prior to disposal. A certain amount of grief was involved in this process. Life had challenged Claudia on many occasions, but embedded in these sometimes overwhelming trials, were many blessings... A favorite quote of Ralph Waldo Emerson's summed it up... "On the debris of our despair we form our character." She knew this to be true as she re-read letters and reviewed mounds of memorabilia... the circumstances surrounding the divorce were painfully recalled... the memory of love was such a sad thing. Then there was the hell she endured with the abuse, the problems with children and the years of recovery were remembered. She had disposed of tons of papers, but still had a great deal more. As she looked around the newly decorated room, she was disgusted with the mess she had created. She picked up a journal from the floor, and began to read. It immediately became apparent that she was not going to sleep tonight, but was going to allow the many memories to flood her mind and emotions. She thought of her favorite poem by Robert Frost... "Stopping by Woods on a Snowy Evening"... his last lines... "But I have promises to keep... And miles to go before I sleep...And miles to go before I sleep." She knew when sleep came it would be for a long time.

BOOK 1

Mr. and Mrs. James Fitzpatrick, III
and
Their Child, Claudia

...and dear God, please help me be a good girl so mother and daddy can love me...

Edward James Fitzpatrick, III, and his wife, Elizabeth [nee Tyrie] were an unlikely couple. Their respective histories had been carefully edited, and none but a handful of trusted lifelong friends were aware of the circumstances of their lives.

Edward James Fitzpatrick, III, had joined his Father's investment firm immediately after his graduation from Harvard Business School. His father, Edward Fitzpatrick, Jr., had been apprehensive about his son's choice of schools...Harvard had just opened their business school and it was not yet ranked as was the Wharton School of Business but the son thought that the reputation of Harvard could be of value. He was proven right year after year as the business attracted the top people of the corporate world.

Edward III (who had been called James, Jimmy, or Jim all his life) was an unusual man in the sense that he had been raised with a great deal of money but was comfortable and able to interact with diverse groups of people. He was a clean shaven, handsome man with finely chiseled aquiline features, and a well-proportioned six-foot frame. His quick wit and charming manner ingratiated him into the checkbooks of many wealthy business colleagues and into the hearts and beds of many belonging to the gentler sex. James exhibited an enviable and pragmatic democratic code of ethics. But beneath his gregarious exterior, no one really knew Edward James Fitzpatrick, III... he had developed an impenetrable shield as a child with eyes that were inscrutable.…. James could laugh, or he could be angry, but his piercing blue eyes showed no emotion. The one person he had deeply loved and trusted was gone… At the age of eight, he braved the suicide of his Mother. He adored her, and knew she was the only person in his young life that could "see behind his eyes."

"You know Jimmy that the Bible tells us that our eyes are the windows to our soul?"

"What does that mean Mama?"

"It means that I can look into your eyes and see right into your soul… into your spirit, and I know what you are thinking!"

"NO, Mama! You're only kidding me, right? You can't really see behind my eyes, can you?"

"Yes, I can Jimmy…God gives Mother's a special gift to be able to see your thoughts! Those enchanting blue eyes of yours are a mirror…they are beautiful and so are you! Don't let anyone else see into your eyes Jimmy… don't let anyone know you except the one who will love you."

"Who will that be Mama? Do you love me?"

"I love you so much Jimmy…I will always love you! Remember that!" They were sitting on a Victorian "fainting couch" in her bedroom. He remembered the day so well… the sound of soft rain falling and the exotic smell of spring. The casement windows were open despite the rain, and his Mama was dressed in what he would remember as a beautiful, creamy white, satin dressing gown. It was Saturday afternoon… She put her arms around him and hugged him close to her. He put his head in her lap while she stroked his hair, the mellow sounds of the opera coming through the large radio next to the chair. Soon he was asleep. When he awoke it was dusk… his Mama appeared to be asleep so he got up quietly and left the room. Two hours later, when dinner was brought to her room, there was pandemonium. He was directed by the tearful servants to stay in his room and, later, when they brought his supper tray they were unusually kind and solicitous toward him, telling him only that his mother was ill and needed her rest. He never knew his Mother was dead until his Father arrived home the following morning. The rest was history to James… it was a defining moment in his life and it created a lifelong, unexpressed dissonance between James and his father that only intensified when his father remarried within eight months to a very young socialite daughter of a multi-millionaire client. A year later, his new "mother" gave birth to twin girls... but James was not around to share in the wedded bliss and birth. With his Father's blessing, he had chosen to separate himself from his father and new family, boarding at the Riverdale Country Day School. James was an intellectually motivated child, and was eventually accepted as the youngest student ever accepted at Choate where he met many loyal people who, later, became loyal clients. Attending boarding school was seemingly a sad thing for James, but in the long run it helped him develop his own persona.... and to develop confidence and a sense of integrity that had been absent in his life. As an only child, he appreciated the camaraderie he was able to develop at both Choate and later at Harvard. For the rest of his life he maintained a cordial and respectful business relationship with his father, but Jim never forgot two important teachings of his mother... "don't cast your pearls before swine" and "don't let anyone see behind your eyes."

When he married Elizabeth, he had few expectations. James was acutely aware of his inability to sustain a deeply abiding, monogamous relationship. After being with "Beth" on several occasions, he knew her "love" was focused on attaining wealth and position... she had been honest about that... and when she announced that she was pregnant he thought that perhaps a marriage to her would be preferable rather than to the usual disingenuous aristocratic society- type of woman he normally dated. He had been angry about the pregnancy, but felt Beth's needs were manageable... She was self-engrossed to a fault, nervous about her lack of education which could be a positive factor. He had thoroughly investigated her background and knew every lie, every tawdry and indiscriminate transgression, every brazen social blunder, but he also knew every act of courage and all the dreadfulness of her life, and he allowed her to be. She served him well, and she was educable. She welcomed his input and knowledge about how things should be done, and so they were courteous, cordial and respectful to one another, sharing the bed infrequently which suited them both.

James had not wanted any children, but when his second child, a son, was born, he was genuinely delighted... yet, he never found the magic formula for establishing a close relationship with this son, who was so fine and caring an individual. When the son, Jamie, died, James experienced another defining moment of his life ... a grief he had not known since his mother's death. In fact, several people who knew him well thought that James Fitzpatrick never really recovered from his son's death. He changed. It might be said that the eyes of his soul closed forever. He drank more, he looked tired a lot of the time, his temper became mercurial, and he was less inclined to his usual expansiveness...in fact he became quiet and somewhat introverted. However, each day he continued to don his impeccable white shirt and starched, detachable collar, one of his many well-tailored suits, his English raincoat and his inevitable hat... the skimmer straw in Summer, and the homburg in Winter. He liked to walk the 2 miles to the railway station where he boarded the New York Central train... the same one that he faithfully rode each day for forty years. In his dark leather briefcase was a daily agenda, carefully written out the previous evening during the train ride to his home. In earlier years, James had often entertained in the city... sometimes with, but most times, without his wife. On the nights he spent without Elizabeth, he would send for his chauffer to meet him in the city so they could drive home his companion du jour. The chauffer would often wait long hours for his master, and on these nights, Jim's energy was sapped but he was emotionally nourished and revitalized. Elizabeth's shrill recriminations could be heard throughout the house after James had been opportunistically photographed with some beautiful companion for the evening, but she would mellow when presented with a beautiful "bauble" that James, in his wisdom, had thought to provide for her.

When Elizabeth married Edward James Fitzpatrick III, she was under no illusion that theirs would be a magical union. "Jimmy Fitz" had a hallowed reputation within her milieu ... his womanizing was legendary, if not somewhat fabled. But Beth's need for security far outweighed her need for moral conventions. She considered it a miracle the night she met James, and instantly vowed to prolong the miracle.

At the age of fourteen, Elizabeth had fully developed both physically and emotionally and she was not blind to the fact that she was a beautiful woman. She had been blessed with skin that was like alabaster and her large, green eyes flecked with brown and orange stared out of an angular face with high cheekbones, framed by a mass of untamed, very black curls that fell randomly and charmingly about her face. She had always been thin, almost frail, but was endowed with good sized, perfectly formed breasts that accentuated her twenty-two inch waist, and her long, beautiful legs were exquisitely shaped. After one of her terrible arguments with her mother, she left the small Pennsylvania town that had become her adolescent prison and went to Philadelphia, known as "the city" or "downstate." She knew several other friends from her town that had escaped the creeping blight of the mining town and they offered her shelter and helped her find a job as a hostess at a restaurant. Along with her beauty, Elizabeth was street smart. She knew how to lie about her age, to flirt with the men and, in time, became highly proficient in manipulation and subterfuge. By the age of sixteen, she had moved to New York City and secured a job dancing at a fairly respectable nightclub... and then the magic happened. In 1918, she had been accepted as a "Ziegfield Girl" and at a private party on opening night of the Follies, she met Edward James Fitzpatrick, III. With her charm, manipulation and shrewdness, she managed to snare the up-and-coming young financier... or so she thought.

Her new lifestyle was a challenge to Elizabeth. She set about reinventing her history... never did she admit that her education ended at the close of second grade, that her father abandoned his wife and children, and that the ensuing divorce caused her mother untold humiliation and shame. Instead, she declared her love for her "wonderful" father, obliterating as much as possible the fact that he had "loved" her so much that he came to her bed at night on a consistent basis, and that she repressed the childhood inner conflicts and endured his alcoholic murmurings so as not to risk being tied to the kitchen stove and beaten with a belt as were her three siblings.   Fortunately, Elizabeth had an innate sense of design and she went about discovering all she could about decorating and entertaining. She was relentless in acquiring as much information as possible about "decorum"… everything that related to gentility, breeding and manners became very important. She spent a great deal of money on designer clothes, on salons, opulent furnishings… anything that would reflect affluence and status. James never demeaned her lack of knowledge, and consistently supported her determination to assimilate the many things needed to become savvy and sophisticated, a haute monde member of the privileged class.

But, in spite of the fact that Elizabeth cultivated as much refinement and culture as she could with a precision that would have made the military jealous, she was unable to purge, completely, the remnants of her humble and painful background… nor could she eradicate the lack of self-confidence she felt regarding her lack of education.

She was crazed when a third child had been conceived. She screamed and cried for days, threatened to abort it, and, generally, was inconsolable. James also did not want another child, and was calmed only by the counsel of his parish priest, who helped him understand that God had a plan for his life, that he had the means to hire help and to give his wife all the support and love she needed at this time. With time, Elizabeth calmed down, but she never fully accepted the birth, which had been difficult and debilitating for her. It was one of the few times that she and her husband were bonded… unfortunately, the bond was born out of shared disowning of their beautiful little daughter…a precious human being, who would be the innocent victim of their abnegation for the rest of her life…Claudia…

1

Claudia began her decent... a "belly flop" on her new "Flexible Flyer" sled... a present from "Grandy,"... her beloved Grandmother.

"Oh how I love this," she thought.... Her eyes were squinted almost shut as the icy wind slashed her face but she squealed with delight. At the age of eight, Claudia had an unrivaled ability for the fastest runs on this hill, the longest and steepest in the upscale suburban town where she had lived since birth.

At the end of the run, she rolled over on her back, lying in the snow for a few minutes then joined her best friend, Joanie, who was sitting in an adjoining snow-bank eating the ice off her frozen gloves.

"You know what I love best about this Joanie? I mean besides the speed and the wind?"

"What?" Joanie had heard this a thousand times before, but she was a good friend.

"I love to feel the cold on the outside, and the sweat next to my skin."

"Claudia, you know we're not supposed to say 'sweat!'... it's *perspiration* and the reason you perspire is because you wear so many sweaters and that silk underwear... my Mother says that silk underwear is the warmest...and the most expensive!"

Claudia knew that Joanie's family talked a lot about how much things cost. Even at her tender age, she was aware of the vast differences that existed between her "station in life" and the "others" as her Mother referred to them.

"Joanie, what are you going to do now?"

"I have to go home. My mother said I had to be home by 4:00. What time do you think it is now? I'm probably late... I guess I'm always late!"

Their other friend, Margie, came bouncing down the hill, turned her sled into the snow bank, and came to a stop next to the two girls. "Uhhhhoooo. I'm freezing!"

"Margie, Joanie has to go home, so I guess we should go too?" Claudia and Margie lived near each other, about a half mile up the hill.

"Yah... I have to dress up tonight 'cuz my Daddy is bringing company home to dinner. I hate dressing up, don't you?"

Claudia and Joanie nodded in unison. They sat for a few minutes giggling and discussing the inevitable obligations that parents force children to observe, and agreed that parents, in general, are "peculiar" and very "illogical" a good deal of the time.

"O.K. you two, I'm leaving... I have to go to the bathroom." As Claudia said this she stood up, grabbed an armful of snow and dumped it on her two friends. They laughed, grabbed her and pushed her into the snow bank. They kept up the antics for a few minutes and then said goodbye to each other with a ritualistic pat on the back and a handshake reminiscent of the "secret" handshake Margie had once observed her fraternity Father teaching her bother.

Margie and Claudia began their breathless trek home, Margie's house was first, and finally Claudia pushed open the gate to the stone pathway that would take her to the back of her stately house. She went to the delivery entrance and was shocked to find it locked. It was imperative that she relieve herself and she quickly tromped down the fieldstone steps to the basement door. It was locked also. Tears began to form in her eyes. She had miscalculated her need and had forgotten that the servants were off today to attend a wedding. She remembered, now, her Mother telling her to be dressed and ready to go to the country club for dinner by 5:00 PM. Claudia sat on the icy cold steps, and the tears were now falling on her cheeks. Being a child who was forbidden to make decisions on her own, she was unable to formulate a plan that would prevent the humiliation that she knew was coming. She sat very still but suddenly felt the warm stream on her thighs, and at that moment knew she would be punished ... shamed and isolated ... it was a frequent part of her life. Through her tears, she gazed up at the sky and began to say a prayer. Claudia was a devout and religious young child. She frequently replayed the memory of being five years old when she was chosen to crown the statue of the Blessed Virgin at the annual May Day celebration in her church. Her Mother had taken her to New York City to one of the designer shops and purchased a beautiful white dress... a white veil had been made and, at the last moment, attached to a row of the ultra- fragrant lily of the valley. Claudia was a shy and retiring child, and on that May day she was very nervous as she walked down the endless aisle, the crown of white roses for the Blessed Mother on a white satin pillow. When she walked up the steps to the altar, one of the priests had lifted her up high to place the crown on the statue's head. She had tilted the pillow, and the crown dropped to the floor... when it was handed to her, she, in her nervousness, had placed it on the Virgin's head slightly askew. She remembered some of the spectators laughing, but what she remembered most was her Mother's outrage at her ineptitude. And she remembered the feeling of loneliness that followed the shame she felt for causing such embarrassment to her parents. She felt that same loneliness now. In truth, Claudia felt lonely most of the time. The servants had been told to keep their distance, and her Mother was gone most of the time. "Appropriate friends" were selected for her and she had learned to lie to her Mother about the time she spent with her "true" friends like Joanie and Margie.

Claudia heard the chauffeur opening the garage door and knew her mother was home. She went around to the garage entrance hoping to shed most of her clothes, but was intercepted by Margaret, the chauffeur's wife.

"What in the world happened to you child? You look frozen to death!" She began to call Claudia's Mother despite Claudia's pleadings not to. And then there she was.

2

There was no mistaking the look of displeasure on her Mother's face. Elizabeth Fitzpatrick was only five feet, five inches tall, but when she was angry, she looked greater than six feet tall. Claudia thought that she did something miraculous with her body to stretch it out as she sucked in her breath. With one impeccably manicured hand she grabbed Claudia by the back of her snow jacket and Claudia stumbled into the house, where she was handed over to Marion, her Mother's "house assistant"

"Take this ragamuffin, scrub her and put her to bed without any dinner! It's disgraceful that she is parading around looking like a refugee from Hungary!"

Marion had been trudging home through the snow and wind, when "Lady Cruel", as she had nicknamed her employer, pulled alongside her and motioned her into the car. Marion had hoped to be home before the lady, knowing that Claudia would need to have help cleaning up. But her train was delayed, and she was anxious about the child. Marion was like a Nanny to Claudia. She loved the little girl, but was restricted in her communication with the child, as it had been made clear to her as well as to the other servants, that they were to have as little direct involvement with the family as possible. Marion had been "chosen" for her position from among many candidates living in the small Pennsylvania mining town… she had been 13 years old and was grateful to be snatched from the intense poverty in her life. There were eleven siblings, and one never knew if there would be food or clothes or a warm place to sleep. "Lady Cruel" had insisted on Marion's family signing a contract with several restrictions and they were glad to do it at the time. The first "restriction" concerned Marion's age, which the family was forbidden to disclose to anyone outside of the family. Other restrictions concerned the length of time of her employment, and specific reasons why she could be terminated, such as gossiping. In the last 9 years, Marion had come to profoundly dislike her employer, but she was without alternatives. She had worked very long hours, especially after Claudia's birth. She learned to do as she was told, not to gossip, and to squirrel away every cent she could in preparation to leave...which she hoped would be soon! She gave Claudia as much love as she could without being obvious. Tonight, she sneaked some milk and scones from the kitchen, watched the child hungrily stuff her mouth (which would have caused the lady a heart attack!), tucked her into bed, and whispered an Irish blessing to her.

■ ■ ■

When Claudia Marie Fitzpatrick was born, the youngest of three children, her Mother was quite outspoken about the "unexpected misconception" and the "painful embarrassment" of bearing a "late life" child. During Claudia's early childhood, she rarely saw her Mother who preferred to spend most of her time craving publicity for the endless amount of charity work she did to insure Claudia's inclusion in the Social Register.

Claudia was almost 20 years younger than her sister, Constance, and 13 years younger than her brother, Jamie (Edward James Fitzpatrick the fourth.) During the lonely hours she spent staring out the windows of their enormous stone house in the suburbs of New York City, or of spending long, isolated hours in their Park Avenue apartment while her parents were socializing, Claudia would think about many things, but always that she never felt connected to anyone in her family except her brother, Jamie, whom she loved very much. She thought her mother was a beautiful woman but that she had an "icy" personality and was very snobby. Her father was handsome and she frequently heard him described as "charming." But she had been on the receiving end of his fiery temper and she did not like his sense of humor because he made fun of others. She knew his job as President and CEO of Fitzpatrick, & Fitzpatrick brokerage company was important, and she knew he spent a great deal of time playing golf and socializing at the country club, but she knew very little else about him. The one bond they shared was going to the German deli near the railroad station on Saturdays to purchase the deli items on a list from her Mother, and while they were there, she was treated to an ice-cream cone...2 scoops...one vanilla and one chocolate for her, and 2 scoops of vanilla for her Father. She always looked forward to this outing ... it was the only hour of the week she would spend with her "Daddy," ... she loved him so much and felt very sad when the hour was over... so, she would muse... "well, there's always next week."

Claudia saw photographs of "Daddy" in magazines and newspapers, and heard the remarks others made about the "beautiful women" hanging on his arm, and, as she lay in her bed at night, garnered first-hand knowledge from the loud arguments between her parents that there was something very wrong with how he entertained many of the female celebrities. She unobtrusively heard several remarks by the servants about her parent's sex life or lack of it... she didn't understand it all, but was bright enough from a young age to know that her Father did things they did not approve of, and she wondered why and what these things were. It made her angry that her "Daddy" was rejected by anyone... Claudia was sensitive to rejection of any kind from a very young age.

3

Within 24 hours, the sled had disappeared. Claudia was "restricted" to her room, which was not at all unusual… in fact she rather liked this discipline. Because she was shy and withdrawn with adults, she welcomed the isolation that spared her having to interact with her Mother or her Mother's friends. She went to school, came home, did her homework, and wrote in her diary which she carefully hid in her closet under her carefully folded sweaters.

This day, Claudia wrote:

> "Dear God… I am so lonely. I don't know why Mother doesn't like me. I try so hard, God, to be good and to do the right thing. I'm glad she didn't find out about my awful accident yesterday… that would have REALLY made her mad even though it wasn't my fault that I couldn't get into the house…When Mother left to go to the Country Club by herself, I wondered why she would rather be alone. I don't like being alone, and I love Margie and Joanie, but I know Mother doesn't like them. Is it wrong God, for me not to tell her I spend time with them? If it is, I'm sorry… but I don't know what else to do. I am so lonely without them. Help me, God, to be good, and bless my Mother,

my Father, my dear Mom-Mom and Grandfather. Help me forget what he did to me, and help me to keep the secret like he told me to."

■ ■ ■

The "camp" in the Adirondack Mountains had been in the Fitzpatrick family since the early 1900's. It had been built during the great camp era when John Avery Rockefeller had developed Camp Wonundra, which had been hugely successful with his upper class visitors. Edward, the elder Fitzpatrick and his partners in the Wall Street Firm, built their summer getaway for both recreational and business purposes. After all, if their wealthy customers were going to Upper Saranac Lake, why not them? So, Camp Daingean (meaning "fortress" in Gaelic), was constructed in record time.

When she was five years old, Claudia was sent with Marion to spend the summer with her grandparents. She had never met her grandparents, and was far too young to understand the dynamics that had prevented her from knowing them. She remembered once that she had asked about them. The family was at the dinner table, and Connie was talking about visiting her friend's grandparents. Claudia had turned to her Father and innocently asked if she had grandparents. He didn't answer her, but instead roughly pushed his chair away from the table and disappeared for the night. She remembered her Mother's reprimand to her...

"Well, Claudia, as usual you have behaved stupidly! Your Father has not been home for over a week to dine with us, and you drive him from the table with your impertinence! Go to your room. Marion will bring you your milk but you get no dessert."

Jamie came to her room later to kiss her goodnight and all he said was, "Hey kiddo, you didn't do anything wrong tonight...Mother was in a bad mood and I suspect Father was in a bad mood, too."

"But do we have grandparents, Jamie? Everyone else talks about theirs, and I don't seem to have any. Are they dead?"

"No, darlin'...they aren't dead. I don't know a whole lot about them, but I know that Grandfather still works with Father, and that Grandmother is a good deal younger... and they have five children... our Aunts and Uncles. And we have cousins, too. But something happened a long time ago between Father and Grandfather, and there hasn't been a friendship since that time. But guess what! I overheard Mother and Father talking with Marion, and I think they are going to send you to meet our relatives this summer. They live in a Camp in the mountains, and you will love it there. I went once with Mother before you were born, and it's a great deal of fun with a lot of things to do"

"Like what, Jamie... what's a camp. And if I go there, who will take me and what will it be like?"

Jamie had spent over an hour with her that night. It always lifted his spirits to spend time with this winsome and exuberant little girl with her green eyes and blond curls. Her cute face was always so expressive when he was with her, and he enjoyed the bright and inquisitive questions she posed as he described everything about the "mountains" and about the "camp" and about the many fun things to do. He explained to her that their Father and Mother were going to Europe and that because he was going to college at the end of the summer, he was going to stay at the apartment in New York and buy all of his needed school supplies and clothes, and work at the "business" part time. Jamie clarified everything so well, that Claudia felt excited about the outing she was about to take. She was curious... a little bit scared but she trusted Jamie, and knew that everything would be alright.

As it turned out, it was the happiest time of Claudia's young life. At first she was shy, but it wasn't long before her cousins and Aunts and Uncles involved her in their games and showed her all the things she never knew existed... the paths winding up into hills, the blueberries, the snakes and spiders which scared her to death... the Lake which was so cold it made her pee unexpectedly, but it didn't seem to matter to anyone... no one cared when she was dirty or if she "perspired"... they all laughed a great deal which was new to Claudia, and before long she had lost her shyness and felt like one of the family. She adored her Grandmother. They all called her Mom-Mom... and she liked all her cousins and loved her two Aunts... they were twins and they took her everywhere... to the village where they shared ice-cream sundaes and to the movies which thrilled her. At night she would curl up in her Mom-Mom's ample lap, and receive many hugs. She delighted in listening to her Mom-Mom tell her how much she was loved. Her Grandpoppy read her books, and took her out in his boat with her cousins. He promised Claudia that when she was ten he would teach her to sail, but for now, Claudia was very content to learn how to swim and to go fishing with Grandpoppy in the little rowboat. Edward Fitzpatrick was a great story-teller who loved to sing the old Irish songs he had learned as a child and at night one of her Aunts would play the piano, and they would all sing. That summer was an amazement to Claudia. She thrived physically and emotionally and was thrilled to learn that she might be going there each summer. She was carefully admonished by Marion not to talk much to her parents about her time at the camp, particularly not to show her happiness to her Father. So, at the tender age of five, Claudia learned to separate her life. She endured the endless lessons in etiquette and comportment at home, and "escaped" in the summers to what she regarded as her real family.

4

When Claudia was seven, several changes occurred in her life. Her sister, Connie, got married in May, and it was the first time Claudia had seen a wedding. She was surprised when Connie "appointed" her as the flower girl. It was no secret that Connie was her Mother's favorite... they were more like sisters than Mother and Daughter... Connie had never been kind or pleasant to Claudia like Jamie had been... she would often go to "mother" with complaints about things Claudia was or was not doing, suggesting various disciplinary actions, and she laughed at Claudia and ridiculed the things she said. Connie was a petite, attractive woman, self-focused like her Mother, with a highly inflated opinion of herself. She felt victimized by a man she referred to as "the love of my life"... a young man who had "rejected" her by entering the priesthood. Now, at the age of 27, she was feeling desperate about getting married and finally agreed to marry a man she had known for several years... Michael was an up-and-coming, nice looking attorney, working for a prestigious Washington, D.C. law firm. He had his pilot's license, and had spent some years in China leading some to posit that he might be an intelligence agent. Claudia would learn years later that Connie had major reservations about his character, but felt she could control the outcome.

There had been months of preparation and many arguments, and although Claudia had been isolated and uninvolved, it was a happy time for her because she could do almost as she pleased ... no one paid any attention to her so she took advantage of this and spent long hours with her favorite friends. They rode their bikes to new places, and explored the woods along the brooks and streams that bordered their property. She climbed trees and played king of the hill, blind man's bluff, tag, and a variety of other games she had learned to enjoy at camp but rarely had the freedom to enjoy under her Mother's usual watchful eye.

The day of Connie's wedding was cool, sunny and beautiful, and she didn't mind much having to wear the frou-frou dress and spreading the flower petals all over the floor of the church.

Then there was the reception that was held at the country club. Claudia loved it! She had been nervous during the ceremony hoping she would not do anything to embarrass anyone, but now at the reception, she was happy as she watched her parents dancing... She knew her Father loved dancing the waltz... everyone cleared the floor, and Claudia heard many remarks about how "beautiful" they were, how "graceful" and the onlookers applauded rather expansively. Later, her Father picked her up ... she put her feet on top of his, and they were dancing! It was a memory Claudia cherished. She had often wondered what it would feel like to sit on her Father's lap and to feel safe like she did with her grandparents. This gave her a small inkling of that lovely feeling, one that was not to be repeated, ever.

In June of that year, Claudia went to Daingean to spend her third summer with her grandparents. The camp had seven bedroom "suites" and Claudia noticed that year, that her grandparents no longer shared a suite. Now Grandpoppy was sleeping at the far end of the camp in his own suite that had been designed with a bedroom, office and bathroom. Claudia noticed that he spent a great deal of time alone in his room, and that several times when she ran to get him to take her swimming or fishing, he smelled funny. One day when she knocked at his door, he answered it completely nude. She screamed and ran away very fast, and heard him laughing so she thought it was just a joke of some kind that she didn't understand. On a rainy day toward the end of the summer, Claudia made her usual trek to his rooms to see what they were going to do. Would they play checkers? Or maybe he could continue teaching her to play ping-pong? And she would love to go into the small town to the ice cream parlor for a super sundae! "Poppy" invited her in and showed her some books that he had bought. They sat in one of the big cushy armchairs by the huge stone fireplace and sitting on his lap, Claudia noticed that disagreeable smell. As he read to her he began to rub her back, which she loved, but it was just a few minutes before he told Claudia that he was not feeling well, and that he wanted to rest. He asked Claudia if she would be his nurse. She liked that idea, and put a blanket on him, got him a glass of water, pretended to feel his pulse and wiped his forehead. "Poppy" asked her to lie on the bed with him.…. He had something to show her, and he took out a small vibrator. He put it on her head and she giggled, and then he put it on her arm and she thought it was the funniest sensation she had ever known.

"Now, I'll be the doctor, and examine you, Claudia… O.K?"

"Hmmm…I don't know Poppy, I don't like doctors."

"I promise that you'll like *this one!*" and with that "Poppy" put the vibrator on her legs and slowly began to move it up toward her thighs.

"Now just close your eyes and relax little one… Pretend you're in the lake and floating on a raft, and I am the little fish who is going to surprise you…" He began to sing one of his Irish lullaby's and was soon touching her and kissing her. He showed her his "little fish" and asked her to kiss it and fondled her with increasing ardor.

Claudia was stunned, confused, scared and very silent. When it was over, "Poppy" said she was a very good girl, and that he would give her something special every time she came to visit him. But…and this was *very* important…she was not to tell anyone about this because if she did she would have to go to an awful place where there were witches and ogres and they would eat her and attack her. "Poppy" kept reaching down next to the bed and drinking from a big brown bottle. She hated the smell, and she hated how she felt. She wanted to leave, but was afraid to say anything. So, she just lay there, until "Poppy" began to snore, and she knew that he was fast asleep. Claudia ran to her room. She saw some blood on her panties, and was very scared… "Maybe I'm going to die!" she thought, but never said a word to anyone that day or any other day that summer.

Claudia's grandmother noticed the child's abnormal irritability and withdrawal during the final weeks of that fateful summer, but the servants were the only ones who noticed the blood-spotted bed linens.

Claudia never saw her grandfather again… he died of a sudden heart attack in December of that year…on the seventh, the same day the Japanese attacked Pearl Harbor. She did not go to the funeral, and she never went to the camp again.

5

World War II did little to change Claudia's life... she was too young to understand what was happening in the world... but she did notice that people seemed to be friendlier, more helpful, and several of her friend's family members had something called victory gardens. Every month she would take her little red wagon and go throughout the neighborhood collecting scrap metal with her friend, Joanie, and she noticed the many flags people had in their yards and windows, and how willing they were to help with her collection. Heard many times were phrases such as, "God is in control," or "the United States is truly a blessed country...God will take care of us," and "God has a plan for our lives."

In January, her older brother, Jamie, made an unexpected trip home from college and announced at dinner that he had enlisted in the Navy. There was a great deal of crying by her Mother and her sister, Connie who seemed to visit a great deal. However, her Father pounded him on the back and made some remark about "being a man" and "doing the right thing." Then there was an argument about whether or not he should have finished college and more arguing about going into "the business." Claudia sank into her own thoughts and began to think about Jamie. He had been good to her. He often interceded for her, intercepted the telephone calls from her "little urchin" friends, took her to the movies and for ice-cream to cheer her up. Jamie was funny... he told her lots of jokes that made her laugh. Claudia loved him a great deal...he was gentle, and kind, and often told her she was a "beautiful little girl" with her blond curls and green eyes. Claudia felt safe with Jamie, and the night before he left she was sitting in his lap listening to a music program on the radio....a man by the name of Mantovani was playing a song that Jamie said was his favorite. President Roosevelt had just given a speech, and although Claudia didn't understand a whole lot about what he said, she liked his voice. Her sister had cried during the speech, and her Mother dabbed at her eyes with the finest Irish linen handkerchief. Her Father had left the room during the speech, saying something terrible about Mr. Roosevelt, and soon her sister and Mother went upstairs to "freshen up." Claudia put her arms around Jamie's neck and buried her head in his chest. She began to cry and to tell him she had a terrible secret but was afraid to tell him. He patted her head and her back and talked soothingly to her, thinking that she had, once again, done some forbidden childish thing with her friends. But what he heard appalled him... he sat upright, startling Claudia who fell to the floor.

"What are you telling me, Claudia...is this true...did you tell Mother about this!"

Claudia began to cry and curled up into the fetal position. Sensing his mistake, Jamie went to her and lifted her into his arms.

"My God, Claudia, I am so sorry. My poor little "Blondie"... it's not you I'm upset with... it's Grandfather ... what he did that worried you... all this time... not having anyone to talk with... Please, my dear sweet little sister, know that I love you and will take care of this... I'll tell Father and Mother... you can't bear this all by yourself!"

"NO! NO! Jamie, you must not tell anyone. You MUSTN'T! Something terrible will happen to me, I know it! Grandpoppy told me that witches would get me and... oh, please, Jamie, don't tell anyone... promise me you won't."

Jamie just held her and soothed her. He promised Claudia he would not tell anyone, but in his heart, he knew that he had to do something. Even though Grandfather had died and would not ever bother his sister again, he knew instinctively that this dear lonely little girl needed some kind of help. He had always tried to give Claudia some of the love his parents neglected to offer her. Well, he would think about it and figure out what he could do... his immediate reaction was to make sure that she was taken to see a doctor, but he was unsure how his parents would handle the situation... they certainly were not understanding nor compassionate towards this sweet little girl. Jamie knew he had to be the one to make the initial call to their family doctor... he was a good man and would understand and be sensitive to the entire situation...Jamie had known him all his life...he would know who to contact to help his sister. Since he was leaving early in the morning, he would call from the base and get things started. Then, the next time he was home, he would confront his parents, discuss this shocking, hurtful news, and make sure that they gave Claudia the love and care that was needed.

But Jamie didn't know that night that plans often change.

■ ■ ■

Jamie was driving the short distance from Virginia Beach to the Newport Air Station at Norfolk, Virginia. He had enjoyed his time off spending a long afternoon and evening with some old friends of the family... probably his last time off before "shipping out" wherever that might be. Of the 72 seaplanes at the base, there was word that three quarters of them would be leaving by the weekend. He loved what he was doing. Jamie had over 100 hours of flight time under his belt, a gift from his Father when he was only 16 years old and continuing until he went to college. When the possibility to fly sea planes presented itself, he immediately grabbed onto the opportunity and was accepted into the program.

The first thing Jamie had done after leaving his home in January was to call the family doctor, Dr. Strickland. They had a long conversation, and true to Jamie's instincts, it was evident that the doc understood the family dynamics... they had a long conversation resulting in Dr. Strickland assuring Jamie that he would handle the situation with great care and wisdom making sure to spend time with Claudia without her parents being present. Jamie's anxiety was greatly relieved after talking with the "Doc," and today he had been invited to spend his last leave with Sean and Moira Cronin, a couple who had close ties with his family and had been at Camp Daingean one time that had coincided with one of Claudia's summer visits. It would give him a chance to further explore the situation.

After dinner, as they relaxed with a brandy, the conversation had shifted to their last visit to the Adirondack's and the death of Grandfather Fitzpatrick.

"How did you like Camp Daingean? Rather a fantastic place don't you think?"

"Moira and I always loved going there! The setting is spectacular and there is so much to do! But, the thing I enjoyed most was your Grandfather's stories!"

"Yes, he was a real raconteur." Jamie's thoughts raced. He remembered Edward's stories about his childhood... how fortunate they had been to have money unlike most of the other Irish immigrants.

"Sean, do you remember what year my Grandfather was born and how it happened that the family came here... to America?" Jamie was now very curious about Edward's early life.

"Oh, I remember everything quite clearly... that's because I wrote a book that dealt with immigration, and I was most interested in his viewpoints and first-hand observations." Sean Cronin was a history professor at the University and had written many scholarly books and articles... He was now on a subject he loved and became quite animated about the subject.

"Edwards's father, your great-Grandfather, was a highly respected barrister in Ireland... a non-Catholic which worked very well to his advantage. He was a smart man in recognizing that Ireland was somewhat doomed at the time in history when he immigrated... the political climate, the economic climate, the long and bitter relationship England had with the Catholics... It's true, you know, that the Catholics were not allowed to own land, and even their church attendance was banned for some time... can you imagine that they were not allowed to worship! The Irish were referred to as 'papists' and therefore enemies of the state."

"Where did that idea come from Sean?"

"It began with the Reformation... that's when the alliance between Rome and the English empire was broken, largely due to the demands of Henry VIII. Since that time there was nothing but suspicion and anger toward the Irish Catholics because of their ties to the Pope. But that's another story, Jamie... let me get back to Edward's Father... your great-Grandfather. It was in 1825... great-Grandfather Edward gave up a very lucrative law profession to come to America with his new, dear wife, who interestingly was a devout Irish Catholic. It was fortunate that your great Grandfather was a Protestant, and had money for good accommodations and a safe passage... the Irish Catholics endured absolute hell on those ships, riding in the belly and being herded like cattle... but in this case, it made no difference... his wife died in childbirth on that wretched ship, and the baby as well. So, great Grandfather Edward Fitzpatrick arrived in America a grief-stricken man, but ready to work ... which he did, and eventually married again...a lovely young woman, I'm told, who was also a Catholic... and she bore a brood of children, your Grandfather, Edward, Jr. being the eldest."

"Hmmm. That's interesting about the religious difference. That must be the reason he was so successful when he came to America. My understanding is that most Irish Catholics who came to America were very poor and were treated horribly. The wealthy Americans were Protestants and that's how my great-Grandfather became so well established. Do you know anything about Edward Jr.'s marriage?"

"All I know is that he was married in 1898 at the age of 30... and the reason I know this is that there had been a huge wave of Irish Catholics emigrating to America because of the potato famine, and he told many stories about how his Father, your great-Grandfather, was able to help these people... which was a great deal... and as a boy he often shared a meal or his bedroom with those needing help. It was a desperate situation! You know, in Ireland, the Irish Catholics were prohibited by the English from entering many professions so they remained dirt-poor farmers. Then, when the famine began in 1845, there were about one million who starved to death in Ireland during the five years of the famine. Ah, it was Ireland's darkest hour, I can tell you. Ships bound for England left the Irish ports crammed with grain and cattle while the farmers died in droves. Some debate the issue that the famine should be considered genocide by the British... there certainly existed an extreme racist mentality. The English people were ambitious and industrious, but they unfortunately believed that poverty was caused by bad moral character and that idleness was the devil's work. They were unable to admit that their political policies and the economic policy of forbidding land ownership by the Catholics was *causing* the problems." Sean paused to take a long swig of his ale and Jamie took advantage of the pause to lead into another question.

"Was great-Grandfather Fitzpatrick ever involved in the 'Young Ireland Movement'?"

"I don't know a thing about that, Jamie, but I do know that when the Irish Catholics immigrated to America it was with some misgivings. Life in Ireland was cruel, but coming to America was a battle for survival. The ships that brought them to America were known as 'coffin ships' and if they survived the crossing, once they arrived here they lived in filthy tenements and damp cellars all of which were vermin infested. And the racist attitude toward Catholics was the worst in the history of this country. Not only that, but there were terrible scams ... They were robbed of the little money they had. No group was considered lower than an Irish Catholic and there were many discriminatory practices. The employment ads in the newspapers read, 'No Irish Need Apply', and the Chicago Post ran a piece that said, '...scratch a convict or a pauper, and the chances are that you tickle the skin of an Irish Catholic...putting them on a boat and sending them home would end crime in the country.' Many Protestants were Puritan descendants and viewed the growing influx of Roman Catholics with great dismay... Irish American Protestants, with the exception of those like your great-Grandfather, went to great lengths to distance themselves from the Roman Catholics... I read old articles about the convent that was burned down in Massachusetts, and saw copies of the nasty cartoons...no pun intended... by Thomas Nast...even the police discriminated against the Catholic immigrants. There was always a positive depiction of English rule and the Irish had no power and no one to speak for them except for people like you great-Grandfather and the Catholic Church both of whom did wonderful things for the immigrants, including establishing Catholic education for the children who were largely illiterate, and providing a safe haven for all."

"This is incredibly enlightening, Sean. I wonder if Grandfather Edward was aware of the things he did when he drank."

Sean was caught off guard. As an historian, he was enjoying the discussion of the Irish immigration, but Jamie's reflection about his Grandfather's drinking abruptly cut into his dissertation.

"That's an odd comment, Jamie. Care to shed some light on your thoughts?"

Jamie looked at Sean a long minute.

"There is something on my mind, Sean, but I am not at liberty to discuss it right now. Perhaps we can get together soon, after I get my thoughts together and we can discuss it then."

"Sounds good to us Jamie… call when you can come again for dinner. Maybe next week?"

"Yup… I'll call you."

But Jamie never got the chance to discuss anything further with the Cronins. Two days later, while on a routine training maneuver, a freak storm occurred that unexpectedly produced massive waves and he did not stand a chance of surviving when the wheels of his floatplane malfunctioned. Jamie's plane hit the water and broke into pieces. His body was never recovered.

6

A pall descended on the Fitzpatrick household after Jamie's death. Claudia was devastated. No one spoke to her... preparations had been made for Jamie's memorial but she was not included in any of the arrangements and, afterwards, the house became eerily quiet. There were many times she was paralyzed with fear, not knowing whether or not she was alone in the house or if the strange noises she heard were from her parents or from the servants quarters or perhaps someone else! She would huddle in her bedroom, pushing furniture against the door, uncertain what to do if she needed help. Her parents had become even more emotionally remote and impervious to her needs. They spent a great deal more time at their Park Avenue apartment and rarely included Claudia in their plans, communicating by notes left on the refrigerator, where Claudia's meals were neatly packed in containers by the cook with preparation instructions taped to the tops of the little glass casseroles. In essence, Claudia spent the rest of her childhood and teenage years alone, and had no memory of having had a conversation of any magnitude with either of her parents.

Marion, who had been her only friend, had left within two months of Jamie's death... it had been another terrible loss for Claudia... she had come home from school looking for Marion but could not find her, and it was only at the excruciatingly sober dinnertime that her Mother broke the news...and, of course, when Claudia broke into tears, she was sent to her room. Marion was not there to sneak her any scones and milk, and that night Claudia was very hungry and cried herself to sleep. She felt ... no, she **KNEW** that everyone she loved would be taken from her.

Marion had cried herself to sleep the night she found out about Jamie. Within weeks, she would join the nearly three million women who worked in a defense plant during World War II, and although she realized how difficult it would be for Claudia, she was happy to be leaving behind what she considered years of repression working for the Madame Cruel. One day while on lunch break at the factory, she confided to her new friend...

"Jamie was the only person in that household who loved that child, besides me... and with him gone...I just don't know what will happen to her. I never seen anything like it... After Mr. Jamie got hisself killed, that lady never touched that child. It were like she blamed the whole world for his dying, and mostly hated the little girl knowing how much Mr. Jamie loved her."

As time passed, Claudia became happiest at her new school. She was very involved in the extra- curricular activities, and was a natural athlete excelling in track events which garnered a good deal of support from her classmates. Toward the end of the sixth grade, Claudia had an unusual experience that affected her for many years. She had always been well liked, sought after as a friend until a new girl came into the class. She was cute, petite and very outspoken but for some reason that always remained a mystery to Claudia, this new girl took an instant dislike to Claudia, and with the most artful cunning, began a hate campaign against her. Within a month, Joanie Finnegan was the only friend who would speak to her.... the others, both boys and former girl-friends, would stand in groups and, as she walked by, they would smirk at her, make faces and for the most part remain silent. It was to be a defining time in her life, particularly where women were concerned. As usual, Claudia had no one to talk with. Mom-Mom had sold the camp and was living in the South with one of her daughter's. Claudia's older sister, Constance, was now living in California and there had been no improvement in the relationship with her Mother.

Between her eleventh and twelfth years, she grew in stature a full four inches, and developed a stunning figure. When she walked into a room, she did so with natural grace and elegance... mannerisms that were the result of the ongoing dance and comportment lessons demanded by her mother.

■ ■ ■

In her junior year at the all-female prep school, Claudia began a "steady" relationship with a young man from a neighboring all-male prep school, who was grudgingly approved of by her parents, since his parents belonged to the same country club and he drove a foreign sports car. Craig was tall, handsome and well built, and Claudia felt safe with him. It was the first time she had indulged in "necking" and since she had never been kissed, hugged, or caressed by either parent, Claudia was astonished at how wonderful the closeness felt. In her first year of college, she took a class ... Psychology 101 and had to read a book by Ashley Montegue, entitled, *Touching.* She was fascinated with Montegue's research on the importance of touch, and realized how lucky she had been to have had the caressing love of her Grandmother and her brother Jamie.

Claudia had been promised she could attend college abroad, but instead, her Father forced her to attend a private woman's college in New York City which meant she had to live at home and commute to the City on a daily basis. Every day she boarded the New York Central commuter train to Grand Central Terminal and from there, disobeying her Father, fought her way into a subway that took her to the upper East side. She would attend a class or two, play bridge and go out to lunch. Her Father gave her five dollars a day.... the commuter ticket was prepaid, and although she had been **ordered** to take a cab from Grand Central to the college, she chose, instead, to spend ten cents on the subway, thirty-five cents for her daily lunch at Schraffts with six of her classmates, and the rest she squirreled away for the little things she needed like lipstick, mascara and cigarettes, a habit she developed that would have caused mayhem at home. It was obvious to everyone that Claudia was not a bit interested in classes.... she attended just enough to get by with Ds, even an occasional and surprising B. Craig was attending a college in the Northeast... they planned to get married after their Sophomore year, and she spent a great deal of time writing him letters and daydreaming about a life away from her parents.

But, for a while, it was another lonely experience. Claudia was the only student from the suburbs, and because of train schedules and parental control, she was unable to participate in many of the social activities that involved the other students. That is, until she began to use the lack of communication to her advantage, and realized she could be independent without divulging much of anything to her parents. She began to maintain her choice of friends without the usual parental interference, and in time, Claudia had several close companions. Shannon's Father owned a great deal of real estate in the Metropolitan area, and she was interesting and assertive, and knew every inch of the City... Mitzi's family owned a 6 bedroom apartment on Park Avenue, and a house in East Hampton, where Claudia spent many fun-filled days and nights, experiences that helped broaden Claudia's knowledge of how to work the social register instead of being a slave to the status quo. Her best friend, Doreen, who was a runway model for a famous dress designer, awakened Claudia's great sense of humor, so, through all three of these women, Claudia expanded her boundaries... instead of her command appearances at the Stork Club or meeting under the clock at the Biltmore, she drank cocktails at quirky bars, explored all the fabulous museums, attended off-beat plays, was thrilled with the operas, ballets and symphonies that she chose to attend, combed the beaches, and began to realize how much fun and distinctively different life could be when _she_ made the decisions for her life.

Then, at Thanksgiving break, Craig ended their relationship, stating he had met someone else at his college. It was another devastating loss to Claudia. She again pondered the question if everyone she loved would be taken from her... and relived the grief she felt when Jamie had been killed. However she was now able to handle these dark thoughts with a more mature attitude, and during the next year, her friends were a support to her and helped her to cultivate a diverse dating life... and a fairly secret dating life that forestalled the usual humiliation of her Father's cultural slurs. She would stay in the City at one of her girlfriend's homes, and even by herself at the Park Avenue apartment, overcoming her fear of being alone. She dated at West Point, met a likeable boy from Harvard, and began to realize that she had something about her that other people liked... but was not sure what it was, and was unsure that it was going to last.

7

In December, 1952, the dreaded day came for Claudia when she had to don the white silk organza gown, the strand of pearls, the long white kid gloves, the white satin shoes, and the little diamond tiara her mother fabricated had been handed down to her by her French grandmother! It was her sophomore year of college, she was eighteen, and even she knew how attractive she had become. Two of her classmates, including her friend, Mitzi, were "coming out" at the "Infirmary" Christmas Ball (the 19th Annual Debutante Cotillion) held, as always, at the Waldorf-Astoria Grand Ballroom.

Since Claudia's early childhood, Elizabeth had worked with her daughter toward this day... not only the dancing lessons, the focus on staying slim, the comportment lessons, but also had educated her about the gossip mongers who provided the press with a steady diet of nasty debutante stories. She harped on the viciousness of the press, their vulgarity and their vengefulness. From time to time, she would pull out her scrapbook of articles about "chubby" Babsy Munroe and the tainted reputation of Mimsy Hanover to prove to Claudia how the press could make or break one's coming out.

Claudia stood in front of the mirror staring at her image... Her dress was quite beautiful, she had to admit... It had a modest strapless bodice embroidered with seed pearls, and layers of organza over the crinoline made her waist look very small. She liked that but she loathed the entire concept of being a debutante! Wasn't America supposed to be a nation of equality? Why should she get her picture in the paper, and become "famous" just because her Father and Mother had money and pushed her into a class of people she found to be highly judgmental, incredibly stuffy and pompous to say nothing about their arrogance and derisive attitudes toward the "lower classes."

"Just look at me!" she murmured contemptuously... and in a mocking tone, went on to say, "Now, remember, Claudia, be sure to bow correctly, be sure your gestures are feminine and proper, and be sure to say 'fiddle-faddle' at least twelve times tonight while fluttering your eyelashes!" The absurdity of the moment made her laugh and at that instant Elizabeth floated into the room, looking radiant and "perfect" in her Molly Parness gown, her perfectly coiffed hair, professionally applied makeup, nails newly manicured and her body still tingling from the most sensuous massage. Elizabeth had been able to determine what the decorations were to be at the Ball... white dipped smilax with pink twinkling lights...and was able to pick out the perfect shade of pink shantung for her dress, a long sheath that accentuated her fabulous and hard won figure. The color warmed her skin tones and intensified the color of her eyes. Her hair was still very black (with the help of her hairdresser) with a perfectly placed white segment framing her extraordinary and wrinkle-free face

"My darling daughter, you are breathtaking! You surely will be the *most* beautiful young girl tonight! The press will not be able to resist your many charms, and I am sure you will be selected to be in Cholly Knickerbocker's column as the deb of the year!"

The positive assessment by her Mother greatly surprised and pleased Claudia and, smiling sweetly, she gave her Mother a very light hug, complimenting her on her beautiful appearance. She knew better than to voice any of her concerns about this night. For years she had suffered in silence through all of the "preparations"...she was aware from an early age that arguing with her Mother made things worse for her... she had never felt part of the family, never felt that her existence was recognized or that her opinions were heard or that they were important. Claudia was highly intelligent, and had become socially aware. The several civic volunteer jobs she did as part of the publicity for inclusion in the social register had been a revelation to her. In one such setting, she helped out in a shelter for unwed mothers, (which was particularly upsetting to her parents) and became acquainted with a plethora of social problems, including poverty, abuse, family dysfunctions that appalled her, sexual practices that shocked her and witnessed a side of life she did not know existed. At home, during the endless formal dinners, she began to talk about becoming a doctor that infuriated her father and she was forced to resign from the shelter and work instead in the office of the local Women's Club where she felt suffocated and useless.

Another of her volunteer jobs included a children's day care. Recently, there had been a dialogue about the kibbutz system in Israel. This led to a further discussion of the Jewish state, and how more than six million Jews had been exterminated during World War II by the Nazi's. Claudia was appalled! She had heard many disparaging remarks about Jews in her milieu... her father referred to them as "kikes" and often said that Hitler was smart. Her teachers and school friends were outspoken about the desirability of excluding Jews from any social affairs. Claudia had always been sensitive to rejection and also to "exclusion" because of what had happened to her in the sixth grade. Almost all the people she knew were White Anglo Saxon Protestants, and as a religious Catholic she was often ridiculed or shunned. She understood that as a Catholic, it was unusual for her to be included in the social register, and remembered many conversations between her parents as to whether she should be presented at the Gotham Ball (which was for Catholics) or at the Infirmary Ball (which had a smattering of Catholics but was largely a WASP organization.) She hated the arguments, but hated the premise of the arguments even more. She thought the whole thing was terribly confusing, because, after all, what difference did it make what religion you were! She often pondered how anyone involved in a religion, believing in the unconditional love of God, could want to hurt or demean another human being based solely on what religion they were. She remembered in prep school, a so-called friend of hers had invited her to a church rally. She was taken to a "bible believing

Christian church" and heard the "minister" refer to the Pope as the anti-Christ, and Catholics as cult worshippers, and Jews as unclean, and anyone who was not "born again" as unbelievers who would burn in hell. Claudia had been very upset about this incident, and sought counsel from a priest, but he, too, denigrated other religions in the lecture to her about staying away from "those fundamentalists" and to regard her religion as the "only true religion", so she decided that she would get to know God on her own terms without the clergy. Her parents never knew of her resolutions, and she obediently attended church outwardly accepting its institutionalism. But in her heart and in her spirit, she began a journey to find a one-to-one *relationship* with a loving and just God.

Elizabeth had finished her thorough inspection of Claudia and announced that the limousine was waiting. *Well, thought Claudia, here goes. It will be over soon and I can begin to live my life differently.... I hope.*

BOOK II

Gerald Parker
And
His Wife, Claudia

...and God, please help me be a good wife, teach me to love my husband the way he needs to be loved.

PROLOGUE

Gerald Parker stood in front of James Fitzpatrick's enormous, intricately carved executive desk in the middle of a vast walnut paneled office with floor to ceiling windows, plush oriental rugs, and large, comfortable groupings of tapestry covered chairs, Queen Anne tables topped with Stiffel lamps...and even Gerald with his limited knowledge of art recognized what he assumed were priceless hangings of well-known artists.

"Good morning, Mr. Fitzpatrick. As you've probably guessed, I'm Gerald Parker." Gerald extended his arm for a handshake and it hung in the air as James stood up slowly, ignored the invitation of a handshake, and waved Gerald to a large chair in front of his desk. As James stretched to his full height, he was aware that Gerald was slightly taller than he was, but very thin and not at all well- built. He was, however, wearing a Brooks Brother suit, and James wondered how he could afford this on such a paltry salary.

"Yes, I'm aware of who you are, Mr. Parker... may I offer you some coffee? A drink?"

"A cup of coffee would be nice... black...please."

James buzzed his secretary and ordered two coffees. James thoroughly disliked Gerald's persona... he was neither handsome nor manly looking... He decried Gerald's impoverished background as nothing more than a ploy to gain control of Claudia's anticipated fortune... He had an aversion to Gerald's chosen profession in advertising/marketing ... but more than all these combined, Mr. Fitzpatrick disliked Gerald's Jewishness. James fervently wanted his daughter to marry within her culture, specifically an Irish Catholic man of *his* choosing. What few people knew about James was that underneath his seemingly profane and nefarious capers, he had an unswerving passion about his Irish Catholic heritage. As a child, he had heard all the stories, and, in some cases, witnessed, first hand, the misery, pathos and intense suffering that the Irish immigrants endured in the face of bigotry and frightening discrimination. He had done an extensive investigation on Gerald Parker... this man standing before him had no depth... he was not a person who could see it to the end.

"Gerald, I suppose I should thank you for coming here this morning. What's on your mind? Your call to me for this meeting was somewhat of a surprise."

"Well, Sir, I guess you know I've asked Claudia to marry me. I love her very much and think we could have a good life together. But Claudia tells me you are opposed to the marriage and I thought if I could meet with you perhaps we could talk things over and you could see that all I want is Claudia's happiness." Gerald had rehearsed this opening speech for days, with input from his brother, his brother's wife and his Mother.

Unfortunately, he did not know that Mr. Fitzpatrick did not give a rat's ass about Claudia's happiness... he was very angry that his expectations were being ignored and Gerald Parker definitely did not meet any of his expectations. After all the money he had spent on Claudia's "gentility" and all the money he spent on his wife's demands for Claudia's climb into the social register, he was not about to relinquish her to this inferior piece of humanity. His daughter was throwing her life away... she had forgotten who she was!

"You are correct, Mr. Parker, in your assessment that I am opposed to the marriage. I don't like anything about you... not your background, not your religion, or *lack* of it... not your career preference, not anything, Gerald. So, I am prepared to give you this check and ask that you completely disappear from Claudia's life." James now extended his arm and pushed a check across the desk toward Gerald.

"This check is for $2500. Is that all Claudia is worth to you Mr. Fitzpatrick?"

James was infuriated... but felt vindicated... all this bastard Jew wanted was money! Without any display of emotion, he reached inside his top desk drawer, pulled out a large checkbook and hurriedly scribbled a check.

"I'm not going to play games today, Gerald... so I'm giving you a check for ten thousand dollars... That's as high as I will go. This has nothing to do with how valuable Claudia is to me, but it has everything to do with what you state is Claudia's happiness. You say that is what you want?"

"Yes sir, but..."

"If you want her happiness, Gerald, take the money. Otherwise she will never see me again, she will receive no inheritance, no gifts of any kind, and that will make her very *un*happy... and possibly you, too, I might add! Do you understand, Gerald?" James eyes were incredibly readable. Gerald saw profound anger and raw power in those eyes, and knew that any further discussion was futile.

"I don't know what to say, Mr. Fitzpatrick. I naturally had hoped for a different outcome. I will talk this over with Claudia and let her make the decision, but no matter what the decision, I will not take your money." Gerald stood, mumbled a "goodbye", and left the office. He never disclosed any part of his visit to Claudia.

James sat there in deep thought for a long time after Gerald left the office. He was not used to "failing" and he was known for his tenaciousness.... So, that day, James made a decision that he would confine his intractability to his communication with Claudia... she was pliable, sensitive and compassionate and he would devise a plan... after all, wasn't he the master of manipulation?

1

Claudia had met Gerald in a most unexpected way. After the years of wasting time in college, her Father insisted that she attend a secretarial school to prepare for a job. She had begged him to allow her to attend St. Anne's Nursing School, but he threatened to disown her if she dared "devote her life emptying bedpans." So, she dutifully took the secretarial course, hating every minute of it, but was surprised and thrilled when she landed a job the next year in an Advertising/Marketing firm. Although she had an active social life, she remained uninterested in the approved list of men she dated... they were pretentious and conceited. So, when she met Gerald Parker at work, it was refreshing... she thought of him as creative, sensitive, humorous and intelligent... and he pursued her purposefully which, to a young woman in such need of love, was quite flattering ... so Gerald became her knight in shining armor.

Three months after joining the marketing firm, Gerald had asked her to join him in having a drink after work. It was the beginning. From then on, always on Friday nights, they would go to a little bar on Lexington Avenue and sit for hours nursing a beer, talking, laughing, telling stories of their childhoods, gossiping about their colleagues at work and analyzing the relationships. Occasionally, if Gerald could afford it, he would splurge and take her to the Copa, or to the Embers to listen to the legendary jazz pianist, George Shearing, sometimes to their favorite Japanese restaurant for sukiyaki, and when he was "flush", they would go to a Broadway show or the ballet. Wherever they would go, it was mandatory to catch the New York Central 1:10 am train... it was the last train of the night and they would hold hands, sitting huddled together on the wicker style seats. Gerald would get off at Mountain Hills, while Claudia went further north to Marindale, usually the only person getting off the train at almost 2 AM, and scurrying through the dimly lit underground tunnel until she finally reached her parked car in the lot next to the station. In the many months they dated, Gerald had never kissed her, nor had he shown any affection, which confused Claudia. She loved to be kissed and cuddled... in the past most of her dates were quite aggressive and she usually ended up fighting them off, and although she was glad that Gerald "respected" her, she felt a sense of rejection... a glimmer of loneliness.

Then, in October their relationship changed dramatically. Her dear friend, Mitzi, had become engaged, and had invited them to the Hamptons for a weekend celebration and party. On Saturday night, while they were dancing, Gerald had begun to kiss her hair, and to run his hands up and down her almost bare back. They went outside for air and standing on the large wrap-around porch Gerald suddenly pulled her close and kissed her passionately for a long time. Claudia was unrestrained in returning his passion and they sat on the oversized wicker sofa oblivious to anything but each other for a long time while Gerald declared his love for her. She felt safe and cared for and lying in the upper bunk of the uncomfortable bed that night listening to her three other college friends snore, cough, sneeze and snort, Claudia silently replayed every moment, every word that was spoken by her new love until dawn began to filter through the Venetian blinds.

True to his decision, James had ranted, railed, cried, cajoled, made financial promises, and threatened Claudia for the next six months on a daily basis. He was a seasoned bully and knew how to ride roughshod over people when he wanted his way. The sessions with Claudia vacillated between loud, angry tirades to sessions of tearful begging... always ending with the phrase, "you will no longer receive a penny from me if you marry that Jew!"

Some who knew him thought that James was reliving his son's death, and did not want to lose another child. Little did they know that it was strictly the challenge that drove him... when Claudia refused his request to break off the relationship with Gerald, it was as if she had thrown down the gauntlet ... he both admired her spirit and at the same time vowed to break that spirit. She sought solace from her parish priest, but he supported her Father, and informed Claudia that he would not officiate at her wedding, nor could any other priest officiate at any marriage to a non-Catholic in *his* church. The problems bonded Claudia and Gerald. Originally, the couple had planned to wait a year after Gerald proposed marriage, but home life was so hellish for Claudia, that they moved the wedding date forward from October to May. In April, Claudia left home and went to live at a hotel until the wedding took place. And then the day arrived... but not before James called Claudia at the hotel with one last ploy.

■ ■ ■

Claudia put the finishing touches on her makeup.... then she put the pearls around her neck... They were beautiful, a precious gift from Gerald. She had seen incredible jewels in her lifetime, even in her own family, but these were so special to her, not at all like the pearls she had to wear as a debutante. Earlier in the day, she had received a phone call from her future sister-in-law...

"Claudia, I'm in the lobby and have a delivery for you. Can I bring it up now?"

"Of course, Sophie... What is it that you have?"

"A lovely surprise.... something for your wedding."

Sophie stayed while Claudia opened the long, thin box. "Oh how beautiful!"

"Ohhhh, they are beautiful," exclaimed Sophie. "I'm so glad Gerald got you what I told him to get!"

The remark instantly stung, but Claudia merely looked at Sophie and said, "Thank you Sophie for bringing these to me."

"Well, you know that the groom can't see the bride before the ceremony!"

Sophie talked in lecture form most of the time, very emphatically and with firm gestures that precluded any disagreement. Claudia wished that Gerald had given her the gift himself last night when he was visiting. But, within minutes she recovered her equanimity and original gratefulness for Gerald's generosity. And now, with the pearls in place, she was ready to leave for the Cathedral. But, at that moment she was startled by the ringing of the phone. Her dear childhood friend, Joanie Finnegan, now her Matron of Honor, put her hand over the receiver.

"It's your Father, Claudia. Do you want to take it?"

Her heart leaped with anticipation. "He's going to come to my wedding", she thought.

"Hello, Daddy..."

"Claudia, I have one last request. Please do not do this." James Fitzpatrick was sobbing, pleading... "Please, Claudia, do not go to that church.... because if you walk down that aisle and marry that man, you will hear a gun-shot in the back of the Church, and that will be me killing myself!"

■ ■ ■

As they stood at the Grand Hotel registration desk, Claudia felt painfully shy and embarrassed. Although she assumed her most sophisticated attitude, she was sure all eyes were upon them and that many were snickering at the obvious newlywed status. While Gerald was registering, Claudia mentally replayed the ceremony. When she had arrived at the church, she had been extremely anxious as she waited quietly and alone with Joanie... her thoughts were chaotic... "What am I doing?" "Where is my Father... is he really going to shoot himself?" "Should I tell someone?" "I don't know what to do..." "Should I go through with this?" "Do I really love Gerald... love him more than my Father?" "Daddy won't do anything bad... I know he won't... he's not crazy, and there must be some part of him that loves me..." "No, he's never said he loves me... he has never even given me a hug..." "Maybe he'll shoot me..."

The first strains of Mendelsohn's Wedding March were then being loudly but regally performed on the massive organ by some stranger she had never met... all part of the wedding "package" the Cathedral had offered her for a what she thought was a very high price. Joanie gave her a hug and whispered, "It's going to be fine, Claud... follow me."

Claudia had meticulously planned every detail of her wedding. It wasn't going to be the opulent occasion like her sister Connie had for her wedding, but she was going to have an elegant and gracious event for the few that were brave enough to attend. She had gone to Saks Fifth Avenue for her wedding dress and chose an ivory waltz length gown of peau-de-soie, trimmed with Belgium lace, and in place of a veil, had a custom made vintage inspired headpiece made of the same lace imbedded with seed pearls with a short face veil. The dress had a full skirt in the popular style of the day covering several crinolines, that accentuated her 21-inch waist, and the softly rounded neck with the exquisite lace trim complimented her lovely skin tones and provided the perfect backdrop for the pearls Gerald had given her. She had chosen the small cathedral Chapel for the ceremony... it was perfect... beautiful, small, intimate and peaceful. Joanie Finnegan's brother, John, had just become a priest and agreed to officiate. She had asked Connie's husband to walk her down the aisle as was the custom of the day, but when he refused, she decided to go it alone! For the "reception," she had coordinated all the details with the hotel management... they would have champagne and hors d'oeuvres, and the suite she was now occupying was large enough for the 15 to 20 guests who would be present. Although all of this was done with a sense of bravado, there were always those nagging feelings of disgrace, the humiliation of being denied a marriage in her own church, the gossip mongers that she knew were busy chattering, but most of all she resented the people who said they loved God but hated a man because he was Jewish. Had these people not made the connection of Mary, the Mother of Jesus being Jewish? Did they think the holocaust she had heard so much about was justified? And, what about Gerald's Mother... this was her son, whom she loved, being mal-treated by these rich Catholic people.

As she began the slow walk down the aisle, her thoughts were still racing, and she waited to hear the gunshot... but then the short ceremony was over and she was aware that everyone was crying, including the priest. "Everyone knows," she thought... "Everyone is crying because of what I have done..."

Claudia was glad to escape into the elevator. When they reached their room, Gerald immediately enfolded her in his arms, and within seconds both were unambiguous in their desire for each other. In the next seven days of their honeymoon they exhausted themselves in each other's pleasure. They were well suited sexually... and this added to the strong bond of friendship that had coalesced in the harrowing months prior to the wedding.

On the last day of their trip, Claudia awoke early and quietly viewed the sun-filled room. It was very large and furnished exquisitely in mauves, blues and ivory... her favorite colors. The hotel had been chosen by the Father of her college friend, Mitzi. As a wedding gift he had paid for the entire hotel bill! Claudia was amazed and grateful not only for the awesome monetary generosity, but for the recognition and silent endorsement of her marriage from a person her Father's age.

Gerald was stirring... Claudia snuggled into his arms and began to weep, softly.

"Thank you Gerald, for the most wonderful honeymoon a woman could have."

"What is it sweetheart? Why are you crying?" Gerald was concerned. What had he done wrong?

"Gerald, I love you so much. I am so happy!"

"I love you more, my darling ... but that's no reason to cry."

"It is for me, Gerald. Promise me...*really* promise me that you will never leave me. So many people I have loved have gone ... I sometimes think I am a jinx. Please don't ever abandon me ... be my friend forever..."

Gerald interrupted her... "Claudia, I've never been happier than I am now... I couldn't conceive of ever leaving you. I will love you forever, no matter what happens. We will always be together and you'll never be able to get rid of me!" He jumped out of bed and caught her up in his arms and they danced around the room laughing and happy, secure in the knowledge that theirs was a love never to be destroyed.

2

The young couple had been lucky to find a studio apartment in Brooklyn Heights, only blocks from the water, for a very affordable rent. It was quite small and very dark, but, in the beginning, neither seemed to notice. Claudia was giddy with her new found freedom. She and Gerald rode the subway together, took long walks near the water, made the rounds of the many restaurants and shops in the area, and on weekends, spent most of their time in passionate love making. In June, Claudia was disappointed when she got her period, and thought a great deal more about her inability to have children. Gerald became frantic when she exhibited two days of intense pain and vomiting. Claudia tried to reassure him that this was normal for her, but he insisted a doctor come and examine her. Claudia was mortified to be causing such a fuss, but was relieved when the doctor lectured her about getting some help. "You don't have to suffer like this, Claudia. I am going to give you some pain pills, and I want to see you in my office when your menses cease." The pills were wonderful... they made Claudia feel happy and without pain... and she wondered why no one had ever helped her before.

Two days later, a development occurred that thrilled and surprised her. Elizabeth Fitzpatrick telephoned her daughter and described a lovely garden apartment she had seen in Eastdale, a small community in Westchester County only a few miles from where Claudia had lived all her life. Elizabeth explained that she felt it would be safer for Claudia to live in this area, that the apartment was large and airy, and that she would subsidize the rent. The apartment was currently occupied by a friend's daughter, who would be moving in three months. "Don't rush to make the decision... You have time to talk it over with Gerald, but I think you would be wise to move from the city."

Claudia was touched by her Mother's concern. It was a new and unfamiliar type of communication, but although it was pleasant, it was also somewhat anxiety producing. Claudia had quickly become disenchanted with the small, dark Brooklyn apartment. There was no air conditioning, and the summer humidity was suffocating... the only window was in the living room and it was smack up against another building. The landlord would not fix the broken stove and she had to cook on a hot plate. And, worst of all, there were bugs in the tiny Pullman kitchen that Claudia had never seen before and they were positively disgusting! She excitedly told Gerald about the call from her Mother. He was silent for what seemed a long time, and then responded that he was at a loss to understand why Claudia would want to live near her parents after the way they treated her. Claudia said no more to him about the call, hoping that he would rethink his answer and that they could discuss it further in the coming weeks.

Gerald's family had a small cottage on the Jersey Shore, and the couple made plans to spend their two weeks summer vacation there. It would certainly be a blessing to get away from the oppressive heat and humidity of the city.

The second week of their vacation at the Shore, there was a family meeting that shocked and angered Claudia. Present, were Gerald's parents, his obnoxious brother Clay and his wife Sophie, his older sister, Rosie and her husband, Tom, and, of course, Claudia and Gerald. Claudia thoroughly disliked Gerald's brother, she barely knew the sister Rosie, and had only met Tom one time at the wedding. The meeting was an "intervention" to prevent Gerald and Claudia from moving to Westchester County, and more importantly, to tell the Fitzpatrick's to "stick it" as far as the subsidy was concerned. Claudia was upset and extremely hurt that Gerald had talked with them about a subject that she felt was a private matter, and that he had not discussed it further with her, but had gone to all of his family and obviously discussed the matter in depth with them. She had been ambushed, and she did not like it. Claudia would soon realize this was the beginning of a pattern in their marriage... Gerald did not like discussing things with her. He particularly disliked delving into feelings and avoided confrontations and despite the group therapy they would eventually attend, this never changed.

The "intervention" had lasted more than an hour. After it was over, everyone went their own way and Claudia refrained from any further discussion with Gerald that night, except to express her disagreement with the outcome.

When Claudia went to the doctor after arriving home from their "vacation," she found out she was newly pregnant. She was thrilled and scared.... now, more than ever, she wanted to be in her old surroundings, have a doctor with whom she was familiar, be around people she knew, have room for the baby, and above all, get out of the dark, cramped, "buggy" apartment. In the following weeks, Gerald was aware of her morning sickness, watching her retch standing between the subway cars, and vomit when they pulled into Times Square being assailed with the smell of garlic, orange juice, popcorn and sweat. It was a very hot summer, and by the end of September, Gerald came to her and said he had thought things over and decided they should move to Eastdale. He had talked to a friend at work who was getting married, and the friend was really excited to sub-let their Brooklyn apartment. There it was... all tied up in a neat package, and Claudia was reminded that this was a final decision and they need not talk about it again. So, the first week of October, they moved to their new, large, bright, airy apartment in Westchester County...they were now officially suburbanites.

Claudia was ecstatically happy and experienced a fledging sense of joy and gratefulness. Her Mother gave them money to buy some needed furniture and carpeting, and they both had fun shopping. Gerald's family bought them a bedroom set and Claudia was most grateful for this. Her friends bought them a baby bassinette and decorated it beautifully and she was treated to maternity clothes, a baby shower and a "used" new car which granted her untold freedom. Teaching Gerald to drive was a chore, but they got through that without threatening divorce. Claudia stopped working the end of December... she was very large and very uncomfortable, and wondered why she had gained so much weight... so far, 60 pounds and the baby was not due until March, maybe the first of April.

It was the second week in March that she experienced the most intense pain ever. She was diagnosed with kidney stones and spent two days in the hospital. The only bed available was in the maternity wing, next to the delivery room, and Claudia listened to the screams of childbirth with increasing fear and anxiety. The "stone" was passed and she went home until a week later, when her first born child, a boy, entered their world.... weighing in at nine and one-half pounds. It had been a 9 hour labor in a dimly lit room with only a nurse monitoring her. After 3-4 hours of labor, they gave her a drug to induce labor which greatly intensified her pain, and finally they gave her a drug that obliterated her memory. The next day when Gerald was finally allowed to see her, he enfolded her in his arms and they cried together from love, relief, and happiness. Claudia still had not seen her baby.

3

The greatest baby gift she received was from her Mother who had hired a baby nurse to assist Claudia for two weeks. It was a god-send! Claudia had never been around a baby, knew nothing at all about bathing or feeding, and would have been awake 24 hours a day monitoring the noises, gurglings and cries of her newborn. At the end of the 2 weeks, Claudia's confidence had greatly increased under the tutelage of the angelic nurse, and she was rested and healed enough from birthing such a large baby so that she could assume the staggering responsibility of her first-born.

Within four weeks, she had regained her marvelous figure. The 78 pounds she had gained during her pregnancy had miraculously disappeared and although she was not at her original weight of 106 pounds when she married, she was pleased to be a healthier weight of 115 pounds which looked far better on her 5 foot 7 inch frame. After the initial shock of responsibility, she was reveling in exploring baby David, voraciously ingesting every word that Dr. Spock ever wrote. She drank great quantities of coffee, realizing it helped to suppress her appetite and helped to keep her awake for the middle of the night feedings.

Five months after little David's birth, Elizabeth Fitzpatrick had her first major heart attack. Claudia was racked with guilt... and the guilt was fed by those family and friends who knew the history of the chaos surrounding "the wedding." Her sister, Connie, flew in from California to take charge and on several occasions made indirect sarcastic remarks to Claudia, which was an established dysfunctional communication pattern within the Fitzpatrick family. With others, Connie was more direct, making judgmental and accusatory remarks about "all the stress Mother endured prior to that ridiculous wedding."

When Connie decided to go home after 2 weeks, Claudia was summoned to the house... it was explained to her that Elizabeth was "frightened" to be alone in such a big house with the fairly new staff of servants. Maida, a recent Latvian immigrant was the part time cook, and Jorge and Maria, were a young couple from Cuba who polished, repaired, cleaned and organized the entire house and grounds. Elizabeth was heard to loudly proclaim, "I am surrounded by foreigners who can't speak English, and I am terrified they will kill me!" To assuage her guilt, Claudia agreed to visit Elizabeth daily, including one day over the weekend so her Father would not miss his golf game.

The schedule was absurd. The "visits" became very lengthy and exhausting. Every morning, after attending to Gerald's minor needs, Claudia would bathe, dress and feed the baby, put baby supplies for the day into her carry bag including the newly sterilized bottles she had made up the night before, then the car bed, the small playpen and toys. The day was spent with her Mother, reading to her, making her lunch (Elizabeth was afraid the "dour and ferocious" cook would put poison in her food), writing letters for her, doing her personal laundry, listening to her tearful stories laced with paranoia and suicidal ideation, plus taking care of her baby, leaving at 3 PM to rush home, shower, redress herself, cook a gourmet dinner for Gerald, clean up their apartment, feed and prepare David for bed, eat dinner with Gerald who usually had too much to drink, and drop into bed at night feeling that there was something wrong but not knowing what. She was bewildered when her sister, Connie, refused to visit in order to provide Claudia with respite care... she thought about how close Connie and her Mother had always been, and was sure that her Mother felt hurt... and she was irritated that her Father never thought to spend more time with his wife, and refused to hire any of the home health nurses that Claudia had located. Claudia could not discuss anything pertaining to the family situation with Gerald... his response was always the same.... criticism or silence and rejection, usually in the form of walking out of the room, or picking up a newspaper to read. She began to feel that Gerald did not value her... he was so uncommunicative... and she characteristically reacted to these negative feelings with self-recrimination, and feelings of inadequacy. She was trying to please Gerald.... she loved him, but recognized, with her, he was becoming more and more remote... she was slowly being excluded from his life, and soon he might leave? On weekends, there were frequent parties, always with Gerald's friends. He lived for these times... he was the center of attention, he and his brother playing off of each other with their humor, entertaining everyone present. Claudia hated the parties... they were boring... everyone making small talk... gossiping...it was all so meaningless... and she hated the copious amounts of alcohol they all consumed. She would sit quietly, laughing at the appropriate times, but underneath the mask she wore, there was a terrible loneliness...she did not feel much joy.

With a few exceptions, she did not like Gerald's friends, and was never able to cultivate any positive feelings for his brother and sister in law. She found their extroverted and frequent humor denigrating toward others.... always directed toward the disenfranchised, making fun of those they considered less intelligent, less sophisticated and urbane and impugning those who had gone to "inferior" colleges. It was the same sarcastic, self-serving humor that was her Father's hallmark. It was made very clear that Claudia was an outsider in this group of fourteen close friends, and although she worked hard to fit in, she often found herself unable to connect with them. Gerald's brother and his wife were the self- appointed "leaders of the pack," and she remembered in later years, the two times that Gerald cried bitterly because he was unable to express his own ideas... he felt overwhelmed by their forceful and intrusive personalities... but that was when he was young, and as he matured, he learned how to repress any feelings that would necessitate change.

Claudia and Gerald also entertained a great deal... she was a gourmet cook, and had great panache as a hostess... she liked being at home so that when Gerald had too much to drink, they would not have to drive. At other times they would go out to dinner, most of the time with the same friends, spend too much money and stop off at a favorite club or lounge for nightcaps that would result in several of the crowd getting drunk... often this was Gerald, who would slur his words, vomit, and become very self- absorbed and introverted.

Claudia was astonished when she became pregnant with her second child when David was 9 months old. Gerald was not pleased, and his drinking increased. Claudia reprised the morning sickness, but continued her hectic visiting schedule with her Mother... she was grateful for the four weeks she spent at home after her second son, Matthew, was born weighing in at just under 10 pounds. Her doctor and hospital experience had not improved with this second birth, and she found out through hospital gossip that her doctor was an "alcoholic." Her labor this time had lasted over 22 hours and Matthew's face was bruised...a blackish eye and cuts on his face which looked quite swollen... and his head somewhat misshapen. When she summoned up all her courage and haltingly asked her doctor about this, his behavior became loud and bizarre and he created quite a scene that frightened Claudia. The same baby nurse was hired by her Mother, which was even more of a blessing than before...Claudia was exhausted and Gerald was very involved at work... he had a new job and needed his sleep to be fresh and bright. The effects of the prior night's martinis were both a blessing and a curse...Gerald fell into an alcohol induced sleep early in the evening... deep and undisturbed by any noise around him... so when he woke in the morning, he was refreshed and ready for his busy days. Any care of the children was left to Claudia... that was the rule of the times in which they lived.

She continued to see her Mother as often as possible, but it was twice as difficult with 2 babies. She continually fought the exhaustion by consuming huge amounts of coffee, smoking incessantly, snacking on high carbohydrate, high sugar foods... and ate most of her meals on the run, if she ate at all. Her whole life was dedicated to being the best Mother she could be and the best wife, and the best daughter...but somehow Claudia felt she failed at all these roles.

When Matthew was six months old, James Fitzpatrick finally sold the huge family home, moved his wife and one servant to a large, rambling apartment on the grounds of his favorite country club. It relieved Claudia from her impossible schedule, but then, when Matthew was just 11 months old, she discovered she was again pregnant.

Gerald hated the apartment, he hated the cramped lifestyle, he hated the responsibility of such a burgeoning family, but most of all he hated the promise he had made to Claudia, when they married, to honor her Irish Catholic mandates regarding birth control... but he didn't have to worry... Within weeks of her diagnosis, she miscarried. There was hardly any discussion of this event...little emotionalism, and possibly a sigh of relief on the part of Gerald.

Two months after her miscarriage, Elizabeth Fitzpatrick made it possible for Claudia and family to move to Long Island, to a tract housing complex like the ones that were springing up all over the Eastern seaboard to house the post WW2 booming population. If truth were known, Elizabeth had grown tired of Claudia and the monotony of the children. It was worth the down payment she gave to Claudia to move the 100 miles to the South.

4

Claudia had never seen houses like the one they moved into. It was exactly like the one next door... and all the way down the street. She worked her decorating magic inside, and wickedly decided to paint the outside a distinctive light turquoise color, which caused raised eyebrows in the neighborhood. She was initially happy to be on her own, and to have a house where she could use her creative abilities. Gerald seemed better for a while... possibly because he left at 7 AM and did not arrive home at night until 7 PM. and his only family "duty" was to kiss the children goodnight.... Claudia had already fed them, bathed them and tucked them into their beds. Gerald was then free to attack his martinis, enjoy the gourmet meal Claudia had prepared, always with a bottle of wine... and regale her with amusing stories pertaining to work. Gerald had become indispensable to his company and began to travel frequently. He loved it... the freedom was exhilarating to him, and each time he scheduled a trip, he would try to work it to be away for at least 2 weeks. Gerald's mother became Claudia's closest companion.... Claudia liked her a great deal, and was grateful for her presence and help with the children. There were several crises with the children... as there always is... and they seemed to occur whenever Gerald was away. The first was when they discovered David had "a hole in his heart" and had to be admitted for testing to the children's hospital in a neighboring city. It was a traumatic time for everyone...

even Gerald who arrived home a week later. The next incident concerned Matthew who was admitted to the hospital because he was bleeding from his penis. Claudia, as usual, drove to the hospital alone while her Mother-in-Law took over at home. Gerald arrived home 4 days later. Then when Matthew had to have an emergency tonsillectomy, Gerald arrived home 10 days later. There were other similar incidents, and Claudia weathered them all with strength, equanimity, and courage... but the incongruity of these incidents only served to increase Claudia's negative self-image... she was not able to see the strength and courage, but instead felt inadequate and lonely. And then, to the surprise of all, Claudia was pregnant again. It was a catastrophic time... Gerald was very unhappy... He handled it in his usual non-communicative manner, and seemed to travel even more. This time, Claudia chose to have the baby at a Catholic Hospital in New York City with a wonderful new doctor in attendance, and she was thrilled and surprised when her delivery room nurse turned out to be an old classmate of hers from Prep School... it was a happy experience, and Claudia enjoyed the pregnancy, which was monitored very closely...especially her weight and diet. On a Thursday night, Gerald helped Claudia check into the hospital at 10 PM for the induced birth. When her time was near, the staff tried to find Gerald who had disappeared, but he could not be located and he missed the natural birth which he had agreed to be part of... it was never clear where he went. Claudia's third son, Zach, made his appearance in the easiest birth to date. Unfortunately, he had a breathing problem, and it was ten days before he was able to leave the incubator and go home. It was an unexpected blessing for Claudia who stayed with him in the hospital during that time, and when she finally arrived home she was well rested and revitalized. From the beginning, Zach was a tranquil, calm and delightful child. Although Gerald had been upset about the baby, he was happy with his job and loved the traveling that afforded him freedom... seemingly, he became more relaxed and content at home.

That fateful day when the assassination of President John F. Kennedy occurred, Claudia was drinking her 8th cup of coffee in the newly decorated kitchen she had designed and executed. She was on a perpetual diet, and was using coffee to quell her appetite but suddenly the room began to spin, her head was foggy and she couldn't think straight, she broke out in a cold sweat, her legs felt rubbery so that she fell to the floor, she was nauseated, her heart was pounding at an odd rate, and she began to tremble. Later, when she saw her doctor, she added to these symptoms that she felt intense inner trembling. After a rather cursory examination, he diagnosed Claudia as being depressed with anxiety and gave her 2 prescriptions.... an antidepressant and a tranquilizer and referred her to a psychiatrist. Claudia did not know what depression was... she told the doctor that she had been feeling good...she was unaware of having the "blues" which was all she had ever heard of "depression." Attempts to question the doctor further fell on deaf ears. His reply to her was that the psychiatrist would fill in the details, that he was only a family doctor and not trained in psychiatric issues. But he was trained to give Claudia the 2 prescriptions? He did mention to her on the way out of the office that the recent birth of her son, Zach might have caused a hormonal reaction that can cause depression.

Claudia dutifully went to the psychiatrist alone... Gerald, as usual, was "very busy"... so she characteristically overcame her fear and trepidation and traveled the 30 odd miles to a neighboring town well known as the "millionaire mile"... and easily found the large Georgian style home. To the left of the circular drive, she noticed there was a separate entrance marked "patient entrance." With a false confidence, she walked up the winding walkway, and reached the door that had a "please enter" sign. No one was around when she walked into the large, light, airy room with floor to ceiling windows, flowery furniture... an oversized sofa, three amply stuffed chairs, a large desk in the corner surrounded by floor to ceiling bookcases. There were several tables with large lamps that cast a soft glow throughout the room, and she recognized the familiar muted music... it was Montovani playing *"Charmaine"*... a favorite of hers that caused an instant memory of her brother Jamie... The doctor entered the room within a minute of her arrival... he was approximately six feet tall, well built, with blue eyes and black curly hair like Jamie had... he was charming as he introduced himself and immediately put her at ease with a calm voice, an easy smile and a fatherly manner, although she was surprised that he was probably close to her age. After a few minutes, he took a short history, and then asked her to disrobe, lie on the couch and submit to a "neurological" exam. It was an uncomfortable moment for Claudia... and she was hesitant... "but after all he is a doctor," she thought, and obediently disrobed, donning a very small, very thin, medical top, and, as instructed, laid face down on the couch. The doctor pricked her entire back and lower extremities with a pin, and then asked her to flip over on her back so that he could do a frontal exam, which necessitated her removing her top... but he did put a thin white sheet over her body which did little to cover her nudity, as he proceeded with his "exam." He talked soothingly to her the entire time, asking her many questions, and when he was finished, and she was dressed, he set up a series of appointments, and then gave her an all-encompassing hug... she could feel his erection, and he deftly removed his penis from his trousers, continuing to hold her and talking to her in soothing tones. He asked her to hold his penis, and in a flash Claudia remembered her grandfather, broke away and ran out the door. She never told anyone about this incident, but decades later was infuriated to read a glory filled obituary, documenting his heroic life and enumerating all his many awards and honors.

When Claudia was finally diagnosed correctly many years later, she would remember this entire period of time... the diagnostic and referral process... as one of the most defining moments in her life... and the most damaging. That day in November, 1963 was appalling... not only for the assassination of her President, but also for the reprehensible misdiagnosis and physician related abuses that followed, that caused many years of physical and emotional pain and suffering, not only for her, but for Gerald, the children and her extended family.

5

Gerald had been doing quite well financially with his company, and even before Zach had been born, they had discussed moving to a new upscale tract in New Jersey. Now, after the incident with the psychiatrist, Claudia pushed for a speedy move and used it as an excuse not to return to "Dr. Love." Within 2 months, they were in their new house... filled with new hope... but life took some bizarre turns that taxed an already fragile family dynamic.

For Claudia, there was a pervasive sense of shame and she wondered if she were to blame for the psychiatrist's sexual behavior... was it really her fault? Had she said something? Had she sent some signals to him? Why hadn't she become angry, or why didn't she let someone know about the incident? Why had this happened to her again... after the "incident" with her Grandpoppy, she began to wonder what was wrong with her... did other people have this happen to them? Was she a sexual freak? The thoughts were reoccurring... she never discussed any of this with Gerald, fearing his possible reaction of abandonment... so, she kept everything hidden within her... it was a lonely feeling.

There was no doubt that Gerald was a workaholic and, at times during the years, showed tendencies toward alcoholism. After the initial years of financial struggles, he was now prospering... and he was "experiencing life," traveling extensively to Europe, wining and dining the foreign haute monde, and specializing in making his sexual fantasies come true. His strategic thinking and "spin tactics" were working for him as well as his rich clients. Claudia knew little of his travels but had spent enough time in Europe to know that beautiful women were made quite available to men like her husband ... Gerald chose to communicate very little to her... and she rarely complained. All of her life she had been programmed to sublimate her needs and it was expected that she would continue to sublimate her needs to those of her husband and children. There was another behavior emerging in Gerald that disturbed Claudia... his non-communicative behavior now encompassed lying... more accurately, lying by omission or for convenience. On a lovely spring afternoon, Gerald arranged for the family to go for a drive. When they arrived home several hours later, a cage full of little white mice that were the children's pets, was missing from the locked garage. Everything... including food, replacement cage items, etc., were gone and the garage was swept clean. Gerald denied knowing anything about it, even though it was obvious he had arranged for someone to come and remove the items. Claudia was not angry, but was bewildered by his denial, wondering why he hadn't just asked her to get rid of the pets if he was so opposed... it was one thing to keep the information from the children, but she was his wife... not a child. She laughed off the incident... it was really not that important, but what was important was the frequency of similar events that occurred throughout the years.

However, "life was good" for the Parker family... there were many times that they enjoyed their life together and Claudia never wanted to "rock the boat." For the most part, they were enjoying their new home and making new friends.

Then, several months after the move, Claudia had another "spell" exactly like the one she had experienced before... the dizziness, the cold sweats, the rubbery legs, feelings of passing out, intense inner trembling and nervousness... and she went to a new psychiatrist. This doctor was on staff of a private psychiatric hospital over an hour's drive from their house.

In the 50 minutes that she was seen by him, it was strongly suggested that Claudia be admitted to the "Clinic" as an inpatient so that she could be thoroughly assessed and to give them time to explore her symptoms and regulate her medications. Gerald assented to this arrangement and seemed to be relieved, while Claudia was terrified, but naturally submitted to her doctor and husband. Within an hour she had "voluntarily" checked in, was assigned a private room and Gerald had left. The next day, Claudia was given tests she had never heard of... an EEG, which she found very interesting, blood tests, an IQ test and some horrible test where they made her lie down and then spun her around and around until she cried out to please stop. None of this was explained to her. The following day, she was informed she had an appointment with her doctor, and he explained to her that he was a Rogerian psychiatrist. Claudia did not know what that meant, and it was not explained to her, but she quickly came to realize what it meant... He rarely participated in the sessions, but sat smoking his pipe... "uh huh, how did that make you feel." His focus was again on her "clinical depression," and Claudia found herself constantly directed into discussing her loneliness, her childhood, her feelings of rejection... but when she discussed her physical symptoms... the terrible fatigue, the mood swings, the very foggy head... it was ignored, and she found herself talking just to use up the time. That morning was pivotal for Claudia. Dr. Uh huh, felt it was necessary for her to undergo electroconvulsive therapy (shock treatments), because he felt she was "morbidly" depressed and the medication was not working as it should. He explained rather vaguely what shock treatments were and told her she would not remember them, and, in addition, might have some memory loss for a short time. Claudia was alarmed. She called Gerald after her session and he agreed to be there that evening to meet with Dr. Uh huh to discuss the situation. Both Gerald and Claudia asked questions... some were answered, and some were ignored... the analytic summation of the meeting was that Claudia had endured a neglectful and abusive childhood/adolescence with the residual result of adult depression. Claudia had done some research on depression since her initial diagnosis from the family doctor, and now discussed her doubts with Dr. Uh huh, telling him she did not feel sad, nor did she experience any of the symptoms she had read about. He countered with describing depression as a very complicated illness that often manifested itself in physical symptoms such as she was experiencing. He explained to her that the shock treatments would erase subconscious memories that were feeding the depression. Gerald interjected that he thought it might be a good thing to try the treatments... it was discussed that there would be six to eight treatments and then Claudia would be re-evaluated.   So, that night, things were set in motion for more years of struggle, distress, heartache and suffering for Claudia, and her misdiagnosis was firmly imprinted within her spirit and her psyche that she was mentally defective.

When shock treatments were given to Claudia, she was lightly anesthetized with a barbiturate derivative, and she was given a muscle relaxant. Electrodes were placed bilaterally on her head, a bite block was inserted in her mouth to avoid any injury to teeth or tongue, and an O2 mask was placed on her nose/mouth. Then a machine was turned on that provided a brief application of electrical stimulus which produced in her a seizure that lasted approximately 60 seconds. There were several other patients in the room where this treatment was performed, and as each was finished, they were taken back to their room to recover. When Claudia woke from the short acting anesthesia, she was extremely confused... she had no idea who she was, where she was nor was she able to identify with what was happening. It was a frightening experience. It took her several hours to begin to remember anything... she wondered if this was what it felt like to die. Electroconvulsive therapy is used when it appears that a person is resistant to orthodox medications... it is very controversial. Claudia was scheduled for 6 treatments but in the end she was given 22 treatments. At the conclusion of the treatments she had lost 30 pounds... she was consistently confused.... she felt unable to react correctly to any stimulus... in effect she felt catatonic.

No history was ever taken by the new Psychiatrist... he used the diagnosis that had originally been made by the family physician months earlier after her first spell. After the shock treatments, medications were increased, changed, withdrawn, re-introduced... Claudia was still very nauseated, and she was sure it was from the medications, but this was denied by the doctor. She was in the clinic for almost 2 months... Gerald visited her each weekend, and he would take her to what became their favorite restaurant in the nearby college town... the ambiance was wonderful... the food divine to Claudia who was tired of the bland, hospital food. In spite of her treatments, these outings with Gerald were happy times. None of the other friends ever came to see her nor did her parents or sister.

When Claudia finally arrived home, it took her many weeks to acclimate... portions of her past memory never did return, and she was appalled when she saw herself in the full length mirror. She was pale and gaunt... almost down to 100 pounds on her five-foot-seven inch frame. Her clothes hung on her emaciated frame, and she felt very unattractive. Added to this was the profuse number of physical symptoms that continued to be ignored.

A new physical symptom that had begun in prior year's, became more frequent and embarrassing... projectile vomiting... and Claudia noticed it usually happened when she ate certain foods... meatloaf, roast beef, scallops, popcorn. On one such occasion, Gerald was entertaining clients and asked Claudia to accompany him. They ate at a gourmet restaurant (Claudia had scallops) and, afterwards, went to the Ballet at Lincoln Center... but ten minutes into the first Act, Claudia had to excuse herself and spent the next hour in the ladies lounge vomiting with extraordinary force... the attendant tried to help her out but she was obviously frightened, and begged Claudia to let her call the ambulance... but Claudia refused, stating that it was "just a bug."

Gerald finally appeared at intermission, and she begged him to take her home... they had a very quiet and tense ride that night... Gerald was very upset that he had to leave his clients without a host. It was a further indication to Claudia that she was a burden to Gerald.

It never occurred to Claudia to discontinue any of the medications... after all, she had been raised to be compliant with authority figures. She would not know for many agonizing years that she had the power within her to change and/or to control the negative and positive outcomes in her life. For now, her only concern was to perform her duties as a wife and as a Mother... and she made a decision to somehow have more joy in her life.

6

Claudia remembered the precise moment she realized Gerald was having an affair with her good friend, Helen, a neighbor who worked as a fashion editor for Sophisticated Style Magazine. It was a Saturday night in October, 1968, at the height of the sexual revolution that was taking place worldwide. Claudia and Gerald had invited two other couples for cocktails and dinner. They were seated in the charming dining room Claudia had so lovingly decorated, enjoying one of her gastronomical delights after a prolonged cocktail hour. Everyone was in a festive mood... they had just enjoyed a delicate curried lemon-ginger soup, followed by a delectable, rolled filet of Dover sole stuffed with a creamy asparagus and crab mixture, tiny red potatoes that had been roasted in their skins to a crisp buttery delight, and they were beginning to savor the dessert... English trifle and Irish coffee. Jokes were made about the English and Irish offerings and then the conversation took an abrupt change to discussing a neighbor who had just sued her husband for divorce because of his adultery. Claudia made the comment that wives always know when husbands stray, although they often do not admit that they know. Helen, sitting to her right, exchanged an imperceptible glance with Gerald, sitting at the other end of the table, and declared in a smug tone, "Believe me, my dear, wives *rarely* know if the lovers are smart about it!" At that moment Helen's eyes locked with Claudia's and Claudia knew

Claudia suffered silently with tumultuous and paranoid thoughts... women of her class rarely discussed infidelity, but as a child, she had overheard enough arguments between her parents to know that it occurred rather regularly, and she felt it was her "duty" to accept it. So, she had not said anything to Gerald, but regarded this infidelity as being quite different from those Gerald might have had in Europe and wondered if Helen ever accompanied him on his trips. Claudia mused, "Helen is so different from me...She is far more confident, and avant-garde...I feel like Polly off the Pickle Boat when I'm around her..."

So, Claudia did what many women of her generation did... she internalized the situation and came up with the result that it was her fault... a popular misconception of that era, as was the belief that infidelity was far more acceptable than divorce which was considered destructive to the smooth running of a society. In the last 2 years, Claudia had been hospitalized three times with the diagnosis of clinical depression. *She didn't feel depressed*, but she was experiencing terrible headaches and debilitating fatigue in addition to the re-occurring "spells." At times she hallucinated which terrified her and added to her misdiagnosis... but the worst was the foggy head and the inner nervousness. She didn't sleep well, and she was on a constant diet... the grapefruit diet, the cabbage soup diet, whatever came out in any of the women's magazines, and of course, at least 12 cups of coffee a day to which she had added at least a pack of cigarettes per day and caffeine-laden diet soda. The psychiatrist she saw once a month, continued to diagnose her with depression and the proliferation of medications also continued. Although Claudia continued to complain about all her physical symptoms, his response was to prescribe stronger doses of the medications, and for each negative symptom, a new pill. Pills to pep her up, calm her down, to make her sleep and to wake her up. She frequently asked the doctor why she was on so many medications given the fact that she had submitted to the shock treatments because the medications were not working. There was never a logical answer.

Gerald was fed up! Claudia could understand why. She thought long and hard about the vows they had taken... "For better or worse, in sickness and in health.....'' and felt protected by these vows, but realized that there was a limit for Gerald. She felt a great deal of compassion for him... he was trying to keep the family together, but Gerald was not a man that could sublimate his own needs to those of his family.... Above everything else, he had an overpowering need to excel financially and he was being drained both emotionally and financially by Claudia's illness. He no longer wanted a traditionalist wife and children who made demands on him ... he wanted his freedom and the affair with Helen was an attempt to secure that freedom.

Gerald left for Europe on the following Monday. It was a rainy day, and after the children left for school, Claudia retrieved several boxes from the garage and sat on their bed rifling through them. She began with an unfinished scrapbook that contained considerable memorabilia from their dating days. They had been everywhere... there were photos from the Stork Club, the Copacabana, the Latin Quarter where, for the first time, she had seen Frank Sinatra, and, of course, a mountain of memorabilia from the Embers. She had been to most of the places in college, but with Gerald, everything was so special. She chuckled when she remembered the strip club they had innocently gone to on their honeymoon, and became slightly tearful when she found the children's little beaded bracelets and newborn photos. There was memorabilia from the Biltmore... "Under the Clock"... the night Gerald had proposed to her and she told him she could never have children. "Well," she thought, "that surely was a poor diagnosis!" Then she found the letters that Gerald had written her in the early years of their marriage.... there weren't many letters, but each one spoke of his happiness being with her, of his undying love for her, of his commitment to her, of her exquisite beauty and her special gifts, and his reiteration that he would never leave, reminiscent of the declaration he made to her the last day of their honeymoon. The tears flowed liberally and Claudia remembered the closeness and friendship she and Gerald had shared.

"Oh God, what has happened! Please, Please, let this pass... help us get through this difficult time and renew our love... Help me get well, and help our family grow stronger and closer."

He was gone for three weeks. During that time, Claudia read a book called *The Feminine Mystique* and decided she should go back to work. She wanted to prove to Gerald that she was strong, and "worth something" ... and she wanted to be able to contribute financially to the marriage. Perhaps it would increase Gerald's love and admiration for her. She worked out all the details and when Gerald returned home, he agreed with her that it might work out. There were a great many details to think about, and Claudia was busy the next several months laying the groundwork. She interviewed 11 women and finally secured a nanny for the children, bought some new clothes, mapped out the area within New York City where she wanted to work. Then she summoned up all the courage she could and went job hunting in her chic new clothes and with her foggy head, her fatigue, her nausea, anxiety and an impenetrable mask she had successfully developed over the years. Within 2 weeks, she had a job working for an advertising agency as an administrative assistant to the president... a glorified secretary but with higher pay. Every day she took a bus from Southern New Jersey to the Port Authority Bus Terminal and walked the 26 blocks to and from her job. Gerald worked only blocks away, but they never had lunch together, and only occasionally did they commute together. She drank gobs of caffeine to ward off the headaches and to keep her energy going, coffee in the mornings, and cola in the afternoons. When Gerald was traveling, she worked late, coming home to sleeping children and a lonely house.

She had begun going to a therapy group after work, where she discussed her suspicions regarding Gerald's affair... the group members agreed that there were definite signs of an affair, but shocked her when they were divided as to whether it was with a male or female... and the psychiatrist and one group member suggested that she take a lover for herself. For her part, Claudia felt betrayed, angry and guilty... the one person in the world she had trusted was now disloyal... it was the worst lie of all... and she began to look at Gerald wondering what other lies and betrayals he had been guilty of. What ever happened to commitment! "No matter what," she thought, "we could work through this." She kept telling herself that things would be better... that people make mistakes and make bad decisions... she wanted to believe in Gerald, and wanted to believe that he still loved her. She put all her energies into her job and made sure the household ran as smoothly as possible.

Then, a new symptom appeared. One morning, walking through the Port Authority Bus Terminal, she began to hemorrhage... Fortunately, it was a morning when Gerald was with her. In the ladies room, she packed herself with paper, and took the next bus home and went to the doctor. Within days, she was having a hysterectomy... she was only 33. However, she was not sad about the surgery, nor did she experience any of the negative feelings regarding her "lost" womanhood that she had read about in so many women's magazines. Claudia had been through hell... her church's teaching on birth control was tearing her apart and having a deleterious effect on her marriage... now she looked forward to a normal sex life with Gerald without his complaint that the condoms he was "forced" to use were ruining his sex life... or without having to endanger her life with the birth control pills. The experience seemed to bond Gerald and Claudia for a time... but the "bonding" was short lived. Within a few months, things were much the same as they had been... Gerald was again uncommunicative, his interest in her sexually had all but disappeared, and he withdrew into his study at night, where he sometimes just sat and stared into space.

Within the next year, they bought a 9 bedroom Victorian house in an upscale beach resort. Claudia felt her New York job was a dead end, and with Gerald away so much and the nannies coming and going at a rapid rate, she found a job locally, working as an orthodontic assistant. It was a small, quiet office with little stress once she learned the routine. She bought herself a little VW bug and had a sense of accomplishment. Claudia was very excited about the move. She had become very involved in the children's lives, and now had the time to drive them to their respective track meets and soccer games. She had also become very engrossed in art... the house was large enough for her to have a studio which she loved! Each child had their own room which greatly contributed to family harmony, and she had been accepted as a volunteer tutor in the first Federal funded program within the public school system designed to help those children who were falling behind. Zach was going to this school and she was happy to be with him as they walked the short distance each morning.

The house required some remodeling which Claudia loved doing, and even Gerald was trying to lend a hand when he could, even though he made it plain that it was not something he enjoyed!

On a Friday night the last day of October, Claudia and Gerald had an extended cocktail hour. Gerald had too much to drink... One drink for Claudia was always too much with all the medication she was on, and she was tired and irritable. She began to rag on Gerald about his lack of communication, and soon they were involved in a heated argument... the first in a long time. It appeared that they both had been saving up all their complaints about each other, and there were loud and ugly accusations and threats. Claudia began to goad Gerald ...

"Why don't you hit me, Mr. Parker... Go ahead... slap me...I know you want to..."

Gerald did not respond... He just grabbed her by the shoulders and stared at her...

"Come on Gerald, get it out of your system... hit me..."

They had moved from the bedroom study into the hallway, and were standing near the stairwell. Before Claudia finished her last sentence, Gerald hit her solidly across the face, unbalancing her and she fell half way down the stairs. She began to cry softly, looked pleadingly up at Gerald, but he stood frozen and said, coldly... "Are you satisfied, you bitch!" He went back to the study and slammed the door, while Claudia limped down the rest of the stairs, gathered her things, and left the house to drive to a friend's house where she stayed until late Saturday afternoon. Gerald was gone when she arrived home. He had left a brief note that he would be home Monday night... and when he arrived about 9 P.M. it was a cordial but unemotional reunion. There were no apologies from either one, no attempts to discuss anything further and he slept on the sofa in his study.

The next morning was Election day and she had the day off. Claudia sleepily said goodbye to Gerald as he left for work... He did not respond.

At approximately 11 AM Claudia went to the kitchen, brought a glass of wine to her bedroom, took 159 Phenobarbitol tablets, slashed her wrists and laid on her bed to wait for the blessing of death.

7

Claudia had died in the ambulance but at the state of the art medical center, they were able to resuscitate her and placed her on a ventilator. She remained in a deep coma for eleven days, and on the twelfth day, astounded doctors when she regained consciousness without showing any signs of the expected brain damage.

Because Claudia lived in one of the six states that considered suicide a crime, she was involuntarily remanded for a period of time to a psychiatric hospital. During this time, she saw three different psychiatrists on a regular basis, all of whom directly and indirectly suggested to her that she should leave her marriage, and make a life for herself and her children. It was shattering to her... she loved Gerald, and considered divorce abhorrent... it was antithetical to everything she had been raised to believe about marriage... divorce was never an option...people stayed together no matter what happened...it was an indication not only of her failure as a wife, but her failure as a woman.

Claudia had lived with her parents and then her husband... she had never been on her own, never had her own apartment, and the only times she had been alone were the times when Gerald traveled, and those times she had either her Mother-in-law or the Nanny in the house. She couldn't imagine raising her children without their Father. The whole idea was repugnant to her, but the daily infusion of the ideas offered to her by the psychiatrists soon began to take shape as a possibility. Claudia began to believe that this idea was possible, that the doctors *knew* that if she returned to the same environment she would again be at risk. What they did not prepare her for was the chaos, the stark reality of living alone with three children, trying to support herself, grieving for a man that she still truly loved, ignoring the reality of her background... a wealthy little girl who had never been allowed to make a decision, who had servants to plan and perform the major household chores, a naive, sweet, little girl who had been ridiculed and rejected for years, who never had the supportive love necessary for ego integration, or the stability of a loving relationship except for the brief love of a dead brother. Added to these staggering considerations were the consistently miserable physical symptoms that Claudia endured and battled every day of her life.

But, in spite of everything, Claudia reluctantly accepted a loan from a family friend... after she drew up a contract and repayment schedule... and bought a small tract house where she lived with her three children, trying on a daily basis to put the pieces together. Gerald had decided to proceed with a divorce which devastated her...she tearfully begged him on several occasions to accept a legal separation for a period of time, but to no avail. He reiterated many times that he no longer wanted the responsibility of a wife and children. Claudia was aware of the feelings once again that everyone she loved would be taken from her.

In essence, Claudia had been victimized by her affluent background, lacking the "survivor" skills that come with learning that life is a struggle. You might say she had been caught in the web of a dichotomous generation, representing a childhood espousing ivory-towered idealism, gentility, delicate womanhood and time-honored traditions versus an adult era of activism, assertiveness and anomalies. In many ways she had broken away from the "time warp" of her childhood but retained too much naiveté to succeed in the harsh reality of the activist age.... the chasm between the decades of the 50's and the 60's was immense.

When her marriage ended, she was adrift. Her responsibilities were great... her supports were non-existent. The alimony and child support she received were a small fraction of what she needed to pay the bills... the

mortgage, household expenses, medical expenses, raising three children...
the bills never ended... they lived a financially austere life. Claudia's Father
had not "*re*-owned" her... he had kept his promise that she would "not
receive a penny"... and in spite of the struggle and hardship she was suffering, he was impervious to her needs, suggesting to her through others
that she go on Welfare like "the others".... whatever that meant. Caring
for three boys, alone, was difficult... and sometimes very perplexing... was
she doing the right things... saying the right things... did she show them
enough love ... or maybe too much... was she too much in control... or not
enough.... did she spend enough quality time with them... or maybe too
much time so that they resented her... The children missed their Father...
The five week intervals that Gerald had established when he would see
them were hurtful to the children and she found herself constantly making excuses to them why he could not see them more often. When *his*
weekend came around, she had to take the children to him early Saturday
mornings and pick them up late Sunday afternoon, a 200 mile round trip,
and they were unruly for days after their visit with Gerald. He had already
become public with Helen, and was truly no longer interested in his own
children... he was busy with Helen's four children! Claudia tried desperately to maintain a positive mental attitude. There were days when she
could barely manage to get out of bed due to the overwhelming fatigue
she was suffering and to combat this, she continued to drink 10-12 cups of
coffee a day and to skip meals to cut down on calories and the food bills.
Most of her friends had mysteriously disappeared and she again found
herself alone and isolated. Perhaps the most discomfiting part of her life
was the lack of intimacy... after so many years of isolation and rejection,
Claudia had established a deep intimacy with Gerald when they married...
not just the sex, but the friendship, the oneness, the connectedness that
she had never knew existed. She begged her sister to come and stay with
her for a time, thinking that they may be able to connect now that they
were older, but the request was rebuffed.

After Claudia secured a part-time job, she went to a new doctor for
help with the many physical symptoms, but after reading her medical chart,
he continued the prescriptions for the tranquilizers, the anti-depressants,

and the myriad of other mind-altering drugs. The brain fog continued... she felt like a walking corpse... and, once again, ignoring her pleas for help for the many physical symptoms she was experiencing, the doctor gave her another medication to pep her up, and before long, the profusion of mind-altering drugs were again increased, generously prescribed by the doctor who was convinced that Claudia was nothing more than a stunning-looking, neurotic, rich, spoiled woman that he labeled to his office staff as suffering from somatoform disorder... a hypochondriac.

The next five years were a blur to Claudia. She felt anxious much of the time... she had lost count of the many doctors she went to that ignored her physical symptoms, and began to think that she was indeed a hypochondriac.... perhaps crazy... so she took the pills like the good submissive woman she had been trained to be... she worked hard at part-time newspaper job, which she thoroughly enjoyed, she cared for her children as competently as she could, but was physically and emotionally fragile, and felt she was doing a poor job of parenting. What she did not realize, was that she was learning to improvise... she had to... money was scarce... what was the old saying... need is the mother of invention? Claudia was becoming extremely creative! For a child who had been forbidden to make decisions on her own, she was now learning to be self-reliant, even feisty at times. She was assailed by those who were judgmental ... the neighbor across the street who spent most of her time peeking out her window to see what Claudia was up to...it was a time when divorce was unacceptable to many, questionable by the rest... she was even denied receiving the sacrament of communion at her church. A social worker from the children's school made several visits to her home to assess her skills as a "divorced" mother, and made recommendations that she and the children enter "family" therapy. No one offered any real help until she met a woman one day at the library. They were about the same age, but "Sarah" was a high-energy person... very upbeat and obviously happy. Claudia was astounded when Sarah began to share her story of depression, her ensuing "addiction" to prescription medications, prompted by her *ex*-physician. She told Claudia of a private "clinic" she had been referred to and the treatment she had undergone. Claudia listened carefully, and for the first time in years she had hope. She made the necessary inquiries and before long had made the decision to go to the Connecticut clinic. A trusted friend offered to care for the children so Claudia was able to stay at the clinic for the required month, painfully withdrawing from her doctor-ordered dependence on the prescription drugs.

It had not been easy when she arrived home...she endured many difficult sleepless nights, and anxious days, but within three months, Claudia was experiencing an improved sense of well-being...for the first time in many years she felt whole... her head was no longer "foggy,"...most of the physical symptoms had either disappeared or had greatly diminished... she was able to concentrate and making decisions was easier... she had more confidence and felt in control of her life. And, the best of all, she never, from the day she entered the Connecticut clinic, had another mind/mood altering medication.

BOOK III

Part 1
Joshua Henderson

...and dear God, my Father who loves me, please deliver me from this abuse, and help me to be a loving wife and to learn to submit to my husband in all things....

PROLOGUE TO BOOK 3 - PART 1

There was an imperceptible hush when Joshua and Claudia Henderson entered the room. Men and women alike were unmistakably attentive to the couple's arrival, some no doubt, agreeably fascinated, and others possibly circumspect in their interest. From an alcove at the far end of the room, Kitty Borg watched with special interest. She had seen them often on local TV and in the society pages of the Los Carmelo newspaper, but found them far more stunning in the flesh.

"Josh," she speculated, had the dark good looks and persona of an iconic celebrity... and his clothes were unmistakably Italian. The luxurious silky, white jacket and light blue gabardine trousers hung effortlessly on his tall frame, and even from her obscure position, the brilliant blue of his eyes was intense, the color enriched by a rather theatrical blue ascot and, of course, the obligatory California suntan. In contrast, Claudia was blond, a natural beauty, undeniably sensual... but hers was a restrained, regal sensuality. She was tall for a woman...5'7" or 5'8", every inch supple and perfectly proportioned, garbed in a softly draped, white Grecian style gown with a high neck of ecru lace. Her green eyes were luminous.... " She's definitely elegant," Kitty mused, "and she exudes class !" She watched with interest as they were greeted by their hostess, Margo Leon, another transplanted New Yorker who wanted to honor Josh on his birthday. Kitty edged closer. Josh had kissed Margo hello and his wife goodbye and was now wending his way toward a small group of men around the champagne bowl, greeting everyone as he went. Margo, who looked all of her sixty-nine years tonight with her overly tanned, leathery skin and ill-fitting, designer frock that looked like a leftover from someone's ten worst-dressed list, had flitted away toward the kitchen where the surprise cake and gifts were stashed. For a moment, Claudia looked a bit lost, a trifle vulnerable?

"Hello Claudia, my name is Kitty Borg... I've been looking forward to meeting you."

"Oh, Kitty," she put her hand out... "It's so good to meet you! How are you? I feel so bad about being so late, but Josh just had to sleep ... you know how drowsy he gets driving. Well, of course you don't know that ...we've just met, but my husband drove up from Los Angeles this afternoon and he was so exhausted when he got home. He just flew in from Florida last night and I think he's still on Eastern time. Are you with someone Kitty?"

"Yes, with my husband... his name is Norman....that's him standing next to the piano....the one with the bald head and earring. He's trying to look like 'Mr. Clean.' " Kitty was glad to see that Claudia was amused. When she smiled the stress lines in her face relaxed. Kitty was surprised at how nervous Claudia appeared to be tonight and detected some redness around her carefully made up eyes, as if she had been crying.

"Kitty..." Claudia hesitated.... "Could we, uh, ... would you have lunch with me next week?" Claudia was intense and spoke in a low tone. "I'd like to talk to you and I don't want to come to your office. Someone will see me and then the rumors will fly."

Kitty looked intently at the woman next to her. There was a sense of gravity in her face and voice. Kitty knew women like Claudia didn't ask for help from strangers until there was a significant difficulty... a crisis.

"Let me look at my calendar tonight when I get home and perhaps you could call me first thing tomorrow morning at the office? O.K. with you?"

"Thanks Kitty. I just feel I need to talk to someone about some things on my mind."

Claudia put her hand on Kitty's arm then made an excuse to move off to chat with others. Norman was immediately at her elbow, leading her outside to the patio for some fresh air. Kitty looked back momentarily and caught a fleeting glimpse of Claudia and her easy smile. She would soon learn this smile belied some dark secrets.

1

Claudia stepped out of the shower, wrapped herself in a soft, thirsty towel and went to lie on the bed while she cooled off. It was predictably hot for July, but today even more so, since there was no sea breeze. She had turned on the air conditioning and bathed early so Josh would have the bathroom to himself when he came in. Several of the other baths were being remodeled, as was a major part of their fifty six hundred square foot house. She and Josh had decided to remodel instead of moving, utilizing more of their nine acres of land. At the beginning, Claudia had thoroughly enjoyed working with the architects and designers; however, it had recently become a nightmare. Even though all the additions and changes had been discussed and accepted by Josh before the remodeling had begun, he was now constantly complaining about the money, the need to "cut back," ragging on her because of her extravagances… complaining about how hard he worked so that she could "just sit and do nothing!" It baffled Claudia … she was involved in many community activities and was developing an educational/marketing program for a business idea she had. Last year she had completed her Master's degree… it was something she had begun just before she met Josh, and he insisted she continue after they were married. She had recognized too late that he was angry and threatened by her education, her friends and her intelligence.

Claudia heard his car pulling into the driveway. "Good," she thought, "it's only 4:00 o'clock. We have lots of time before the party." She pulled the towel from around her and snuggled provocatively under the satin sheet, hoping to entice him when he walked in. Josh enjoyed her playfulness ... but today, when he walked in, he threw his briefcase across the room... came to the side of the bed started right in. "Well, don't you look like a fucking whore!"

She rolled over on her side, pulling the sheet close to her. Claudia knew what was coming and immediately felt a surge of foreboding and helplessness.

"I suppose you spent the day in the pool and turned on the air conditioning just to show me how much money you can spend in one day. And where did you get these sheets?"

With that Josh ripped off the sheet from around Claudia, bent over her and with his finger in her face began yelling obscenities. " You fuckin' bitch, don't you think it's about time you get off your ass and start pulling your weight around here? I'm sick of your crazy ideas that cost money. You're nothing but a cock sucking whore that's bleeding me dry."

"Get away from me... Please, Josh, get away.... stop this!"

Her mouth was dry, her voice was hoarse and shaking...she was frightened, childlike, while pleading with him to leave her alone.

Josh picked her up. She was kicking and crying, begging him to put her down. He whirled her around the room and then threw her on the bed with such force that she bounced off and landed on the floor.

He came over to her naked, sobbing body, looked down at her and yelled, "Oh you're so damned dramatic! You're nothing but a C-rated movie queen." As he said this last thing, he kicked her in the thigh and walked out to the back yard, stripping off his clothes as he went, throwing them in her direction. He threw his shoes at the wall. They bounced off and grazed her head. Claudia laid silently on the floor, curled up in the fetal position facing the wall.

Then, by the grace of God, he was gone and she heard him dive into the pool. Like a wounded deer, she crawled into the bathroom and locked the door. She knew from experience that he might come back and finish off the argument and the bathroom door had the only lock that Josh had not broken... Not that he hadn't tried. Claudia grabbed another towel... she was lying on the floor, her naked body heaving with sobs. "Oh, God, why does this happen! Please...let me die, let him die. Please God, deliver me out of this hell. Oh, Josh, why can't you love me! I try so hard to please you! What is it that I do...why can't I make you happy? Oh, please God, let this end!"

Twenty minutes later Claudia began to get up from the floor. She knelt in front of the sink... turned on the cold water... soaked a wash-cloth and held it to her face. She was shivering and the tears continued to run down her cheeks. Mechanically, she kept ringing out the cloth, applying pressure to her face to ebb the flow of tears and to prevent any swelling from occurring. She continued this ritual for several minutes but was so cold that she tentatively opened the bathroom door to see if she could get to the closet for a robe. Josh was not there. She quickly moved to her bedroom closet, pulled out a thick terry cloth robe and wrapped herself in the comfort of its soft folds.... then went to the French doors leading to the pool. Josh was lying in a chaise lounge and she knew he would be asleep, relaxed and emotionally removed from what had just happened. She stared at his tanned, muscular body. He was beautiful ...tall and perfectly proportioned. A towel flung care-lessly over his naked body did not quite cover his ample genitalia. He was proud of his body, working out what she thought was a bit obses-sively. He enjoyed his nakedness and flaunted his attributes. Now she looked at him with a profound sadness.

Claudia crawled into the disheveled bed, emotionally spent. She pulled her robe around her, then the blanket and two pillows. She needed the comfort and security.

■ ■ ■

"Claudia.....Claudia....."

She awakened with a start. Josh was kneeling at the side of the bed. She instinctively drew away, but he put his hand on her arm.

"Claudia....please....don't pull away from me. Darling, I'm sorry. I can't imagine what happened to me. I love you sweetheart....please.....forgive me."

Josh enveloped her in his arms. He was gentle, tender.

Claudia opened her eyes and stared at him. Josh was weeping, shaking his head in bewilderment.

"Darling when I was driving home today, all I could think of was holding you, swimming with you and making love to you. I got so sleepy driving that I stopped and got some strong coffee with lots of sugar to pep me up. I think I had a bad reaction to the caffeine and sugar. Darling, please ... this won't ever happen again. Please know that I love you."

He slid onto the bed, holding her close to him. Claudia began to weep softly.

"Josh, I just can't take any more of this! This is not natural."

"Darling it isn't going to happen again."

Josh slid his hand inside her robe, running his hand down her body and became instantly aggressive... Claudia was familiar with his tactics... It had been a long time since there had been any true intimacy in his lovemaking... He was extremely narcissistic, and she recognized his need for control and domination. She felt manipulated but, knowing the consequences, was too frightened to resist.

"Oh, damn, Claudia, I came too soon."

Josh was lying on his side, his head cupped in his hand. He looked into her eyes and smiled his most beautiful smile.

"Darling, you are just too beautiful... I can't contain myself."

With that, he rolled away from her and she knew he would be asleep within minutes

Claudia grabbed her robe and went quickly into the bathroom. She locked the door, solemnly looked at herself in the mirror, and then vomited.

2

Josh looked at the clock. It was 5:30. He knew that they were supposed to be at Margo Leon's party at 6:00. Well, they would be good and late. He heard Claudia running the shower, and was slightly annoyed when he went to the bathroom door and found it locked. He decided not to make an issue of it. Instead, he went to his closet and very carefully chose his clothes for the night. Clothes were important to Josh. He had abandoned his English tailor's conservative drab and somber materials and now embraced the new Italian "Continental" look which featured rich, luxurious silk-blends and cashmeres. Josh had a broad build and was happy with the relaxed, columnar look of the Milan tailors that swept away the sack-cut look of the Ivy Leaguers. It made him look slimmer and taller. He smiled as he thought of Jake Wexler's alcohol induced revelation three days ago at the men's club that Margo was going to "surprise" him at tonight's party with gifts and a cake for his birthday. Josh wanted to be particularly well groomed because he knew that he would be in the "limelight"... possibly he'd have to make a speech. He wondered if any of them knew him...

■ ■ ■

Joshua Henderson was a highly successful businessman but it had not always been like that. His early life had been impoverished. When his

Father had been sober, he had worked diligently at the woolen mill in the small northeast English town where they had lived their entire lives. But sobriety was a rare occasion in his Father's life, and the meager wage he earned was made worse by Josh's perception of his Mother's extravagance. In Josh's view, she spent money on all the wrong things. He remembered the old piano she had bought from a neighbor and books she thought the children should read. She would buy expensive material and make ridiculous frocks for his sister and herself. He recognized at an early age that if the money had been used differently, he would not have suffered some of the shame that plagued him well into his adult life... this always angered him. His "mum" was an American with a misplaced maverick spirit that made Josh feel different from the other childhood lads. Their Mother's stayed at home, were plump and homey, wearing the customary black dresses and white aprons, baking and cooking, canning and raising farm animals to feed their families. His Mum was different. She was slim, with creamy, soft skin and dark curly hair that framed a tired look-ing face with piercing blue eyes. He heard others refer to his Mother as "beautiful," and "enchanting," but all he knew was that she didn't stay at home. Every day she would ride her horse around the valley in which they lived, talking to the wives, "ministering to their needs," it was said, and teaching the children that could not go to the small, country school. She was the official midwife, the unofficial "doctor," and a teacher in great demand. Many nights she never came home, and his sister would find some snacks that served as dinner while their Father drank himself into a stupor, mumbling that their Mother was taking care of the Lowry child, or that she was helping the damn Denfield woman deliver her baby. Josh knew his Mother had gone to University in America, and he was told one time by his Father that she wanted to be a doctor and had gone to Medical School for a year and a half...an unsuitable role for a woman to Josh's way of thinking. When his Father would work overtime at the mill, his Mum would tell stories of her experiences in America, of the "wonder-ful" educational courses she had taken and of the "fascinating" things she had learned. Often, his Father would come home in the middle of the stories, smelling of drink, and in an unpleasant mood. His Mum would become instantly silent, and Josh and his sister would know that it was time to run to their room to escape the ensuing argument which would ultimately become either a verbal tirade or physical beating to his mother. Josh was glad he didn't have to listen anymore to his Mum's scholarly lectures. He hated school and particularly hated the regimentation and "closed up" feeling he would get in school. He wanted to be free to roam, and he liked to spend hours taking machinery apart and reassembling it. Learning about dead people who wrote poems and how the little, blimey, French prig, Napoleon, wanted to kill the Russians was meaningless to him. But his Mum was intent on him getting an education... she had big ideas of him going to Oxford or Harvard in America, but by the time he reached his teenage years, he had had it with school. Even his Mum recognized by that time that he needed to do something else. So, by the time he was fourteen, it had been arranged for him to go and live with his Aunt and Uncle in America, Holly and Lucas Connolly. They lived in a "small upscale town" in New York, and supposedly their only child, a girl named Melinda, had died when she was six or seven years old.... he couldn't remember... probably another boring story. Mum had shown him photographs of where his Aunt and Uncle lived... the house looked very large... and so was the bedroom that would be all his. It would be the first time he would have an indoor bathroom with a shower and a toilet! His sister Sandra told him that Uncle Lucas was "filthy rich," and that she thought he was involved in the Federal Government, "something to do with immigrations or something like that." In reality, Lucas was an enormously successful attorney who had diversified his wealth into real estate, international banking and corporate holdings. In 1946, President Truman had appointed him as one of the 11 members of the Interstate Commerce Commission.

"I envy you Josh," Sandra whispered to him one evening as they sat around the fire after supper.

"I'd give anything to get out of this place, to experience life in the 'big time' ... but I guarantee you that I'll be out of here not long after you! Mum is sure I'll make it into the University and when I finish there I'll have it made!"

He and Sandra had been through a lot together. When Josh was five and Sandra seven, his Mum had again become pregnant. She was 46 years old, and he had heard she was having a "rough time," whatever that meant! She had to remain in bed, and it seemed to Josh that she cried all day, every day... She did not want to see anyone and food had to be forced on her. When she wasn't crying, she would just stare into space and not even respond to him or Sandra when they went to give her their dutiful good night kisses. At other times she would call the children into the room and have them pray over her, saying that the devil was coming to take her baby. After one such episode, Josh and Sandra walked in from school one day and found their Father and the "real" Doctor sitting at the supper table talking in hushed tones.   His Father had been working extra hours to earn the money they would need for the new baby, and Josh was surprised to see him home so early. He felt scared and went to the room he shared with his sister, laid on his bed and stared at the ceiling. Pretty soon Sandra came in and told him Father Quinn, the local parish priest, had come, too. They were sure their Mum was dying. When they were called to the table their Father told them that their Mum was sick but "not the kind of sick when you die or go to the hospital." He went on to say that because he was never home and there would be no one to watch over them or to take care of them, that it had been decided they would go and live at the "convent" until Mum was well again, probably two or three months.

"Well if Mum isn't really sick, what's the matter with her?" Sandra asked the doctor in her most grown-up voice.

He took her hand. "Well children, it's hard to explain. Your Mum is having a spell... What I mean is… that because of her age… and with the baby coming…. You do know your Mum is having a baby?"

They nodded in unison

"Well she's worried about the baby. She wants it to be born healthy......"

Their Father cut in.

"Children, when you are older you'll understand everything. For now, I want you to be good, obedient children and do what you are told."

With this statement, their Father went to their bedroom asking them to follow. He picked out the things they would need and put them in an old cardboard suitcase. Things moved quickly and soon Josh and Sandra had said good-bye to their unresponsive Mother and were in Father Quinn's old rig being taken to the Lutheran convent about an hour from home.

They were there for almost two years. Josh rarely allowed himself to remember this experience. He'd rather remember that rainy day in April 1947 when he got on the ship headed for the United States. He was fourteen and a half but not at all scared. The war years had taught him to repress most of his feelings but he did allow a measure of elation to be leaving England. His parents were now in their late fifties. Mum had had several other "spells"... one, he was told, when she lost the baby, and on another occasion, after learning that her parents had been killed in a gruesome automobile accident, they found her wandering along the railroad tracks, disheveled, and confused, talking about things that people were telling her to do. It was humiliating to Josh as everyone in the Valley was gossiping about it... as usual, the other lads made fun of him which made him crazy with rage. Another time, just before he had left for America, she had locked herself in her room, slipping notes under the door stating that someone was trying to kill her. The doctor came and this time told them that she was going through some "hormonal changes." Mum had stayed in her room about four months with the blinds drawn, seeing no one, not wanting to eat and staring at the walls. It had been an unpleasant reminder of the "spell" she had had when he was five years old and he had been sent to the orphanage.

Since the day he left his parent's home for America, he had never gone back to England... not when his Mum died five years later and certainly not when his Father died 15 years later.

3

"Well, I'm ten minutes late," thought Kitty as she entered the dimly lit restaurant. "Claudia will be waiting!" The hostess took her to a dark corner where Claudia had selected a table hoping they would not be spotted. After apologizing for her lateness, Kitty began chatting about Margo's party. They took a moment to order lunch and while they ate kept up a running flow of trivial chatter. Kitty was pleased to note that Claudia relaxed during this time, knowing that her guard would be relaxed as well. After the dishes had been cleared and ice tea served, there was an awkward moment.

"How are you feeling today, Claudia? You looked a little tense when I first came in."

"I was...I am! I think I'm always tense these days."

There was a long pause with Claudia staring at the tablecloth.

"Kitty..." she hesitated momentarily looking at Kitty intensely... "I need someone I can trust.... Desperately! I know we've just met, but Margo has told me so much about you and your reputation for honesty and insightfulness... I'd like to see you professionally ... I can pay you whatever you want... but I can't come to your office. Can we work something out?" Claudia was almost breathless as she finished her sentence.

"Claudia, why don't we start at the beginning and take this one step at a time. I'm very flexible and can work out a lot of things, but I need to know what's bothering you first. Are you in trouble?"

"I don't know how to begin, Kitty. You're not going to believe what I tell you."

Kitty covered both of Claudia's hands with hers. and looking into her eyes, she saw the pain and in her voice she heard the familiar and compelling need to be understood.

Claudia began haltingly. She spoke of the "arguments,"... of the times when Josh threw things... food, chairs and other objects... of the times when he would pick her up and throw her around, how he would put his first through things, and always threaten to put it through her face... of the degrading verbal obscenities and the continual degrading assessments of her as a person, such as telling her she was a "crazy person," and he had been an "asshole" to marry her... his continual statements that he hated her and was going to divorce her... how he would restrain her if she tried to leave the scene or break down doors if she locked herself away from him... She spoke rapidly, nonstop, for about 5 minutes.

"Claudia.....Claudia dear, I'm going to stop you at this point because I have the picture and this is a public place." As Claudia related the beginning of her story, her body had become painfully taut, her voice hoarse and tears were beginning to spill onto her cheeks.

" I want you to sit back against your chair, have some tea, and take some deep breaths. I'm going to get the check and we'll go to your house."

"I am crazy, aren't I? Just like Josh says I am."

"No Claudia, you are not crazy. You are a woman who has suffered a lot of pain at the hands of another. You're going to be able to get rid of your pain, but it's going to take time and we can't do it in a restaurant. So, right now, I'd like you to drive home and I'll meet you there in a half hour. Is that O.K. with you?"

"I feel like I'm taking up your time. I'll be O.K., Kitty. I...."

Kitty interrupted. "Claudia, please don't retreat. I have a clear calendar this afternoon and I *want* to be with you. So, let's go!"

■ ■ ■

Kitty slowly drove out of the parking lot and turned west on Junipero boulevard which ran parallel through the town along the water.   Los Carmelo was a beautiful city situated above the sloping green hills along the Pacific. As Kitty drove down the wide boulevard, she was impressed with the job the City Council had done over the years keeping the architecture true to the Spanish Colonial style... the whitewashed buildings with red tile or multicolored domed roofs.   Huge palm trees, Palo Verdes, and other lush greenery and profuse patches of flowers adorned the sidewalks of the many upscale restaurants, boutiques. specialty shops and high end art stores and antique shops.   Driving along this boulevard, one could easily become mesmerized by the glistening blue/green of the water on the left... the gently sloping hills overlooking the craggy rocks below and the brilliant white sand beaches jutting out from their protective coves... but this afternoon, she was not focused on the beauty before her.   Kitty's head was spinning.   After her talk with Claudia, she knew this lovely woman was experiencing the classic symptoms of spousal abuse...she had seen it so many times!   Josh's perfectly controlled public personality, the flawless charm, the ingratiating way he had, particularly with women...   Kitty recalled her initial feelings on Friday night at the party and thought again about Claudia's "red eyes"... she could understand Claudia's fear to become ingenuous, vulnerable...her need to remain aloof, which many mistook for sophistication, even snobbery, and her seeming shyness, which in reality was her fear, her guilt and severe lack of self- esteem.   Kitty knew her intuition on Friday night had been right on target.   She reminded herself to pay attention to the exceptional... almost psychic... instincts for which she was well known.

She turned North onto Manzanita Trail, one of the many winding roads that led into the magnificent Western Hills area where large Mediterranean estates could be glimpsed though the profusion of white pines and diverse species of trees that were indigenous to the West. She felt her usual sense of challenge that came with each new client and said a customary prayer as she drove up the long, winding driveway to Claudia's front door. It was the first time she had seen the Henderson's house... a two-story Spanish revival mansion, a style popular in the 1930's. It was imposing in its grandeur… "I'd say this could qualify as an estate," Kitty thought as she regarded the priceless, panoramic view of the Los Carmelo hillside

4

"Hello Kitty, welcome to the chaos!" Claudia opened the door for Kitty to enter. She had already changed into a pair of shorts and silk shirt. Kitty noticed the imperceptible aloofness as Claudia greeted her at the door and knew enough time had elapsed for Claudia to "regroup" and become less penetrable. It was 2:30 in the afternoon. Claudia had told her that Josh would be late tonight.

"Every, Tuesday he goes to the club after work and gets home late. At least that's where he tells me he is!" Kitty knew she had plenty of time to do a good, initial assessment this afternoon and to evaluate the potential for harm. It would be important to protect Claudia for now, and to begin to plan for the future.

They were standing in the reception area... Kitty first noticed the spiral staircase that seemed to be suspended in space. Claudia's house was white... not a stark white, but a soft, creamy white. The cool, slate floors were covered with plush, oriental rugs...the artwork covering the walls was magnificent, and there were large arrays of fresh flowers and greenery everywhere. Oversized skylights provided natural light to every room, and even though the house was in a state of chaos, there was a tranquil, reflective ambience that prevailed throughout. Kitty was given a "tour" and it was explained that the remodeling, which seemed to be in most of the house, would add several features they had wanted for some time.

Claudia led her outside, and Kitty was impressed with the architecturally stunning pool area which incorporated a large waterfall, and unusual rock formations. Large, glass walls from the master bedroom, which was on the first floor, provided views of the surrounding hills as well as the cascading water in the pool area.

Claudia explained that Josh wanted an indoor lap pool so he could swim year around... "like his Uncle Lucas had in his house.... and we decided to add a small fitness center, a media room and an art room for me, and, thankfully, to update the bathrooms. It's been moving at a snail's pace... I'm sorry we ever started the project."

"Uncle Lucas...?"

"Yes, the famous Lucas Connolly? He was a well-known attorney back East."

Kitty was stunned. She knew all about Lucas Connolly and was shocked to learn that he was the uncle of Josh Henderson.

"Yes, he died around the time I met Josh." They were in an indoor courtyard now, next to the master bedroom, overlooking the pool area. Claudia motioned to Kitty to sit in one of the plush recliners. There was a table with a large pitcher of frosty ice tea and as Claudia filled the glasses, she talked of Lucas Connolly.

"Lucas was very important to Josh... But, a strange thing happened." Claudia seemed to be lost in thought. Kitty waited for her to continue.

"When I met Josh he never said anything to me about Lucas' death.... I knew about it but didn't make the connection to Josh right away. Everyone knew that Lucas had a huge estate, and that Josh was the expected heir, but when I flew out here to get married, I asked Josh on the way home from the airport if he had heard anything about the settlement and he got very upset and angry... it was such a surprise to me because he had never been that way with me. Well, as time went by I learned that Lucas didn't leave his entire estate to Josh. He left the automobile dealerships but left the major holdings to charities and to several obscure people ... and that's what Josh was so angry about... the money was left anonymously and the attorneys wouldn't tell Josh who the recipients were. Josh felt he had a right to know... he was *very* upset!"

"Hmm. That's very interesting Claudia." Kitty said nothing to Claudia about her knowledge of Lucas, but instead prodded her to start at the beginning ... "Tell me how you met Josh... how the two of you got together." Kitty was aware of the sound of water from the many fountains and reflective pools. It was restful and meditative.

"Well, let's see, Kitty... I was living on the East Coast ... in the suburbs outside of New York City. I had been divorced almost six years... a single Mother of 3 children, working part time." She looked out at the water with a far-away look in her eyes. "I had landed a job I enjoyed working for a newspaper and needed a bigger car both for work and for the children ... my little and old VW bug was just not making it... so I had traded it in for a used Ford sedan that gave me trouble from the start. Every time I put it in for service it would be OK for about three days and then the trouble would start all over again....and several times I had gotten hung up without transportation which was dreadful with my job! So... I wrote a letter to the president of the dealership... that was Josh... And he made an appointment to see me. I remember how irritated I was when he was an hour late for the appointment but he was extremely charming and apologetic and made arrangements to have his 'best mechanic' take care of the problems...without charge, of course! And that was that, except a friend of mine who was the self-appointed town crier, called me two days later telling me about this 'absolutely gorgeous man' she had met, and how he had 'just arrived from Palm Beach... newly divorced,' and 'wouldn't it be wonderful' if the two of us....he and I...would 'get together.' I must confess that I did fantasize about this for a day or so, but then put it out of my mind. Then, two days later, I received a dozen white roses with a note that said 'there's a rainbow in your future.' "

"A *rainbow* in your future?"

"Well, Kitty... you have to be up on your commercials... I know it was a bit of a corny play on words... you know... 'there's a Ford in your future'... you have to understand he knew I had been in the advertising business... and I thought it was kind of cute... and romantic!"

"So then what happened?"

"Well, several weeks later we met at a dinner party and I fell madly in love with him after the first five minutes. He was a perfect gentleman, sensitive, attentive, not at all aggressive and seemed to reflect similar values. We talked for hours, and it was very comfortable. I *really* liked him and thought he felt the same, but three weeks went by and I hadn't heard from him. I thought I would die... but finally he called and from then on we saw each other every night"... Claudia paused... "And in three weeks he asked me to marry him."

"That was fast. What was the rush?"

"Well.....he told me that he was on his way to the West coast to open several new dealerships. He was in Westchester only to check up on the dealerships he had there. He said that he and his wife had been separated for over two years but that the divorce was only recently final. He talked a lot about his ex-wife and I hated the things he said about her... it made me uncomfortable that he would talk so negatively about the Mother of his child... someone he had been married to for so many years."

"What kind of things did he say about her?"

"Hm...well... he said she was a clever, conniving, pathological liar... that he never wanted to marry her but that she was so aggressive that he didn't know how to get out of it... this had been confirmed by a couple who had been friends of he and Monica... that's his ex-wife's name. I met this couple before we were married, and the wife told me that Monica used to call her and tell her terrible things about Josh... and she knew they were lies because Josh was such a 'peach.' He also discussed his suspicions of Monica's fidelity, and his doubt about being the daughter's biological Father. He was angry about her 'avarice' towards money, and implied that she was 'bleeding' him financially. It sounded like he hadn't lived with her for a long time in any conjugal way... he made it clear that he had no intention of meeting anyone or remarrying ... but when he met me he was 'smitten'"

"How did you react to that?"

"It's hard to put into words the love I felt. In the beginning, Josh treated me like a queen. He lavished me with gifts and flowers ...he was so... attentive... and so caring! He was kind to my children, and that was important to me."

"How did your children feel about him?"

"Well... as a matter of fact, they didn't like him, but I thought that was only because they felt I was betraying their Father. And...Well... David... you know, he's my oldest... said a couple of times that he thought Josh was a 'phony.' But I thought that was because he was ... well...that he was a tad jealous. David had been pretty much in charge of things since the divorce... he was so mature and had assumed so much responsibility with me working and going to school."

"How old were the boys... when you met Josh?"

"Well... let's see... David was seventeen, in his last year of high school... Matthew was almost sixteen, and Zach was ten and a half ... I miscarried after Matthew... and it was a mystery to me how I got pregnant with Zach... but I'll tell you all this later... I tend to get sidetracked, Kitty, so keep me focused!" Claudia giggled at this, and Kitty smiled and waited a bit before she continued.

"Claudia, what I'm hearing you tell me is that you were a single Mother of three boys... you were lonely, overworked, probably worried about finances... and then this knight in shining armor comes riding into your life, sweeps you off your feet and in three weeks falls in love with you and your three children and wants to get married. Did that seem strange to you? Did you question why a man as successful as Josh would want to take on a ready-made family?"

Claudia visibly stiffened.

"Ah..." thought Kitty, "I've hit a nerve."

"So you feel like my Father and everyone else... I just wasn't worth it and I'm still not worth it!"

"Claudia, you are worth far better than you got. You are an intelligent... beautiful... caring... and sensitive person. What I'm intimating is that Josh targeted you."

"*Targeted me!* What the hell does that mean, Kitty!"

Kitty sat upright, looked Claudia squarely in the eye. "Claudia, Josh has done before what he is doing to you now. What he targeted was your class ... you would be an asset to him. He targeted your sweetness, your loyalty, your altruism and empathy. What men like Josh look for are women like you who are kind, naive, submissive and honorable... almost virginal."

"Hmmm. Funny you should use that word, 'virginal.' Josh was adamant about not having sex before we were married, and on our wedding night he had a very difficult time ... you know ... he couldn't get it up, and then when he finally did, he came right away. He told me it was because I reminded him of a virgin and because he was raised to revere women... so, he was going to have to reprogram his head... meaning that now we were married and now it was O.K. to have sex."

"What else did Josh say on your wedding night?"

"Well, I remember that when he couldn't perform, I was very loving to him and he cried and said that no one had ever been that kind to him, that his ex-wife used to ridicule him."

"Josh's problem isn't that rare... especially if there has been a great deal of stress... but you're telling me that he said it was because you were virginal, and then he's saying his impotence and premature ejaculation problems were historical?"

"Well, no....I mean he said that he never had this problem before. He made it sound that his ex-wife was just so demanding... and that he had not had sex for so long that it was going to take time."

Claudia put her head in her hands. "You know Kitty, now that I'm talking about it I felt there were a lot of inconsistencies. I didn't want to face it... but when I came back home after the wedding to sell my house, I called a good friend and discussed things with her... It wasn't just the sex... that was the least of my concerns, but it was the feeling that Josh was lying to me about a great number of things... I felt confused... but I couldn't put into words what was going on... things just didn't add up... kind of a gut feeling."

"Tell me about the wedding."

"Well, I agreed to marry Josh, but, as I told you, his plan was to leave for the West Coast in three days. So, we discussed the situation and decided that he would go ahead, find a place to live and then I would join him and we would be married there. He felt it would be better if the children were not present so we could have time for ourselves. The night before he left, we were at Marios restaurant, very romantic and very in love. He began to talk about premarital agreements. I didn't know anything about them at the time... then he took this big document out of his jacket pocket and explained to me that it was really for my protection since my Father had so much money. I was stunned... it didn't make sense to me because Father had disowned me years ago. But Josh patted me and just talked away all my fears and concerns. So I signed it and gave it to him to take with him. To make a very long story as short as possible, Josh called every night and said he was looking for a house... a mini-ranch... but after a month, he couldn't find anything... he was anxious to be married, and after a lot of back and forth, I decided to go to the West Coast, get married and take a week looking for a house with him. So I made all the arrangements... you know, I had to find a nanny, get my airline tickets, have a dress made, get things organized... and I was to be there within two weeks. His job was to plan the wedding.   I'll never forget the feeling I had when I got off the plane in San Francisco ... I've never been so in love."

"You went to San Francisco?" Kitty was surprised. She had surmised that the Henderson's had lived in Los Carmelo from the beginning.

"Yes. Josh never said it, but I think he originally went to San Francisco to wait for the inheritance from Uncle Lucas. He had opened some dealerships there and I remember him telling me in letters... this was before we were married... that we might be there for a year or two... until he could get ahead financially." Claudia stopped for some minutes and sipped her tea. There was pain and hurt on her face, and Kitty leaned forward in her chair and patted her hand.

"Go on Claudia."

"We drove home to his condo ... He insisted that I sleep in the bed, and he slept on the sofa. The next day we drove to a beautiful town north of San Francisco, to a picturesque church... I was in my beautiful designer dress and he wore an old turtle neck sweater and a tweed jacket. No one was at the wedding except this woman from his work. She was coarse with a very filthy mouth that really turned me off, but Josh said she was the only one he could find that could take the day off from work. After the ceremony he had planned *nothing!* I asked to go to a restaurant and he took me to a cheap coffee shop and then we went home. I was inwardly upset but didn't say anything, because later he said he didn't make any plans because he wanted me so badly. And, as I told you, when he tried to make love to me he couldn't perform sexually ... and then he began to cry saying how much he loved his Mother and how she had been mentally ill. He again spoke of his ex-wife never understanding him... he says this often... and reassured me of his love ... as a matter of fact I remember him saying, 'I feel more loved by you tonight than any night in my life.' But then the next day he went to work! I was really surprised and felt abandoned. He gave me a hand-drawn map, the name and telephone number of the real estate woman he had been dealing with, told me to contact her and was off! That's essentially the way it was all week. We never went out to dinner, we did nothing except sit in the condo at night and *try* to make love... he was always satisfied and I wasn't, but he frequently explained that it would "take time." During the day, I looked at real estate, but every time I found something I liked, he would find some flaw. Finally, on Friday, the Realtor took me to a house that I thought was pretty tacky and in a somewhat run-down neighborhood. The Realtor said she had shown this property to Josh several weeks ago and that he liked it. We talked about it that night and Josh said that he felt we should get it because the down payment was pretty low, and that I was going to have to come up with the money because he had had to put all of his available cash into the new dealerships. He also liked it because the children's rooms were on the opposite side of the house from the master bedroom and bath, and the house was 'remote'...set back from the road and well removed from any neighbors. When Josh wants something to happen he always makes things sound logical, and he's so charming about it that I end up wanting to please him. So, I got on the plane that Sunday with misgivings and a bank account that hovering around zero. We had already gone to contract for the house. My job now was to sell my house, pack, hire movers, drive across country with the children and when all my assigned tasks were accomplished, we would be together. I was home a week before I realized that Josh had made no provision for any financial support for me. There was no more alimony, I was no longer working and had used up my savings for the down payment. I was horribly embarrassed, and somewhat frightened, but talked to Josh about this on the telephone. He told me to send him a budget, a list of my expenses and that he would take care of things."

Kitty was completely astounded at what she had just heard, but remained composed and focused on Claudia.

"Were you comfortable with this?"

"I had a lot of mixed feelings. Kitty, I don't know how to explain it... I know I'm intelligent... but when it comes to men and finances I am absolutely incompetent!"

Claudia leaned forward and was intense. "Things can be fine one minute and in the next he is in a rage. Like last Friday before Margo's party." Claudia told Kitty what had happened when Josh came home, how she had tried to be playful and how it had backfired. "It's so frightening to me and so confusing. I never know when he is going to laugh at things or when he's going to throw me against the wall!" Claudia began to cry silently at this point but was encouraged by Kitty to talk more about the confused feelings she had toward her marriage and her husband. Kitty then refocused Claudia and asked her to describe her early childhood and memories she had concerning her family of origin.

As she spoke, Kitty got a clear picture of a woman who had been raised in a stern, patriarchal, sheltered, parochial environment, ill- equipped to deal with the serious psychological dysfunction she was unintentionally painting of Josh Henderson. Hours had flown by, and it was time to end the session.

"Claudia, I must be going, but the one thought I want to leave with you is that these are not 'arguments' that you are having with Josh. *This is clearly ABUSE!*... both physical and emotional. *You* are not responsible for it, you are *not* 'crazy' and *you* cannot make it better. You have been emotionally isolated through intimidation and fear and you have most definitely been physically abused which is not your fault and certainly not acceptable! It must stop. Listen to me carefully... I believe everything that you have told me today... I understand that you have been effectively convinced to believe that you are responsible for everything that happens between the two of you...." Claudia interrupted her.

"Kitty I don't know that 'abuse' is the correct word... Josh is not a monster! He's not always 'abusive,' as you put it. He can be so gentle at times, and truly loving. Josh has some very good characteristics!"

Kitty anticipated the defensiveness. It was part of the abuse syndrome. It was also part of the most confusing part of abuse... the reason for mis-understanding why women stay in the relationships. Kitty acknowledged this to Claudia, and then made a move to end the session.

"Claudia, you've done a great job today. Before I leave, I need to ask you one very important question, and before you answer, consider every-thing very carefully. This is the question... do you feel safe being in the house with Josh... Do you know that he will not mortally harm you?"

Claudia put her head down and closed her eyes. Soon, tears appeared under her closed lids and silently slid down her now pale cheeks. In a few moments, she looked very directly at Kitty.

"I feel able to handle whatever happens. I don't think Josh will harm me at this time, but I do believe that things are getting worse, and I know that I am going to have to make a change." Her voice did not waver. Her gaze was steady.

"O.K., Claudia. I think that's a well thought-out answer. And I think we need to work on *what* changes you can make, *when* you can make them and *how*."

Kitty stood to leave, then sat down again. "I have to discuss some-thing else with you called 'dual relationship'. Very simply put, it's a legal obligation I have not to mix socialization and professionalism... that is having friendships or non-therapeutic relationships with any client. So, right here and now, I must tell you that I will be happy to be your thera-pist, but we can't hang out together. We have some of the same acquain-tances.... and might meet occasionally at the same parties or at the same meetings... and when we meet, I might seem somewhat distant, but that is to protect your confidentiality. Is this acceptable to you?"

"I don't have to think about it, Kitty... I want you to be my therapist. I've been to my pastor, and to two male psychologists, and all three of them asked me what I was doing to make Josh so angry. It's been a long time since I've had anyone talk to me as if I am a human being! I need you Kitty. You understand what's really happening!"

Kitty knew this was a difficult request for Claudia. She was not a person who felt comfortable asking for help. She knew that Claudia's sense of worthlessness prevented her from feeling deserving and that her sense of guilt... the guilt that came from being programmed that the abuse was her fault, had led to her keeping the abuse as a hideous secret.

Kitty set up another appointment with Claudia. They would meet the following Tuesday for three hours in the afternoon, again at Claudia's home.

5

Kitty drove home in deep thought. Claudia had touched an empathic nerve in her. She was drawn to Claudia's simple honesty... uncorrupted by the Machiavellianism that often plagued her class. Contrarily, she had felt uneasy around Josh . She thought back to the party on Friday night. She and Josh sat opposite each other at the dinner table and she intuited that he was *too* charming, *too* perfect. Everything about him was rehearsed, planned. His manners were impeccable, his taste in clothes was flawless. Obviously, he was smart and successful, yet he put on an air of the "poor English farm boy," a *false* humbleness and innocence, she thought. And there was something else about Josh that Kitty had noticed. Those gorgeous blue eyes could become frigid within seconds. She recalled that at one point in the conversation at the table, Claudia disagreed with something Josh was expounding upon, and his eyes became like icy glaciers, "fulminating into her psyche," she thought

Kitty had treated many cases of spousal abuse ... if she printed a list of people just within this affluent city there would be a gasp of disbelief. Of course not one of these people came to her for "abuse" issues. The rich did not believe that abuse was allowed to happen to them. When they viewed cases of abuse on television or read about it in the newspapers, it seemed to the elite that "those people" resembled the characters caravanning across of the pages of a John Steinbeck novel. It was not relevant to them. A few well-heeled, well-known women had come out in the media discussing spousal abuse. They were crucified! Not only by the media, but also by their cronies, especially their social "clubbies"... women who felt instantly threatened. Indigenous to their culture was an unspoken taboo against exposing this historically silent crime. She knew from her session with Claudia, today, that no one in this upscale community would suspect what was happening at the Henderson house. To the outside world, Josh and Claudia were a couple to be envied. Josh... Rich, handsome, a bit flirtatious and playful with other women, and Claudia, an undeniably beautiful woman, who had the reputation for kindness and patience... and who never said a word to anyone about her real life.

Kitty was puzzled by the judgmental attitude of women toward other women... specifically, condemnation of the women who suffer from spousal abuse. How often she heard..." Why don't they leave!"... "How can they be so stupid to go back!"... "Why should I feel sorry for them... it's their choice!"   "Blaming the Victim" was a nasty pastime of many people who seemed to be ignorant of the intricacies of the human condition. Kitty thought how well Claudia unknowingly suggested an answer to this issue today when she defended her husband during the session... "He's not a monster... he's often gentle and loving."

"There are so many complicated ingredients in this issue," Kitty reflected. She thought about the book she had written several years ago about spousal abuse in which she had traced the history of the male dominance of women... the *"ownership"* attitude that pervades this *crime*. She had learned through research that among early civilizations, marriage was considered a social contract, with arrangements made by families. In the theocratic Jewish society, there had existed a highly patriarchal system in which the father had absolute power over his daughter and the word for "wife" was "beulah" meaning "owned."   The woman was the "chattel" and was to be ruled over. In the Athenian societies, only wealthy women could escape the cruelty or the degenerate behavior of their male spouse but if she left, the children were always given to the father. The early Christians abhorred divorce for any reason and there followed centuries of unresolved theological debate as to the intent of Christ's teachings, so that by the 16th century, during the Protestant Reformation, there was fertile ground for marriage and divorce revisions. It was then that women were granted separation status but only for adultery and cruelty or malicious or prolonged desertion. In England, until 1857, the sole relief obtainable by women in the courts was the ecclesiastical decree of separation, which became America's heritage.

The early American settlers, primarily devout and religious Protestants, retained a patriarchal structure in which the wife and children assumed subordinate roles. Legally, when a woman married, she became a "femme covert," meaning a *legal non-person*, living under the husbands "protection." Known as "coverture" and fraught with legal disabilities, these laws were not removed until the mid-19th century. In spite of the fact that the Colonists declared in ringing tones that "all men are created equal", there had been a stratified society from the moment of our birth as a nation, carefully cultivated by the white, male, Protestant ethic that quickly became the ruling elite. "Independence" did endow certain *men* with "inalienable rights" but women remained largely in the feudal world subject to the man whose castle was *his* home. It was assumed that the husband was head of *his* family and the legal assumption was that women were "property" with the unspoken expectation that they would be subject to restrictive behavior and abide by a double standard. These assumptions became firmly entrenched in religious teachings with the result that women who are abused... verbally decimated... physically battered... emotionally fragmented... and financially bereft... are sent home, admonished to be patient and long suffering, and to pray for their husbands to become the holy head of the household. Kitty had an impassioned disregard for professionals and clerical advisors who had failed to address spousal abuse with any consistent, or in some cases, accurate teaching. She was appalled to hear that Claudia had gone to her pastor and to two male psychologists none of whom showed any compassion or understanding of the problem... and adding to the dilemma, she was aware that research showed that often, these same "professionals" were abusive in their own relationships. According to law we are prohibited from using racist words, or committing hate crimes and if we continually used filthy and demeaning language in public, or attacked our neighbor there would be some sort of criminal charges... but it's still acceptable for a woman to be on the receiving end of a tirade of demeaning and humiliating language from her husband on a regular basis, and she is expected to be submissive to him. Kitty pondered the immeasurability of spousal abuse. She knew that family violence was pervasive in the United States, with several million American women abused each year. There were no good statistics and she knew one of the reasons for this was underreporting due to *shame*... and the fear... not necessarily physical fear, but the fear that results from the brainwashing that... *it is their fault.*

And so the women hid in the pews of the churches hoping to salve their inappropriate guilt, praying for deliverance from the insanity of their homes. No one was asking the right questions, namely...*why don't the courts consider this horrendous crime on a par with non-spousal beatings and batterings?* .... *why are men allowed to abuse and get away with it? ...why do we, as a society, tolerate it?*

And then there were the children...Kitty could not deal emotionally with the abuse directed toward the children of such marriages, often brutally beaten and emotionally annihilated. She had tried her hand at counseling the child of a local pastor, a young, good-looking man who believed he was god's gift to the world of women and went about proving it while systematically abusing his children and perennially pregnant wife. The incident proved to be a professional turning point to Kitty... She never counseled children again, but began to dedicate herself to helping abused women extricate themselves from their perceived prisons.

She made a mental note to question Claudia about Josh's ongoing relationships with her children... She was reluctant to open this up, but intuition told her that it would be a necessary component of Claudia's decision to leave Josh... And Kitty knew without any doubt that it was necessary for Claudia to leave... and soon.

6

In her second session, Claudia continued relating to Kitty how she had met Josh.

One of Claudia's remaining friend's had invited her to a dinner party. It was difficult to say "yes" to the invitation... she was always so tired when she got home from work and the children had so many needs...but she also recognized her need for some diversion. She went out so seldom... and thought she was becoming too quiet, too serious... possibly boring. So, on this beautiful October night with a large harvest moon, Claudia had chosen a chic winter white 2-piece lightweight wool and linen blend Chanel suit left over from the good years of her marriage. A long turquoise silk scarf from Hong Kong... a gift from her Mother... hung loosely around her neck and she chose her Australian fire opal earrings as her only piece of jewelry. She knew her legs were shapely, and the sandal style heels accentuated her trim ankles. Claudia kissed the children goodnight, gave instructions to the baby-sitter and drove the 35 miles to the elegant East side apartment of Jodie and George Reeves. She eased the car into the curb... Bill, the doorman, gave her a toothy grin... she left the car in his care and rode the elevator to the penthouse, aware of her usual nervous anticipation. Jodie and George Reeves, Jr. had been good friends to her... they welcomed her now with enthusiasm.

"Come in, come in, dear friend. Oh, it's so good to see you! You look gorgeous, but then you always do!" Both Jodie and George hugged and kissed her, pulled her into the living room of their sumptuous apartment.

"Look who's here everyone!"

Claudia went around the room, greeting people she knew and shyly introducing herself to those she did not know. She was only half way around the room, when dinner was announced by Stuart, the Reeves very old butler. George took her arm, walked with her to the dining room, led her to her chair, and as Claudia sat down, she looked across the table into the incredible blue eyes of Joshua Henderson.

"Good evening, Claudia." He rose quickly from his chair. "How is your car?" He reached for her hand across the narrow table.

"You've met each other Claudia?" asked George hovering over her chair.

"Yes... Mr. Henderson was kind enough to help me with my car repairs several weeks ago."

"Yes, Mr. Henderson is always there with a helping hand. Isn't that right Josh?"

Claudia was flustered but even in her anxious state of mind she thought she detected some uncharacteristic sarcasm in George's voice. As he moved away he said over his shoulder,

"Enjoy your evening Claudia. We'll keep our eyes on you."

"You look quite lovely this evening, Claudia. And please call me Josh. Mr. Henderson makes me feel like your school principal." His smile was warm and inviting. His eyes were captivating.

"I will, Josh... And thank you again for the beautiful roses... It was poetic of you!"

Before long, Josh and Claudia were thoroughly involved in small talk and she felt an electric current of sexuality pulse through her. He was humorous and low key... and so very charming. The evening was one of those moments ... time passed unnoticed as they locked out all other distractions. It was late when the guests began to leave. Josh, always the gentleman, asked if he could accompany her to her car. In the elevator he stood close to her, staring seductively into her eyes...then he took both her hands in his… her heart was beating wildly, and her legs felt weak. When the elevator doors opened, he led her outside and they stood close together with both his arms around her waist, while Bill went for her car. Josh was asking her a great many questions about the children and inquiring about their ages and relationship with each other and she hoped her answers were coherent. The car was there… Josh opened the door, tucked her in and lightly brushed her lips with his. She put the car in gear, gave what she hoped was a regal wave and eased out into the non-existent traffic. When she was on the expressway, she began to laugh at her absurd teenage behavior, gazed in the rear-view mirror, and said to herself, "I am absolutely captivated! Oh, God, I've fallen in love!"

She didn't hear from him for three weeks… She felt foolish and was quite irritated. At the end of the third week, his contact came in the form of a huge box of white camellias sent from Hawaii. The note said: "These remind me of your delicate beauty. It was a memorable evening." Two days later he telephoned, and they saw each other every night for the next several weeks. He took her to every wonderful place she had not been for years. On the weekend, Claudia hired a babysitter and she and Josh drove to the mountains in Pennsylvania… they took long walks in the woods… Josh disclosed a bit about his work, but they were quiet a great deal of the time… a tranquil, serene silence. They dallied with each other with long, lingering kisses, and they watched the sunrise, while declaring their extraordinary love for each other. He continued to send her boxes and boxes of flowers, beautiful little gifts of earrings, elegant silk scarves and finally a ring … a simple emerald cut diamond… given to her at the top of the empire state building… he remembered that her favorite movie was "An Affair To Remember." Three days later he left for the West Coast on business.

7

Kitty had been seeing Claudia for two months... She was a little late as usual. Although it was a cool, shady day, Claudia had opened the umbrellas at pool side and the customary frosty ice tea pitcher was on the table, with some little finger sandwiches thoughtfully provided knowing that Kitty frequently had little time to eat. While Kitty was munching on the delicious cucumber sandwiches, they exchanged some pleasantries. It was evident to Kitty that Claudia was very tense this afternoon.

"What's been happening since last week, Claudia?"

"Actually, I've had less fear. But it's been a bad week. Sometimes I think Josh has hidden tape recorders in the house. He seems to sense when I am trying to do something for myself. Kitty, I've done a lot of thinking since last week, and, as you suggested, I started trying to chart the abuse... I can say that word now... and what I came up with is that it began three months after we were married... it seems to happen approximately every three weeks. There have been times when this is not the case, but usually we have three weeks of really good time and then I can feel the tension building for about two to three days, then the explosion, and then after a day or so of hostility he comes and cries and begs my forgiveness....."

"And tells you it will never happen again, that he loves you and then crawls into bed with you and makes love to you in an aggressive, possessive and unsatisfying burst of power, and it's all over in two minutes?"

"Oh, God, Kitty, how did you know!" Claudia clutched her head in her hands… "I just can't stand it anymore … I am angry that I allow myself to be treated this way…I want to yell at him to leave me alone … but I'm afraid to refuse him. A couple of times I tried to say 'no' and it only infuriated him again."

"So you submit to him to keep the peace." This was a statement that Kitty knew to be true. .. And she knew that it was a common trait of the male abuser, demonstrating power and not love. In addition, Kitty was sure that if she could look into Josh's childhood and sexual orientation, she would find a history of sexual abuse or ridicule or possibly violence of some sort. However, now it was necessary to deal with Claudia's stated feelings of fear, her heightened frustration and her intense desire to give up the victim role.

"Claudia, how angry are you?"

"Angry enough that I recognize that it's time to end this… I have to get away from him, Kitty… I don't want to be a victim any more… every time he begins with the finger in my face and uses his filthy language, I want to hurt him."

"Have you? Have you hurt him?" Kitty was calm and very composed. It was important that Claudia not feel threatened by her question.

"Yes… I've slapped him… Last month, when we got into it, every time he called me a filthy name, I slapped his face… then he slapped me back so hard he knocked me down. I went outside and when I came in to use the loo, he was in there… the door was open…he didn't see me…he was squeezing his cheek and using a nail file to injure the skin! I was fascinated… He had actually made his face bleed! Then I found out he had an appointment with the Pastor and I guess he prepared his face to elicit sympathy. He never knew I saw him and lied to me, telling me that I had done this to him. Anyhow, Kitty, I blew the whole thing, and forgot your admonition not to be drawn into his verbal attacks… to *detach!*"

"Well, Claudia in most areas you've done so well! No one is perfect you know, even though you try so hard to be perfect, you must realize that is you childhood heritage. But it is disturbing that you have reached the point of retaliating…everyone has a breaking point and that can be a dangerous place to be..." Kitty paused … it was important to see where Claudia was in her goal to leave the marriage.

"So, you think you're ready to leave Claudia? Let's discuss it."

"I want to leave, Kitty... I don't know if I'm ready... but the newest thing is that recently Josh has been absolutely ugly about Zack... telling me he was going to end up in jail because of his laziness and miserable attitude...it really triggers my anger...but the worst was when Matthew came to visit last week… we were discussing my return to school and some art classes I took with a live model… Josh became unglued about this, and Matthew made a comment to him to calm down and he literally picked up Matt by the collar, pushed him against the wall and smacked him across the mouth while threatening him."

"There it is!" Kitty thought, knowing that it probably wasn't the first time this happened. For the next hour, the session focused on Claudia's plan of action... where she would go, how she would survive financially, who she would engage as her attorney, what she would do if Josh became remorseful and begged her to come back, and more importantly, what she would do if Josh galvanized his entire repertoire of vindictiveness. They had discussed these issues before but Kitty felt that today was the day of decision! The responses from Claudia were well thought out and resolute. She was able to formulate a good plan… with the exception of what to do about the children… that had been an ongoing concern to Claudia.

The youngest boy, Zach, was now eighteen and would be graduating from St. Francis prep, in Alasek, the small mountain community next to Los Carmelo. He would spend the summer with Claudia before going to the University of San Francisco in the Fall. David was 25, living in New York City and was getting married in Washington, D.C. in August...Matthew, 23, was living with his girlfriend in Connecticut but would also be going to the wedding... Claudia was planning on going to the wedding also, then expected to spend some time in New York visiting friends.

"Claudia, why not call Gerald and see if Zach could visit for the summer… I know you would rather have him near you for support, but don't you think it would be wise not to involve him right now? You'd have all your energies for yourself."

"It's the damn loneliness thing, Kitty." Claudia was sad. "I've had so many years alone... there's been so little stability in my life...except for Zach."

"Claudia, I'll be here for you. And there's great therapy in work... you're on the verge of getting a great job, and you will have a great deal to organize and many decisions to make in the coming months... "

"You're right, Kitty. I am so blessed. I have so much more to help me get through this than most women do... When I was at my support group last week, I met a woman... her name was Laura... sixty-eight years old, frail and nervous. Her husband is military, a lieutenant colonel, I think... Anyhow, he has a new young girlfriend, and sued for divorce... the judge awarded Laura five years of 'rehabilitative' alimony. Can you believe it! Sixty eight years old with no education to speak of... and the judge says, 'get a job like everyone else does.'"

They exchanged some other stories and then Kitty refocused the session.

"Claudia, I don't want to keep dwelling on the sexual nature of your relationship, but has Josh ever told you anything about sexual abuse or violence in his background?"

"Hmm. Josh hates to talk about his childhood. But his sister, Sandra, told me about the time they had to go to an orphanage and how unhappy Josh had been while they were there. She said that he used to go into 'rages' and that she would have to sit on him to calm him down..." Claudia paused for a thoughtful moment, then, added, "Josh has made several remarks during our marriage about being humiliated and ridiculed when he was young but never went into detail. He did tell me a terrible story of how he and several other boys... I think they were all about fifteen to seventeen years old ... well they took this girl into the woods and gang raped her. I was horrified at the time to think that this man I was married to was capable of this. He tried to tone it down when he saw my reaction, saying he just watched... but when he began the story he was laughing and saying this girl was a 'retarded fat pig.'... It really frightened and disgusted me that I was married to a man who would commit rape, especially on a vulnerable, handicapped young woman."

There was a long pause before Kitty spoke. "What do you know about his parents?"

"Only that they were poor and that he resented his Mother... he's made remarks about his Father being a 'weakling.' But Sandra told me that the Father 'ruled the roost' and would never give their Mother any money. She had to plead with the shopkeepers to give them food, and she made some sort of arrangement with them... like teaching their children, and being some sort of a mid-wife. I think his Father had a problem with drinking and a couple of times he said things that leads me to believe his Father was physically abusive to his Mother."

Kitty was interested in what Claudia was telling her. It followed the established pattern of the abuser. She wished she could have known Josh's family and wondered if she could have unlocked any other patterns of behavior.

Their session ended with Claudia agreeing to call Gerald about taking Zack for the summer, and to put most of her plan into action.

8

Margaret Connelly, called Maggie all her life, was born into a genteel Boston family on May 7, 1895, and enjoyed a recognizable favored status in the household. Her Father was a successful physician, and although they were not filthy rich, they were extremely comfortable. The Connolly's were Irish immigrants, coming to the United States at about the same time as the Kennedy's, who at that time were far less affluent than they were in later years. A sister had died before Maggie was born... a brother, Lucas, was ten years younger... he adored her and they were always very close to each other. Maggie was the apple of her Father's eye from the moment she was born. She had the lush Irish beauty of his ancestors, the flawless white skin with blue eyes and black curls, and a great wit that belied a sensitive heart... and a brooding that she kept deeply hidden within her. Outwardly, Maggie was always spirited... a consummate extrovert, being the first in the neighborhood to welcome newcomers, or helping her Mother pass out pamphlets for women's rights on the street corner. As Maggie matured, like her activist Mother, she had yearnings to do "something great" in her life. She earned an RN but felt there must be more she could do, and at the urging of her Father, enrolled in medical school. However, after a year and a half, Maggie began to feel suffocated in the overwhelmingly male world that treated her intellectual aspirations with contempt. It was 1917, and on April 6th, the day that President Wilson finally declared war on Germany which paved the way for America to enter the great war, Maggie, like many maverick women of her day, wanted to be involved. She garnered her parent's approval and before long was on her way to join the American Ambulance of Paris, a privately sponsored military hospital run by volunteers. The hospital, located on the outskirts of Paris, had been headed up by an old school chum of her Father's, Robert Bacon. His wife, who was now living in New York, and Maggie's mother, living in Boston, spearheaded funding drives for the Ambulance. The first American troops arrived in France on June 26, and Maggie was right behind them. On the ship to Europe, she had shared a cabin with three other American women volunteers and they had bonded quickly, sharing their excitement and fears about the great adventure they were about to undertake. Little did Maggie know that this "adventure" would change her life... forever.

The American Expeditionary forces had considerable casualties and her hospital was one of many that received the wounded. They came to her in pathetic condition... mud-spattered, torn uniforms, festering wounds filled with maggots, bodies covered with flies and a stench that she would never forget. There was camaraderie and teamwork among the staff that sustained them all and enabled them to give their full energies to the needs of their patients. This esprit-de-corps also helped to dispel the constant veil of fear that hovered over all of them... one never knew when a bomb might destroy their hospital, or a stray bullet might end a life.

Three months after settling in with her duties, Maggie met First Lieutenant Harrison Bradley, attached to the 132nd Infantry Medical Corps. "Harry" had been born in the United States, but his family had moved to England shortly before the war had begun. Like Maggie, he had a burning desire to get involved in the conflict. This day, he had accompanied several of his wounded men to the hospital, and there was an instant attraction between the two that blossomed into a love affair within a short time. The horrors of war brings many things into focus. Each moment is savored, each good-bye brings an unremitting sense of anguish, and then the joy of reunion dims the sordidness and depravity.

Toward the end of that year, Harry took some shrapnel in the leg. It was not a serious wound and it gave them time to be together. On New Year's Eve, they welcomed in the New Year, 1918, with hope and an announcement to their friends that they were now officially engaged. Harry had given her a small emerald and diamond ring... a design he had sketched and sent off to a jeweler in England. Maggie was touched deeply that he remembered emeralds were her birth stone and her favorite gemstone. Each time she looked at it, it reminded her of the warmth and love that she and Harry shared instead of the vileness and horror she saw each day. The first week of May he was there with her again, in the little pension they had rented close to the hospital. They made beautiful love for three days... celebrated her 23rd birthday by drinking too much French champagne... voraciously ate some black market lamb and pate Harry had scrounged up and vowed they would never be apart for even one day after the war ended. Then they were saying good-bye, and the unuttered foreboding began for Maggie. There had been some terrible battles...

On August 11, 1918, dawn broke early - even during the night at this time of year there was little darkness. Maggie dragged herself out of bed. It was hot and humid and she had slept poorly. After splashing cold water on her face at the small sink next to the bed, she peered out the narrow window and stared at the drizzly rain and muddy streets. It had been a harrowing week. The "second battle" of the Marne was being fought in an area known as the Ile de France, between the Marne and Vesle Rivers, from Chateau-Thierry to Soissons and Fismes, and the small hospital was overflowing with the wounded. She said a quick prayer, dressed hastily and was on her way to minister to the many needs of these gallant heroes, now casualties of an insane war.

At 8:30 AM that morning, Harry heard that a squad leader of his pla-toon had been severely wounded while attempting to capture an enemy machine gun nest. He requested permission to go to the rescue of his friend. There was heavy artillery and machine gun fire, but Harry confidently worked his way forward and located his friend. Hoisting him upon his shoulders, he was instantly killed by rifle fire. It was three months to the day before the Armistice was to be signed. An article that appeared in the December issue of the *Atlantic Monthly* described this battle saying, "It was said that in this soul-stirring struggle, the young American troops played their part with heroism and success."

Maggie was overcome with grief. It shocked everyone because she had always been so vibrant, a dedicated and feisty leader always in control. Now, she felt her life was over and no amount of comfort from her friends could penetrate the desolation she felt. She had to get out of France... she hated it now, and wanted the comfort of her parents arms and the cleanliness of her bedroom and fine linens. But Maggie was slightly more than three months pregnant. Harry's remains were to be interred in his hometown in the English countryside. She could not bear to be separated from him, so she made arrangements to go to England, and became a member of a London Voluntary Aid Detachment [V.A.D.], a rest station providing food, beverages and kindness for the trainloads of returning soldiers. It was here that she ran into an old friend of Harry's ... his name was Angus William Henderson. Maggie had not known "Will" very well, and what she knew she did not particularly like, but when she saw him, her heart jumped ... here was a connection to Harry! They began to see each other frequently... Will accepted the fact that Maggie was pregnant without judgment... within five weeks he proposed marriage knowing she did not love him... but he needed someone to care for him. It was a marriage of need for both of them, as Maggie did not want a fatherless child. They drove out to the English countryside and were married in a small Anglican church, a fact that Maggie never told her staunch Catholic parents. Will had worked in a woolen mill before the war and was able to get his old job back... and they settled in a modest three room cottage that Maggie fixed up with the generous amount of money they received from all her friends and relatives in the States. Within a month, Maggie knew she had made a dreadful mistake. Will was having difficulty fitting into normal society again... he had frequent nightmares and unresolved anger toward the "powers that be" ... the ones responsible for sending him into war. He drank copious amounts of alcohol and would become abusive when drunk. On one such occasion, Will pushed her with great force, causing her to fall heavily over a chair. Maggie lost Harry's baby two days later and sank into an irreconcilable depression. In the ensuing years, she performed her "wifely duty" without emotion, and bore two more children.... Sandra, her firstborn, and two years later, Joshua... neither of whom fully extenuated the melancholy experienced with the loss of Harry's child.

9

Josh finished his elaborate lunch with gusto. He liked coming to the Windward Hotel...the view... the smell of the sea air... and particularly the attention he received from the staff. God, how he loved the prestige! He never realized how differently the rich are treated... the eagerness with which they are greeted at the best places, the imperceptible rush to cater to their every need...sometimes it bordered on the embarrassing ... people almost bowing and scraping, anxious to please and craving recognition, so they could go home to their families and say, "Guess who came into the store today?" And then there would be an exaggerated story that would enliven their monotonous day.

His companion du jour was not yet finished her meal. He knew they were going to bed and he had to contain the familiar irritability that was gnawing at him... Josh had no talent for intimacy... it bored him, but he loved the provocation... the defiance of convention... he was a philistine living a counterfeit life, but he thought just about everyone he had ever met was just as fraudulent.

Look at what Lucas had done to him! He had worked hard to please Lucas and Holly... learned all they had to teach him, did everything he was told...knowing that if he secured a place in their hearts, he would secure a place in their checkbook. He had even trusted Lucas... there were times he even imagined that Lucas loved him... whatever love meant. Shit... He remembered having some tender feelings toward Lucas and Holly... but then Lucas had betrayed him... and he never even knew it until he and Claudia were getting married... God! What a jackass he had been getting himself all tied up again with someone who had no access to money... Well, he had learned his lesson and had shown everyone... "I made it on my own... I didn't need Lucas, and I don't need Claudia Fitz*prick!*"

Josh looked across the table at his companion. She fit the pattern that he usually chose for these trysts. Long-legged, slim, sultry, dark hair... "But this one is too chatty," he thought impatiently. He barely listened as she twaddled...

"I'm really into self-actualization, you know... I met the most *wonnnderful* professor when I was taking this class..."

"Sweetheart," Josh interrupted with a smile he did not feel, "I'm getting turned on looking at your gorgeous body... eat your lunch so I can have my just desserts."

They walked arm-in-arm to the private "cottage" Josh maintained on the Windward grounds. He made several calls while she showered and when he heard the water stop running he opened the bathroom door, gazed at the lithe and graceful body, the sizable breasts ....Within seconds her wet body was on the bed and his mouth was exploring her soft skin... But Josh had already lost interest ... It was the challenge that excited him, and knowing that he could not maintain an erection, his women got fast, rough sex, with little foreplay... There was no lingering on his part, and less sentimentality.

10

"Abuse! Come on Kitty, Josh Henderson has a reputation for being as charming and kind as anyone could be!"

"Exactly! If it's too good to be true it usually isn't...true, that is. You know that's the profile of the abuser, Sid!" Kitty was sitting in the stark white, messy office of her mentor, Sidney Strauss, M.D., L.C.S.W.. D.S.W., located in the neighboring town of Metcalf. She had obtained permission from Claudia to discuss her case with him, reassuring her that Sid was very reputable, and would protect her confidentiality at all costs. After her last meeting with Claudia, Kitty felt she needed some objectivity.... She wanted to make sure that she had not interjected too much of herself into the decisions Claudia was making.

"Sid, you know as well as I do that it's really difficult to discern the truth in cases such as this. But, I guarantee you that this woman is being systematically abused by her husband, that it has been going on for over nine years, and that the reason she can't do anything about it is because no one believes her, or hasn't, up to this point, and because there is this code among the wealthy that you don't squeal, no matter what!"

"There's more than 'charm' involved in the profile, Kitty. What else do you see?"

"Well, we know that Josh's Father was abusive to the Mother and we have to suspect that there was abuse to the children as well, or that he saw and heard the abuse to the Mother."

"And?"

"And we know that the darkest side of what happens in family abuse is what happens to the children. Did you know, Sid, that juvenile offenders are four times more likely to have grown up in homes with violence and five times more likely to become abusers? Sid, every day four women are murdered as a result of domestic violence and the number of women who have been murdered by their intimate partners is greater than the number of soldiers killed in the Vietnam War! And ...it's thought that two-to- four million women are battered every year... that's one woman every *nine seconds*... think of it Sid... every nine seconds! But... the worst part of this is that abuse is a grossly underreported crime...and no one has any idea of the prevalence of verbal and emotional abuse!"

"So why aren't the hospitals, doctors and therapists doing more?"

"Well, Sid, you're a doctor... You tell me why?"

"Claudia, you know as well as I do that spousal abuse is a very complicated issue. I'm subject to Mandatory Reporting Laws, and I'm also subject to the HIPAA laws and they do not always benefit the patient. Suppose a woman comes into the ER after being beaten by her husband, and I attend to her injuries, and she wants to go back to him... I want to report him as I should, but I also wonder what will happen to her when she goes back and he finds out when the police come to the house that she told someone... will I have made things worse? Will I have protected her?"

"I know exactly what you are saying, Sid. There's a lot of cynicism and frustration because there is such a misunderstanding why women go back to the abuser. My opinion is that there are poor solutions to the issue. We have the laws, but we also have very poor training among the agencies that enforce the laws as to the best manner to handle the perpetrators. I also think that because the reporting rate among low-income families is 5 times higher than in other income levels, there is a snob reaction... kind of a deep sigh and a shake of the head... with the 'well, what do you expect' kind of attitude... and in addition to the ambivalence and hypocrisy that exists, people just don't want to get involved... it is a private matter... and most people experience some fear of the whole issue... it's easier to blame the victim and move on."

"What about Claudia's friends and family? Can they or would they help?"

"That's another whole bag of tricks, Sid...Claudia has never had any family member help her... and most of her friends are pretty affluent and abuse is handled differently..."

"How do you mean... are the affluent exempt from abuse? How is it different?"

"Sid, you know that we have seen a great number of abuse cases right here in our valley... but have you ever seen any of these women in the ER? I doubt it! Here, among our wealthy patients, when the abuse occurs that needs patching up these women call their private physician and nothing gets reported nor is it ever talked about. Money has its privileges, Sid, and at a certain level of achievement, people tend to know each other all over the world, and they maintain an unspoken code of behavior."

"What else do you know, Kitty?"

"Well, I don't *know*, but suspect that Josh fits the disturbed sexual pattern often seen in the abuser." Kitty related to Sid what Claudia had told her about Josh's traumatic separation from his parents at age five when he went to the orphanage, of the rigid, abusive environment he had both at home and at the orphanage, and of the rape incident when he was 17. "I strongly suspect that Josh most likely frequented prostitutes."

"Why?"

"From things Claudia tells me, Josh suffers from consistent premature ejaculation which could fit the pattern of a man who has most of his early sexual experiences with prostitutes who demand that the sex act proceed quickly... Also, I get a picture of Josh as the male abuser who performs better sexually after an episode of anger, and you know that this can indicate a man with conflicting feelings toward women, with the greatest sense of sexual pleasure, and often of greatest sexual performance, being enhanced when the woman is degraded. And the thing that concerns me so much is that when someone is willing to degrade and humiliate another to the degree that Josh has done to Claudia, it's not a big leap to murder... whether by accident or intent."

Sid and Kitty discussed this for a bit, agreeing that in spite of Claudia's feelings that she was safe that there *had to be a change... and soon!*

"Are there any other disorders that you've discussed with Claudia? What about her?"

"The usual problems of fear, zero self-esteem and an inability to make decisions due to a lifetime of being told how stupid she is!... which is tragic, because Claudia is a truly intelligent, insightful and gifted woman... it is amazing to me that she is as integrated as she is given the degree of neglect and abuse she has endured throughout her life."

"What do we know about Josh's life at the orphanage?"

"Claudia said that Josh hasn't wanted to talk about it, but his sister told her some stories that sounded pretty terrible. First, she told Claudia that Josh frequently had uncontrollable outbursts of rage during his life and that she... the sister's name is Sandra... that Sandra would have to sit on him and hold him down... those were her words..."hold him down"... to prevent him from harming himself or others. Sandra remembered that when they first got to the orphanage... now remember that she was only seven years old and Josh was only 5 years old... well, she said that during the night Josh became what I would term "wildly agitated"... he was yelling obscenities ... at age five... he was throwing things, screaming and crying and hitting his head against the wall... Sandra said she didn't know what to do... she was afraid the sisters would hurt him or make him leave, so she sat on him until he calmed down."

"Sounds like a brief psychotic episode... also could be IED* although there is so little known about this."

"Yes... I can see both..." Kitty paused in thought... "Sid, did you ever hear of Lutheran nuns?"

"No, can't say that I have... Why?"

"Sandra told Claudia that... well apparently this orphanage was run by a group of Lutheran nuns that escaped from Germany during World War I and settled in England. Well, when they were sent there... to the orphanage... the other children made fun of Josh. His hair was long and curly and for some reason he wore girl's underwear... I suspect there was no money available and the clothes came from donations. He apparently suffered from enuresis, and he was humiliated beyond words... it was discussed openly in front of the other children, and they shamed and degraded him relentlessly."

"So, Kitty, what is the plan?"

"Claudia has decided to leave. I didn't tell her what to do... she's really given this a great deal of thought, but I'm worried... Josh has all their finances tied up and he's the only one that can get his hands on any money... Unfortunately, Claudia signed a prenuptial agreement, and put all her money into their joint accounts, co-mingled it, so she is legally bound to split everything with Josh. She does have some money squirreled away ... it gave me such joy to know this... but it's not going to last very long."

"Where is she going when she leaves?"

"She has a friend in Palm Vista she's going to stay with after Zach graduates from St. Francis Prep, and then she's going to Washington for her son David's wedding... she hopes to be able to see some friends in New York while she's back East.,, and my understanding is that she is going to look for apartments while she's in Palm Vista... it's a good place for her to live... in addition to having a friend there, job opportunities in that part of the State are excellent."

"So, what are you worried about?"

"The time element, Sid. No one can predict how Josh will react... he can be very harsh and vindictive. He could also drag this on forever, and then finances would be a problem."

"Can't Claudia work?"

"Yes... absolutely. I guess I was thinking of Claudia in a shelter... my God Sid, can you see Claudia Henderson, the debutante of the year, in a shelter!"

"Kitty, it sounds like you've done some good work with Claudia... I've known you for many years and believe you are an excellent diagnostician and have a unique ability for observation and are very solution focused... follow your instincts... Claudia is a survivor. She has been through bad times and has persevered. Continue to connect her with the strength she's displayed previously... she will be able to make it."

"It's going to take time, Sid."

"No one has invented a magic pill, Kitty. Working out painful situations always takes time... but you know as well as I that every positive outcome increases self- esteem and especially increases our wisdom... who can ask for more than that?"

When Kitty left Sid's office she decided as long as she was in the vicinity she would drive over to the Windward Hotel to make reservations for Norman's parents who were arriving from Switzerland the following week. Sid had massaged her ego... she was grateful for him over the years for keeping her on track ... but right now something was nagging at her... she wished that she had been able to have some sessions with Josh. It was usually her custom to do this, but when she had suggested this to Claudia, the idea was met with negativity. "Josh would never come to see you, Kitty. You represent a world of women that he doesn't like." There was truth in what Claudia had said, but Kitty felt that things would be easier for Claudia if she had made an overture to Josh... she liked to hear both sides of the story. If she could see Josh and determine the pathology, she could help Claudia with her responses, and possibly help Josh with his destructive patterns of behaviors. Kitty felt compassion for him, knowing the background... she could imagine the suppressed feelings of anger and frustration. In recent years, she had become a proponent of Cognitive Behavioral Therapy* (CBT) and knew there had been some good outcomes with its use in cases of IED* (Intermittent Explosive Disorder) ... if that was Josh's problem, perhaps he could be helped. At the same time, she surmised there was a genetic component to his pathology... "Well," she thought, "I can't allow myself to become a clairvoyant... Claudia is my patient, and I need to focus on her and her needs."

Kitty was in such deep thought that she almost passed the entrance to the hotel. She hit the brakes and backed up a bit, but as she was about to make the right hand turn off of Huntsville Drive into the hotel driveway, a car came barreling down the winding road, going the wrong way on the one way street. The driver slammed on the brakes and made a wide swath to avoid hitting her. They were both stopped now, and Kitty glared furiously into the eyes of Josh Henderson who was laughing and at the same time, closely hugging his young, glamorous passenger. Josh showed no recognition, made no apology, restarted his car and sped away, spewing gravel and grass as he went. Kitty hit the steering wheel with her fists uttering appropriate expletives. "Well, so much for thinking I could have a session with Josh," she said wryly. She continued to wind her way up the driveway to the hotel. "But I'd sure like to know more about his life with Uncle Lucas!"

11

It was going to be a bleak winter in Marindale. The town was stunned. There had been no headlines, no publicity, but its image had been sullied and the name of Marindale was now bandied about with a kind of sneering acrimony by those "outsiders" who had been on the receiving end of ethnic slurs and class rejections.

Marindale had always been regarded as the jewel of suburban New York. The community was unique in its beauty, from the elegant main streets with its conclave of ultra-expensive boutiques and quaint antique shops to the formal English gardens and carefully manicured parks. Within the mansions hidden behind the high stone walls and protective gates leading to the long driveways, residents of this sophisticated town had always prided themselves on safety, security and a legacy of gentility that precluded any violence. It was a WASP town, infused with uncompromising values…family and hard work… A town that was solid rich with the "old" money of the rail barons and financial gurus … no new money millionaires here! The clubs were restricted, and that's the way they wanted it. They had their own sense of order and their own sense of justice, and that's the way they wanted it.

Glenwood was a town next door to Marindale. It was far from a slum…. the houses were small, neat and clean with well-kept gardens and flowers.

However, it was a separate world from Marindale. It was 'blue collar".... low socioeconomic status.... with many of its residents offering services to the residents of Marindale....chauffeurs, maids, handymen, roofers, gardeners...people the English would refer to as the "downstairs" people. Most residents were of Irish or Italian decent with long histories of large families, loyalty to their employers and strong political views. They were good, church-going people and they knew that what had happened was a "terrible incident that went horribly wrong.".... The reality of it all cast a pall over the approaching holiday season.

■ ■ ■

Lucas Connolly was sipping coffee in the day room. He loved this room with its large gothic style windows that revealed the magnificent gardens of his estate from every angle. It was 5:00 pm....barely dusk. Captain Duffy sat across the table sipping tea...coffee seemed to exacerbate his ulcer symptoms, so he now drank his tea like his Irish mother... with lots of sugar and thick cream. Duffy liked the English marmalade he had liberally spread on his scone.... "Most likely left over from the Missus afternoon tea," he thought. Duffy was very well acquainted with Lucas Connolly and knew beyond a doubt Lucas was one of the most respected attorneys in the State...hell in the country! Lucas was tall...six feet five inches....he was a sober person, not at all ostentatious with his money like some of the residents of Marindale. It was common knowledge that Lucas had "diversified" and was now one of the richest men in the United States... maybe in the world! He owned banks, a helluva lot of real estate, and who knew what holdings in how many corporations? ... And in the last 10 years had bought out dozens of auto dealerships... "most probably for the nephew" he had heard. Duffy often said that the thing that set Lucas Connolly apart from so many other stinkin' rich was that Lucas has risen to his state of affluence and power without destroying anyone on his way up the ladder. Duffy liked Mrs. Connolly, too. She was not a social climber, and had the reputation of being "a good and kind Christian lady...not snooty or judgmental." He knew his mission here today was a mere formality. Duffy had earned the reputation of being a pragmatic man and realized that there was an historic, unspoken rule here that would prevent any backlash against this family. Duffy also knew there would be no trial because trials are more concerned with evidence, and less concerned with truth, and the evidence in this case was almost non-existent as far as the nephew, Joshua Henderson, was concerned. Everyone would believe Josh's story and believing him would serve many purposes….it would make all of their jobs a lot easier, but more important, especially to Duffy, it would preserve the status quo. As a matter of fact, Duffy mused, Joshua would somehow come out of this looking like a hero. But he didn't mind this time. He owed Lucas Connolly a great deal, and he would prove his loyalty.

■ ■ ■

It was 8:30 p.m. Holly had left the house that afternoon, after an organizational tea for one of her many charitable endeavors. Lucas was glad that she had left before Duffy had arrived in the afternoon, and tonight, Lucas had asked their cook, Alia, for a light supper... a sandwich and a glass of beer. He had munched on it with little zest while reviewing the documents and photographs that Duffy had left with him. A few minutes ago, Lucas had asked Josh to come to the library and he and Josh were now sitting in the cavernous library room opposite each other in overstuffed sofas. Thick oriental rugs covered an unusual slate floor, while hundreds of books lined the shelves of beautifully carved built-in floor to ceiling bookcases. There were exquisite antiques, an eclectic gathering of chairs and tables, two huge desks and the "the everlasting fire" burning in the enormous stone fireplace which gave everything in the room a warm, burnished glow. It seemed to Josh that the fire was infinite... perpetually lighted and kept tidy by the unobtrusive but ubiquitous houseman. Like the rest of the house, there were the oversized gothic-style windows that gave unobstructed views of the splendid grounds of the estate. Tonight, the lavish drapes were open revealing the myriad of lights that illumed the frosty, snow-laden trees and shrubs.

Lucas thought Josh looked vulnerable tonight, "a rare thing," he theorized. Since Josh had come to live with he and Holly, what was it? 2 years? "No... it's more than that....it's been 28 months." As Lucas gazed at his nephew, he thought him to be an extremely handsome young man. "His frame has filled out this past year...he doesn't look so bony." Josh had the characteristic barrel chest and broad shouldered look of the Connolly men. He was wearing the usual casual clothes, the "uniform"...khaki trousers with a blue shirt. Lucas noticed that Josh often wore blue to accentuate his blue eyes, the only clue he had that told him Josh recognized his good looks. He remembered the day Josh had arrived in the United States... dirty and disheveled... his skin so pale against the cheap, rough fabric of his dark blue suit. The kid had looked like a ragamuffin, so he didn't mind the great amount of money Josh had spent on clothes. He was glad that despite the lad's rather crude upbringing, that he had an innate air of refinement... most definitely acquired from Maggie.

Lucas removed his glasses, took his handkerchief from his jacket pocket and studiously began to clean them.

"Josh, tell me exactly what happened today with that girl...give me every detail."

Josh stared at his uncle for a long moment. He opened his mouth to speak and stopped. Tears welled in his eyes....they didn't spill out onto his cheeks, but stayed obediently within the confines of the orbit. In this moment, Josh realized that this was *the* most important performance he had yet to give in his seventeen years of life.

"We got out of school today at 11:30..." Josh paused, and cleared his throat, a mannerism he often employed when he was lying. His voice was unsteady, and his hands were clenched in front of his chest. "For some reason, Julia, that's the name of the girl that was ..." He paused again, cleared his throat, "well, you know what the guys did to her?"

"Yes, I know what they did, Josh... please continue."

"Well, for some reason she...Julia... missed her bus.... I saw her walking and I know she's retarded and shouldn't've been walking home alone, so I stopped when I saw her and offered to drive her home. She knew me from school. There's a couple of retards in the school and they all take a bus every day. Julia tried to tell me something about having the trots, being in the bathroom and missing the bus, but I couldn't make out everything she was saying....I guess someone told the bus driver that her Mother came and got her." Josh took a deep breath and reached for the coke he had brought with him to the library.

"So, you gave her a ride. Were you going to take her immediately home?"

"Yeh! Sure... I was going to take her right home. I already knew where she lived cuz one day Frankie Fahey and I drove past her house ....at least he told me it was her house." Josh stopped and took another swig of coke and then cleared his throat. "So anyhow, I was going to take her right home and then I saw the two guys...."

"Two guys, Josh? I thought there were three boys involved in this?"

"Right! But first I saw Frankie and Manny, you know, Manny Carmango?"

Lucas had made it his business to know the friends that Josh was seeing. He did not like these boys... not because they lived in Glenwood, but because he knew their reputation for being "tough guys"... each of them had been arrested for malicious mischief, and Frankie, in particular, had been a regular visitor in the court system. Lucas knew that Josh had trouble making friends so he hadn't interfered... but this was an unsavory trio... they used Josh for his money and influence... for some reason they appealed to the baser nature that Lucas had observed in Josh. He knew, now, it had been a mistake to allow the association.

"Where did you first see them?"

"Uncle Lucas.... Am I in trouble?" Josh was pale and obviously scared. "I know Chief Duffy was here this afternoon when I was up in my room. I'm scared....What's going to happen? Do you believe me that I didn't do anything...that..."

Lucas interrupted. It was fundamental to his style of initial probing that he temper any display of emotion. From years of interrogating he had learned the art of what his Chinese friend, Leo, would refer to as Asian inscrutability.

"Josh, you come to me with a very disturbing story….."

"It's not a story Uncle Lucas! It's the truth, I swear to you…."

"Let me finish, Josh. My choice of the word "story" is not good. What I want to convey to you is that I know how much you have been through in your life. I am not only your Uncle but your friend and I want the very best for you in life. But Josh, this is a bizarre and tragic happening that you have witnessed. I need to know everything so that I can help you….so that I can handle the details of what needs to be done. Do you understand? I'm not your enemy…I want to make sure nothing happens to you. So please, continue giving me the details. We were talking about you driving with Julia in the car and coming upon Frankie and Manny."

"O.K…..O.K…." Josh put his head in his hands, then took another swig of soda. "Frankie and Manny were coming out of the corner store and I saw them as I was driving by. I stopped to talk to them and they got in the car….I was going to drop off Julia and then we were going to go shoot some baskets. Frankie said we should get Pudgy Wilson…he's this dumb fat kid at school …. I think he's only 15…..and I think he's somehow related to Frankie….like a cousin or something…..anyhow then we went to get Pudgy and then….." At this point Josh sat back and closed his eyes. He seemed to sink down and become part of the chair. "I can't think straight any more. I'm not sure exactly how the rest happened….it was so fast….We were driving and then we were at the abandoned mill… you know, the old abandoned mill on the south side of Glenwood?"

Lucas nodded his assent.

"Well, when we got there the guys got out of the car and Julia got out….she was laughing and seemed to be having fun and they walked to the woods and disappeared… and then I heard her screaming….I thought at first she was just having a good time….but when I went into the woods they were there… doing it… I didn't know what was happening at first… it's all a blur after this… I know I told them to stop… I know Frankie and I got into a fist-fight… and I think Manny ran away and Pudgy was looking for his pants. I got Julia into the car and drove her home… fast. She was crying and saying, "The exercise hurt." She looked pretty awful but I didn't know what to do except to drop her off and I saw her go into her house… her Mother was waiting at the door and she began to scream. I got so scared that I just left and came home." At this point, Josh bent over and again put his head in his hands. He kept saying, "Oh God, I'm so sorry this happened… Oh, God, Uncle Lucas… please help me… please let this be over."

Lucas went to him and put his hand on Josh's head. "Josh, I have to make some phone calls. Why don't you go to the kitchen…get a snack and go upstairs… try to sleep. We'll talk again tomorrow morning. You did well, Josh. Everything is going to be fine and you will not have to worry."

Josh grabbed his Uncle's hand and with tears in his eyes, he gave his Uncle an unprecedented hug and left the room.

Lucas went to his desk. He was not only one of the wealthiest and most respected attorneys in the country, he was also a shrewd judge of character and knew in his heart that he had just witnessed a theatrical moment. He was used to this. Many of his clients were pathological liars…brazen liars with no boundaries. He was repulsed at what had happened, but learned long ago that with the right set of circumstances people are capable of everything. Lucas and Holly were steadfast in their commitment of love to Josh, and love to Lucas meant helping someone reach their highest potential. Now, in retrospect, Lucas realized the cultural chasm between rural England and the urbanity of New York City and its environs was deeper than the ocean between them. Somehow they had all failed Josh. He blamed himself for failing to understand the enormity of the emotional, the mental and social metamorphosis that Josh had to make. A conversation he had with Holly flashed into his mind. It was an unseasonably hot and humid day in May, a month after Josh had come to live with them. They were sitting in the day room, finishing breakfast and discussing what had seemed to be a long, tense month.

"He's really green Holly… and pretty arrogant. I'm surprised at how quiet he is… and sullen! He's shown almost no enthusiasm for anything, except sitting in his room building model cars."

Holly put down her cup of tea, and looked at Lucas with concern.

"He needs an epiphany, Luke. It's our job *and our responsibility* to find out how to give him that."

"I know it's our responsibility... I just don't know what makes him tick!"

"Well, one thing I'm sure of, Luke... I think he feels very intimidated socially as well as intellectually."

"Darling you are so wise. From what I know, his home life with Maggie and... and ...what's his name..."

"Angus... "

"Angus! My God, I cannot understand why Maggie married him! An abusive alcoholic for a Father... And his Mother... my poor Sister... a broken shell of a woman. I think what I'll do today is to call Phil Markowitz and get his advice about how to proceed with our 'parenthood.' I love you Holly... we'll get through this."

Phil Markowitz, Ph.D., was a good friend. Lucas had used him as a sounding board many times when dealing with difficult cases and they had become very close to each other when Melinda had died. Phil specialized in adolescent psychology, and that day, sitting in a dark, back booth at Isabella's restaurant, nibbling on their antipasto, a plan was formulated to help Josh. Lucas was to engage a tutor until September... not the usual kind of tutor, but someone who would be compatible with Josh and could teach him not only educational things, but also cultural and social mores... how and what to eat, how to dress, tour the museums, introduce him to the right newspapers and books. In short, help an almost-fifteen year old leap into the present century. And for his part of the plan, Lucas would begin to counsel Josh about financial matters. After all, the lad had to learn the enormity of the estate he would eventually inherit. When Lucas spoke to Josh about the plan, it was met with the first demonstration of enthusiasm since his arrival in Marindale. Lucas remembered feeling relieved, pleased and satisfied. "It's what Holly said... Josh is having his epiphany." But tonight his heart was heavy... he was experiencing unaccustomed queasiness. "Did I teach him the wrong things? Was it all too late?"

He picked up the phone and for the first time in his life, Lucas felt compelled to use his power and position. He made three telephone calls and then left the library secure in the knowledge that he would continue to support Joshua Henderson in his search for integration. As he climbed the stairs, he was aware of how spent... how exhausted he was. He would wait for Holly to give and receive love ... a nightly ritual that gave great meaning to their life.

12

Most small towns have an active gossip track. But, among the elite, gossip goes underground when a member of their ranks is threatened and they close ranks around one of their own. There is a great emphasis on surface serenity in Utopia… "It's important to get along" …and differences are often subdued and not discussed, at least not openly. There were some comments… "There was a lot of blood"….. "I heard the girl was half dead"…. "Wel-l-l, she *was* retarded"… "It was those 'commoners' in Glenwood… sometimes they are so vulgar and obscene"… "The police said the attack was brutal…" Well, she probably didn't know what happened to her… you know… because of the mental condition…." So, for the most part, the community rallied around Lucas and because of him, around Josh. And they rallied around each other by regrouping into a disciplined, sentient reserve that seems to be a requirement of the aristocratic genetic code.

■ ■ ■

Four days later, Josh was standing at the rail of the ship, the Bermuda Queen, on his way to visit a relative in Bermuda. His Aunt Holly and Uncle Lucas would fly over in a week after "some details" were cleared away. He thought of the last time he had sailed when he came to America…

and how things had changed for him. That had been a rough crossing for him... not only the sea sickness, but as the ship drew closer to the United States, he became highly anxious. For the first time in his life, he had become aware of how disreputable and shabby he was in his homemade suit and farm boots. He had a heightened sense of embarrassment and his self-confidence waned. When the ship docked, he stayed on deck per his instructions. And then Uncle Lucas had loomed in front of him, a very tall, slender man, black curly hair interlaced with gray topping a finely chiseled face... but it was the eyes..."they're the same color as mine... I look like him!"

"Hello, lad, how was your trip?"

Before Josh could answer, they were walking quickly off the ship, some man in a uniform carrying his meager belongings.

"I've arranged for you to be expedited through customs," Lucas was hurrying, "just follow me and don't say anything, I'll take care of everything."

They entered an office marked "Private" and before long the three of them were out in the street, getting into a large, black automobile, the man in the uniform was in the front and Josh and Lucas were in the back and there was a window between them. Josh was overcome with anxiety. Everything was so foreign! The oppressive stagnant air, the acrid smells, the throngs of humanity and the clutter and noise of the traffic. It was overwhelming and paradoxically exotic.

They talked some, but mostly Josh had sunk back into the warm comfort of the seat, trying to assimilate the myriad of new sights and sounds. Sometime later... maybe an hour and a half... the driver turned into a small road behind a high stone wall. He flashed something out the car window.... a massive iron gate opened and they drove through it, up a long, winding driveway. Josh had seen photographs of his Uncle's house but was unprepared for the actual magnificence of the Connolly mansion. It was a rambling, 2-story fieldstone structure set on 6 acres of lush, rolling gardens... Josh thought it looked like a castle. He remembered the tour Lucas had given him later that day, and was particularly impressed with the indoor, heated pool. He soon learned that Lucas was extremely health conscious but was obsessive about his privacy. He and Holly would swim almost every night together. On several occasions, Josh voyeuristically invaded their privacy as they swam naked, engaging in extensive and pleasurable foreplay until later, after hot showers and herb tea served to them in bed by a bashful servant, their love culminated before they succumbed to "sleep, the most gentle sleep."

As Josh leaned against the rail, of the ship, he fidgeted in his inner jacket pocket for a pack of hidden cigarettes. After lighting up and taking several deep drags, he leaned over the railing, watching the bow of the ship slice into the rhythm of the waves. He was alone on deck…it was too cold and too early in the morning for the other passengers. The sun was about to appear on the horizon, and this panoramic backdrop made him feel powerful and in control.

Josh had fallen in love with money. It was seductive and he didn't mind his insular existence or his paucity of insight. His internal approval came from the status he had achieved. He feigned sympathy and empathy but could not really understand or tell anyone what those words meant. He was shallow and grandiose but did not know it. He was a pathological liar but he did not know that either. He had the capacity to talk himself into believing his lies and he played scenes repeatedly in his mind accompanied by an inner dialogue that became real to him, obliterating any fear he had of being caught in his lies. He had learned the art of being disarming.

The sun began to rise, streaking across the sky. Josh had a moment of discernment, and he said out loud to no one, "Sometimes I can't believe my luck!" Marindale was a far cry from the gray, gritty English mill town in the middle of nowhere where he had spent his formative years. He had hated the people with their crusty exteriors and bad teeth. "After such a pissy childhood, I've finally made it." He began to shiver as he thought of what had almost happened. "You almost blew it, you jerk! And for what! For a fuck with some retard? Hell, I'll bet I can have any woman I want." With this, he vowed to himself to be smarter in the future, to learn everything he could to secure the fortune that would someday be his.

■ ■ ■

Josh didn't return to Marindale. At the end of January he was sent to Palm Beach, Florida directly from Bermuda. Lucas and Holly preferred to avoid Palm Beach and its dynastic families, but they thought Josh would fit in perfectly. With his good looks and youthful panache, the women would devour him and the men would temper him with their relentless counsel. Holly's avoidance of the Island centered on what she termed "the hidden agendas" of this enclave of WASP pedigrees…meaning the loathsome racism that was abetted and sanctioned in this one square mile of megamillionaires and titans of industry. However, both she and Lucas had realized the growth potential of the Island and had invested heavily in real estate many years ago. In the 1940's, when automobiles were first allowed on the Island, Lucas was characteristically astute and opened several auto dealerships to supply the Rolls Royce's and Bentleys that would be parked in front of the dazzling couturiers on Worth Avenue. He had hired Sam Johnson as his manager… a good man…who was exceptionally smart and loyal, with uncommonly honorable values. He would be a perfect mentor for Josh and would teach him first-rate skills.

Josh arrived at the height of the season in Palm Beach. He was not yet eighteen and immediately felt "green" and out of place… the familiar insecurities that had surfaced upon his arrival in Marindale. Sam Johnson had been a needed friend… at his side to instruct and teach him. Sam had helped him settle into the Connolly's chic, tastefully furnished condominium, which was larger and far more resplendent than Josh had anticipated. "I should have known that Lucas does everything with class and with an investor's eye," he had commented to Sam who remained discreetly quiet.

Josh had been pretty pissed off when he learned he was "being sent away," but later realized the benefits of his uncle's support… Ultimately, it would assure him of increased power and privilege. Besides, he thought

Palm Beach was quite exceptional, surrounded as it was by both the ocean and Intracoastal with fabulous beaches and water sports. Florida was still enjoying the burgeoning opportunities of a post-war economy and the thriving night-life of the Palm Beach aristocracy captivated him. With his young, virile good looks, his "old money" connections, and the English accent he had so aggressively protected, his assent into the Palm Beach social scene was rapid. At the same time, Josh learned a great deal about the business world from Sam who consistently introduced him to many business contacts. People had faith in Lucas' integrity, and Josh benefited from this legacy.

Josh spent twenty–two years in the Palm Beach area, more or less. At nineteen, he was married briefly to a vulgar, second-rate "show girl" he had met in a Miami bar... she was twenty-nine, and looking for security. After getting very drunk, they had eloped to Hot Springs in Arkansas. The volatile three-month marriage was a financial disaster to Lucas who bailed him out of the ugly situation with the admonition... "No more, Josh... you are now on your own in that department!"

What Josh lacked in formal education he made up for in business acumen. Sam was amazed from the beginning at his shrewdness and resourcefulness, information he passed on to Lucas. However, he withheld his knowledge of Josh's amoral and somewhat salacious personal lifestyle, as well as his nagging concerns about some of Josh's questionable business practices that he had observed first hand.

After the Miami show girl, Josh had become a hard partying playboy... for several years he was a companion, simultaneously, to several wealthy widows... but eventually tired of the charity parties and the dowager adoration, and married a woman who had partnered with him in developing some real estate deals for Uncle Lucas. They were not well suited to each other... Monica's personality was too strong for him and he resented her. They had a daughter together, but Josh scarcely knew her. He had become a workaholic, buying, selling and developing real estate and acquiring a bevy of auto dealerships west of the Mississippi, most notably in Texas and Illinois. Josh managed enough charm to forestall any thoughts of divorce. Monica's business in the Palm Beach area continued to be successful and she had a loyal following all of which generated a substantial amount of money to finance Josh's acquisitions. Monica adored him... she pushed aside the rather serious "physical confrontations" that were part of their marriage. "After all," she often said to herself, "we're not together that much, and Josh can be so very loving and gentle." She was unaware of the extent to which Josh had been unfaithful and disingenuous during their entire marriage, and she was unaware of other things about her husband.

Josh had acquired the Palm Beach attitude that to be visibly rich you've got to spend a lot of money... and he spent more than his share! Life for Josh was overcoming the challenge of balancing accounts... particularly the hidden accounts he secretly kept in foreign countries. He never wanted to relive the poverty of his childhood. Lucas and Monica unknowingly paid for the many prostitutes, the copious amounts of alcohol he consumed, the expensive gifts he bought for himself and others, and the immediate gratifications that were so much a part of his life. Josh felt bored a good part of the time, and at the end of the twenty two years he was feeling suffocated by Monica and the unending parties in Palm Beach that, despite the millions of dollars raised for charitable purposes, were shrines to hauteur and pomposity. He was searching for a new place to live and had been attracted to the West Coast. It would be a realistic time to end his marriage to Monica and to transition into new challenges. He was unaware of how the next few months would affect these contemplations.

■ ■ ■

The death of Lucas and Holly Connolly was stupefying! How could this happen again to the Connolly family... a drunk driver ....slick roads during a snow storm. Lucas hung on for 30 hours, and then silently embraced death to join his wife who had died instantaneously at the scene of the accident. It was a difficult time for Josh. He had never faced the death of anyone close to him. His feelings for Lucas and Holly were the closest thing to love he had ever known. Now that was gone ... anger welled up in him and all the childhood rejections and insecurities floated to the surface. He hated his return to Marindale and the profound loneliness of the big house. He had walked through the maze of rooms... such memories... sitting at the counter in the large kitchen watching Alia, the cook, perform her magic... the intoxicating smells of home baked breads, fish and meats in sauces he never knew existed, listening to her laughter as she told him stories of her childhood in Bolivia. In the living room, he recaptured his first American Christmas... the huge tree, almost touching the twenty foot ceiling, filled with exquisite decorations, the steamy hot, spiced cider, delectable confections and tartlets made especially for him. It filled him with nostalgia and a sense of yearning. Later, he stood still for a very long time in the library recalling every minute detail of "that" night... Lucas had shown him love ... a profound love... in his customary resolute way. Standing there looking at the vintage desk, Josh felt a momentary pang of shame. Had Lucas known?

The funeral was a somber affair in spite of the hordes of people in attendance. Afterwards, Josh found himself in a state of intense melancholy. Monica had been at his side during the difficult days of the wake and the funeral, and his sister Sandra had arrived unexpectedly from Canada where she was teaching school. But neither their support nor the thousands of consoling and affectionate expressions that surged forth from friends, acquaintances and well-wishers from all corners of the earth, could assuage the loss he was experiencing. It was a defining moment in his life.

Josh stayed in Marindale for three weeks after the services. In addition to visiting all the auto dealerships, he made pilgrimages into New York City visiting museums and performing arts that he had been introduced to when he was a teenager, trying to pass the time, knowing that he would be enormously wealthy sometime in the near future when the rather large assemblage of attorneys settled the estate, but none of this eradicated his sadness... until he met Claudia.

■ ■ ■

In the weeks and months following the deaths of Lucas and Holly, Josh was more in touch with his sentiments than he had ever been. Perhaps it was his anticipation of being a billionaire that he found himself susceptible to acts of kindness, and there were times he experienced warmth and tenderness. Claudia was the recipient of this "new" personality definition (which, unfortunately, was short lived.) From the first moment he met her at the car dealership, he wanted more of her. She was soft, kind, and very vulnerable... and also quite beautiful... quietly regal, really. So different from the excessiveness of the Palm Beach women with their limitless plastic surgeries, their bony bodies, their flamboyance and flagrant aggressiveness. Claudia was so natural. She was reserved, almost shy, and looked clean and honest. He wanted to do everything for her. She touched the part of him that had been abandoned, that had been brutalized by the indifference and the abuse of his childhood caregivers. He loved her childlike delight when he had sent her flowers. "Oh, Josh, no one has sent me flowers in years! They are so gorgeous, so fragrant"

After their first meeting at the dealership, when he had helped with her car, he made the decision to pursue her, and without Monica's knowledge, had begun divorce proceedings in Florida. He knew Monica would be stunned... they had some very good sex during the weeks Monica spent with him at the funeral... but that was her problem. After he met Claudia again at George and Jodie Reeves dinner party, he decided to wait until he was in Florida again to tell Monica about the divorce. There was property involved and he needed time to unleash his attorneys... to give them time to wrap everything up... It had taken him three weeks to set everything in motion, He had known George Reeves ever so slightly from the Marindale Country Club ... they hadn't liked each other. Josh had very few friends in Marindale... he felt that in the land of sheep and goats, he had, at best, been viewed as a goat, despite Lucas' popularity and prestige.   At the wake for Lucas, Mrs. Reeves had mentioned the dinner party, and suggested to Josh that he call her son, George... it would be good for him to see some of his old friends from Marindale. So, on impulse, he had called George, and learned that Claudia was to be among the invited guests. Josh didn't care about the bias George had toward him and had accepted the lukewarm invitation to attend the dinner. He had to see Claudia in a public place and woo her in front of a lot of people.   His charm aggrandized in a public arena.   The evening had been a huge success for him and he knew that he would ask Claudia to marry him... and soon! But first he had to figure out what to do about her children.

BOOK III

Part 2
Joshua Henderson and Claudia Henderson

And Lord... I place myself in your mind and trust your plan for my life.

1

It was a beautiful Saturday morning in June. Josh was working outside on the car... his favorite pastime. Claudia had done some gardening, and was in the process of arranging the daily arrays of fresh flowers throughout the house when Josh came in. She heard him rooting around in the kitchen and knew he would be looking for lunch. She sensed he was "building" and was trying to stay away from him, but thought if she went out to the kitchen and made him lunch it might make him happier than he had appeared earlier.

"Hi, dear ..."

"Haven't you made lunch yet?" He was quite irritable and was throwing things onto the counter.

"I didn't know what you wanted... but there's some delicious bread I made yesterday, and some tuna fish. Would you like me to take over here and make some sandwiches?"

"Yeh... I need to wash up."

She heard him go upstairs to use one of the bathrooms that had been completed. While he showered, she made sandwiches, some cucumber salad, and got some beer out, knowing Josh would have at least two with lunch as an appetizer for the heavier evening "happy hour." She took the food on a tray to the patio, waiting for Josh to join her. When he walked through the door she was struck by his beauty... his black hair was made curly by the steamy shower, and he wore nothing but a small towel that snapped at his waist… she always hated it when Josh came to the table without being dressed, but sensing the growing tension she said nothing.

"I'm going to have to spend some big bucks on Zack's car." He proceeded to tell her in great detail what parts he would have to install, and all the time it was going to take him. She knew he would simply take it up to Al at Art Breen's auto shop on route 33… but he had to fabricate the details… it was a prelude to something more, and she could feel her body getting tense.

"We're cash poor right now. All this remodeling, your air fare back East, the insurance on the dealerships… and I don't know why the hell Zach can't buy his gas for cash instead of putting it on the credit card… I just don't know where it's all going to come from!"

Claudia had heard this litany of "poorness" on a regular basis. It had nothing to do with money. Josh was looking for an excuse… she needed to tread on safe ground.

"I know I've not handled things well this year so far, Claudia… I just need you to understand that we are in a temporary slump."

"I do understand Josh… why don't you let me help… I could handle the finances…." The words were not even out of her mouth before she realized that what she had said was a mistake.

"You know, your royal highness, I break my ass going to work every day to keep you and your brats happy… and what gratitude do I get!"

Josh was suddenly on his feet, the chair toppled over… his eyes became wild, his nostrils flared… his finger was in her face, his body bent toward her in a threatening manner…

"You started this today, you selfish bitch! Get up!" He pulled her hair, forcing her out of the chair onto her feet.

"Get in the house you mother fuckin', cock-sucking whore!" He was pushing, dragging her through the door into the bedroom.

"Get over there or I'll smash your face, you miserable woman… you're not even a woman… you're a god-damn fuckin' lesbian cunt… how did I get mixed up with you! You're crazy… you belong in an institution…"

He threw her on the bed... then began to rip at her blouse. Claudia rolled away from him and landed on the floor. He was standing over her.

"Get up... get up I said!... Now you're going to do what I say!" He grabbed her arm and threw her against the wall. Claudia tried to fight back and caught him solidly in the face...

The hit intensified his fury, and he smacked her with the back of his hand on her face and eye, knocking her down to the floor.

"You're a miserable woman... You disgust me..." He spit in her face. "I can't stand the sight of you, you fuckin' bitch... no one likes you... they can't stand you because you're just a stupid, ignorant nothing... a nothing.... Do you hear me? You're a rotten Mother and you're a rotten wife and I can't stand the sight of you!" As she lay on the floor, he put his foot on her hip, cleared his throat and spit out the thick phlegm into her hair with the precision of a bullet.

"Oh! Look at her... poor little girl... putting on your act again... James Fitzpissy's little actress! This is your fault, you bitch... you're nothing but a ball breaker, and I'd like to break you in half!"

"Josh, please... please stop this..."

"Yeh... now you want to stop it you fucking whore. You're responsible for this... You always start it." He suddenly backed away from her...

"I'm leaving... I've had enough of you... get out of my sight, you filthy bitch!"

He gave her one last kick in the kidney area, then turned from her, went to the closet and began throwing clothes out onto the floor. It gave Claudia the chance to run from the room, and on her way through the kitchen grabbed a bottle of water that had been left on the counter. She left the house, got in her car and drove to a deserted spot in the mountains. After a time, she finished crying, collected herself and began her ablutions with carefully chosen products from a "care bag" she had dutifully stashed under a blanket on the floor of the back seat... moistened wipes to remove the spittle and to apply to the wounds on her face, particularly around her eyes, a small brush for her hair, a little makeup hurriedly applied, and a flash of lipstick... She drank the water in huge gulps, took some deep breaths and drove to Margo Leon's home.

2

Kitty and Norman had just returned from "depositing" Mom and Dad at the hotel. It was Saturday afternoon, a time they always set aside for themselves. Their plans for today were unexpectedly interrupted by a phone call from Claudia. Norman had taken the call and as he handed the phone to Kitty indicated in pantomime that she was upset.

"Yes, Claudia…"

"Kitty… I'm so sorry to call on a weekend… but Josh and I just had a terrible fight…he tore the house apart… he slapped me around pretty hard…."

"Claudia… Claudia dear… do you need medical attention?"

"No, I don't think so, Kitty…My face is messed up a bit but I can take care of that. What I really wanted to tell you is that I ran out of the house… you would have been proud of me… I didn't get involved in his madness, but took the first opportunity I could to escape and went to Margo's for about three hours and when I got back to the house Josh was gone! I mean really gone…all his clothes, his personal effects, even his tools from the garage. Kitty… he's gone! I'm free!"

Claudia was slightly hysterical. Kitty rolled her eyes at Norman… he smiled and then silently mouthed the words, "Go to see her." But, Kitty had a better idea. It was time Claudia began to come to her office and she made arrangements to meet her there in half an hour.

Norman held her... "I begrudgingly let go of you... Hurry back! I need you, too."

Kitty drove the short distance to her office. She and Norman had bought this small house near the beach, right off Junipero Blvd.. The upstairs had been remodeled as an apartment and was occupied by a young married couple... the wife was from Vietnam and the husband from China. Both had tragic backgrounds and had been sponsored to be students at the University. They lived here rent free in exchange for cleaning the first floor where Kitty had her office and group rooms, and also kept the yard and pool in good shape.

Kitty and Norman had many properties like this one, some occupied by elderly with no families, some occupied by single Mothers with young children. Many years ago, Norman had been surprised by a substantial inheritance from an unlikely source. Since they knew that Kitty was unable to bear children, they made the decision to use the money to benefit others as much as possible. It seemed that the more they gave away the more their assets multiplied and before long they had bought many "fixer uppers" in the burgeoning Los Carmelo real estate market. The years had been good to them in other ways. Norman was able to pursue his artistic talents, becoming a recognized sculptor, while Kitty had returned to school to pursue a doctorate in psychology. She had chosen private practice psychotherapy fifteen years ago... loved her work and she and Norman enjoyed a close and loving relationship.

■ ■ ■

Kitty let herself into the office through the side door. She loved walking in here. The house was the popular Spanish mission-style so prevalent in the nineteen twenties and thirties. She and Norman had renovated extensively so that it was now open and very light, incorporating many arches. They had used the Mexican Saltillo tile for the floors throughout, which gave the house a nice sense of continuity. Kitty had decorated in neutral tones with highlights in the desert mauves and purples. The overall ambience was tranquil and chic.

In the kitchen, she hurriedly made some tea… while it was brewing, she closed the French doors of the group room, switched on the computer in her custom-designed office… turned on lamps in the therapy room, fluffed the pillows on the sofas, lit the fireplace, and then heard Claudia at the door.

Claudia hugged her with uncharacteristic abandon. In that moment, Kitty was the Mother Claudia never knew, the husband that never loved her enough, the friend she needed desperately and the therapist she had come to trust.

"Kitty, thank you so much for seeing me. I just can't believe what's happened!"

"Claudia, let me look at your face… it's pretty swollen… does it hurt?"

"It's a little sore, Kitty, but I'm fine… emotionally unstable, though… one minute I'm crying, the next I'm feeling relieved, and then I get angry… overall I'm scared as hell."

They had moved to the therapy room and were sitting on facing sofas. Kitty noted Claudia's motor tension… the shakiness, and rapid eye movements… she was also experiencing shortness of breath, so Kitty ritualistically poured two cups of Chamomile tea, allowing a long pause to help Claudia relax. The ugly, large welt on her right cheek indicated a hard, back-hand slap… she was going to have a black eye.

"What are you most afraid of, Claudia?"

"Mostly about financial things… how am I going to survive? How will I be able to pay the bills? Will I be able to get a job at my age?"

Kitty again noted that Claudia's speech was now considerably less pressured. The shock was beginning to stabilize.

"Legitimate fears, Claudia… what else?"

Claudia put her head against the back of the chair and closed her eyes. "I don't know how to tell the children… I feel so guilty about them… I guess my biggest fear is wondering what Josh will do… he can be so vindictive… you know one of his favorite sayings is… 'I don't get mad, I just get even!' "

"Well, we can assume half of that statement is true." She and Claudia grinned ironically.

"My feelings are so mixed, Kitty... I don't want him back at this minute, but knowing how I hate to be alone, I wonder what I'll feel like if he calls and promises it will never happen again." She paused again, and Kitty allowed her the time she needed to sort out her feelings.

"You know, Kitty, there's part of me that loves Josh... I know it sounds crazy, and I'm sorry... I just can't help it!" Tears filled her eyes as she shook her head to emphasize her confusion.

"You don't have to apologize, Claudia... you're a person with a great deal of compassion and your ability to forgive is enviable. Another thing I know about you from these past months is that you are amazingly non-judgmental and usually see both sides of an issue." Kitty learned forward for emphasis... "But in this case, Claudia, I want you to stay angry! Instead of dwelling on all the good things about Josh and your marriage, I want you to remember the bad times... I want you to remember the infidelities... the lies... the times he threw things at you... spit on you... kicked you ... hit you and threatened to put his fist through your face... picked you up and threw you across the room... the filthy language... the threats and manipulations of your money... and especially all the times he told you what a 'miserable woman' you are ... how he was 'fed up' and going to leave you. I want you to remember all of it and write it all down, so that when you are tempted to go back to him.... And you will want this, Claudia... but if you can remember the hurts, the frustrations, the years of pain... then you will be less likely to go back."

"You're right, Kitty... I'll have lots of time now and I know writing things down is good for me."

"As far as the children are concerned... I'd like to devote an entire session to this on Wednesday. For now, call them, try to remain calm when you're speaking to them and make it short and sweet. You really don't know what will be happening, so tell them you will update them when you have something more definite. Let them know you are going to need their love and support but that you are in control. Now... have you contacted the attorney you wanted?" Kitty wanted to refocus the session on crisis intervention.

"Yes, I see him next week. And as I sit here I realize that I've squirreled away enough money to tide me over for a month or two. And Margo offered help, although I know that she is loyal to Josh and I've decided to put some distance between us."

"Claudia, here's the telephone number of the women's shelter…just in case you need it. If you call them, talk to Myrna …Tell her I told you to call and then explain your situation to her. Then I want you to call a locksmith and have all the locks changed… today! Call your security company and have the code changed… today… and make sure that it's working properly. Be at the bank first thing Monday morning, and make sure that your joint funds are still there and then withdraw half of the money… call your attorney's office today and leave a message that there's been a crisis and you need to see him as soon as possible. Call the phone company first thing on Monday and have your telephone number changed, and when you call the children set up a telephone code with them… like two rings and hang up and then call back or something like that."

As Kitty was talking, she was writing down each item knowing that Claudia would not remember. Claudia was quiet… she was smart and knew Kitty was effecting a crisis plan to insure her safety. It scared her. Reality began to encroach into her agitation and initial animation, and Kitty became aware of a drastic change in her affect.

"Claudia… things are going to be fine… but it might be awhile before there's any stability. I think it would be a good idea if we had three half-hour appointments next week. If you need more time, we'll work that out… but the most important thing to remember is that you are strong… that you will have temptation to go back to Josh… I'm sure he will try to engineer this… but if he asks, I hope you will discuss it with me first…"

"I won't go back to him, Kitty. This time it's really over."

Kitty knew that Claudia was referring to the time eight years ago when she had left Josh. It had been dramatic… after one of their "arguments," Josh had left and gone to Florida where he proceeded to have a sexual encounter with his ex-wife, Monica. Matthew, who thoroughly disliked Josh, had talked with Josh's daughter, who laughingly described how she had served them breakfast in bed. When Josh arrived home, Claudia had changed the locks throughout the house, and had put his belongings in the driveway. She had been seeing a therapeutically educated priest at the time that was savvy enough to recognize the pattern of systematic abuse and had encouraged Claudia to leave the marriage. She impulsively sold the entire contents of her home, all the things dear to her, and moved to Arizona. It had been a lesson in courage for Claudia. For the first time in her life she took things into her own hands and made a decision. As is turned out, it was not a lasting decision... Josh went to therapy for 2 months, and they were back together in eighteen months. Claudia had failure feelings...she had not planned things at all well for either financial or social support. At that time, she was unable to find a job and her savings were quickly dwindling... which is the primary and ongoing problem for all women suffering from spousal abuse... and neither the government nor society had good structures in place to alleviate the situation.

"Claudia... I know you're very sensitive to this, but perhaps it would be a good idea if you would make a police report... I know your attorney will say the same thing."

Claudia shook her head no... "I can't... I think it would infuriate Josh so much that it would only inflame the situation." She stopped, closed her eyes and pursed her lips... "If you remember, Kitty, I did that once before, and the police were really crude. One of them actually asked me how long it had been since we had sexual intercourse... and the other thing they said was that I had no bruises... let's face it... they just don't want to get involved."

Kitty couldn't argue with her. Professionally, she knew that Claudia should make a report... if she ever had to go to court, a police report was mandatory... but the reality of the situation was that spousal abuse was only evolving as a reportable crime, and that there was little sophistication or desire on the part of the police to handle the complexity of this family dynamic... it could be a very dangerous involvement. Sadly, statistics for spousal abuse among police officers has been shown to be twice that of the rest of society presupposing that professional neutrality could be compromised. Claudia was right about another thing... this was one of the rare times she had a visible bruise... Josh knew exactly where and how to hit and kick so that there would be no apparent bruises… at least none you could photograph… but what about the emotional bruises?

Often, there was irreparable damage from verbal and emotional abuse… these bruises do not show, but are more insidious and more difficult to heal.

"One more word, Claudia. Please don't be shy about asking for help this time… promise?"

"I do promise… and Kitty… Thank you so much. I am so grateful."

As Claudia was leaving, Kitty took her hand, and gave her a therapeutic hug. She closed the door and was aware of the queasy feeling in the pit of her stomach. She had been through this many times with women… "Well," she thought, "as someone once said, 'buckle up… it's going to be a bumpy ride!'"

3

Claudia was in a high state of anxiety... she had expected Josh to return, full of remorse, as in the past... but, thankfully, he did not call, nor did he return. On Sunday, Margo dropped by bringing lunch for them both... She was a kind and thoughtful friend, but after she left, Claudia knew she had to avoid her as much as possible...Like so many others, Margo was too captivated by Josh and could not understand the situation... which heightened Claudia's anxiety and frustration. Another friend, Anna Lee, had stopped by late Saturday afternoon, unaware of Claudia's current situation. Claudia and Anna had been fellow artists for several years, but Claudia had purposely not discussed Josh with any of her friends. Now, as they sat in the imposing, sunken living room, sipping white wine, Anna was astounded at what she was hearing... and what she had witnessed when Claudia had taken her into the master bedroom suite. The damage was shocking.... the door was hanging off its hinges, molding had been ripped from the doorframe and there were large holes in the walls. Claudia's clothes were strewn around the room... shoes had obviously been thrown at the mirrors, as they were lying in the midst of the glass that had fallen to the floor.

"My God, Claudia, did he use an ax in here and destroy this or what?"

"I don't know... it was like this when I came back home... fortunately, I was able to get out of here before he began to destroy the place... I've been seeing Kitty Borg... you know, the psychotherapist off of Junipero Avenue? She helped me prepare for this kind of a situation, and I had a car key hidden outside the house and have been parking my car in the turnaround for a couple of months. I told Josh it helped me get exercise by walking up to the house... I think he'd have killed me if I had not left." Anna detected a tremor in her voice.

"I noticed your face... did he do that too?"

"Uh huh... I've become his favorite punching bag... but it won't happen again!"

The two women talked for over 2 hours. To Claudia's amazement, Anna disclosed to her that her ex-husband had been abusive, and shared many things that she had learned from the experience... one very important component was that Claudia had to stop being intimidated by Josh and never to embrace the victim role... like cowering in the corner as Claudia had often done, or crying and pleading for Josh to stop ... a stance Claudia almost always took. And, if he called or wrote and began dictating what she was to do, practice the Alanon solution of "detaching"... not easy to do but necessary to do in order to decrease the power women so often give to the perpetrator. The most important thing that Anna stressed that day was that Claudia had to stop wearing a mask... she had to begin to tell people what Josh was, and what he did. "Tell everyone, Claudia... don't be embarrassed any more... we cannot continue to enable these men... and that's what we do when we pretend our husbands are wonderful."

It had been a valuable afternoon for Claudia... she felt a sense of freedom in sharing with a friend who actually believed her ... and gained information that would become significant in the coming months.

Before she left, Anna vowed that she would be supportive of Claudia and marked her calendar so that they could spend at least two hours a day exercising and swimming with each other.

"It would be good for both of us, Claudia. I've been looking for a buddy to motivate me, and this is the perfect opportunity." She gave Claudia a hug and was gone, promising to see her Monday afternoon.

Early Monday morning, Claudia followed Kitty's instructions... it was both humiliating and highly unnerving when she discovered Josh had withdrawn all but $100 from their accounts. Her heart was pounding... she left the bank in a state of increased apprehension, wondering how she could possibly manage without any money, feeling helpless, angry and frantic, all at the same time. However, she immediately recognized her need to retrieve her initial resolve and courage.

On Tuesday, she met with her attorney, and battled the immediate negative thinking and the intimidation induced by his aggressive and rather dogmatic personality. His remarks were insulting and sarcastic, but Claudia pushed this aside, concentrating on the details he discussed. They agreed that Claudia would file for separate maintenance, and not pursue divorce at this time, a decision that Claudia had prayed about and brooded over extensively. A good deal of the hour was devoted to a detailed discussion of his fees, which were exorbitant. She wrote a check with the funds she had squirreled away, severely depleting her ability to be independent. He asked her to write a history of the marriage, and dismissed her with a wave of his hand... "that's it for today... see my secretary to set up an appointment for three weeks."

When Claudia arrived home she found the first letter from Josh. Her stomach did some somersaults, and when she read it, she could feel the pounding in her head from the anger. The letter outlined the financial provisions. Claudia was flabbergasted! It never occurred to her that she did not have to abide by his directives... not until she saw Kitty on Wednesday and reordered her thinking. However, nothing was helping her anxiety. Kitty had offered a referral to a psychiatrist for medication, but Claudia refused. Instead of medication, she pledged herself to the vigorous exercise schedule with Anna, and launched a committed program of prayer and meditation... it was a time of renewal.

■ ■ ■

Josh moved into his cottage at the Biltmore for the next two days. He swam, had a massage, and on Sunday drove to his office to review financial records.

While there he decided he would write a letter to Claudia…. he'd give her some money for a few months, "but I'll be damned if she's going to bleed me!" Josh was angry… at his Father, at Lucas and particularly at his own stupidity for leaving a bruise on Claudia… and for the damages at the house.

He poured himself a drink and plunked down on the extra-long leather couch. He didn't know how smart Claudia would be. Last year, his attorney had outlined some scenarios to Josh. California had become a "no-fault" state in 1970, which meant that he'd have an easy time getting a divorce. No longer would Claudia have "grounds" of adultery. He had learned that no-fault had a sole standard… "irremediable breakdown of the marriage." It assured him that the old provisions necessary for divorce such as adultery or desertion, would not be a consideration in the property settlement or the alimony payments. Hell, they'd only been married for ten years… maybe he'd get off with some meager settlement. "I've got to be careful… my image is very important right now…" Josh sat up and said out loud, "Remember, jerk, the boat to Bermuda! Don't be an ass and throw it all away. Take it easy… think it out before you say or do anything rash." He went to the bar and poured himself another drink… "Remember the charm, Joshua Henderson…and stay in control of the situation"

With that self-admonition, Josh sat at his massive desk and wrote the first of many letters to Claudia.

> "Dear Claudia:
>
> I've decided to move up to Alasek to the Murray's guesthouse. They're gone for several months and it's near the spa… I'll need treatments with this added stress in my life. After that, I'll let you know where to reach me… until you get on your feet, will provide the following:
>
> - Up to $350 for rent – when the house is sold and you move
> - Up to $100 for utilities, including phone – while at Carmelo house

- Up to $40 month for medical/prescriptions/ vitamins
- Up to $50 month for your car expenses
- Up to $200 month for food and sundries…I left $100 in our account for the remainder of June
- Up to $100 month for personal needs and necessities.

I will contact the designers, and expedite the whole operation so that we can finish this fuckin' remodeling project and get the house on the market. I have every intention of remarrying and intend to support you only until you get on your feet.

I think this is very generous of me, considering your unending requirements of me and the impossible conditions you have put on our relationship. It has come clearly into focus for me that there is NO way to satisfy you, and I have finally lost the desire to try. Furthermore, I believe that I have tried much beyond normalcy. I also know that you now have what you've been working toward with that fraud you refer to as a psychotherapist. It simply will not work anymore."

J

"P.S I have cancelled the charge cards, but left the Preserve account intact for your trip to the wedding in August. I believe there is just enough in there for your airline tickets."

Josh sealed the letter. He wanted Claudia to know that he was going to be the one in control. He had offered her more money than he was willing to pay her, but would wait until next month to decrease the amount. He picked up the phone and called his playmate of the month… had one more drink and drove back to his secluded love nest.

4

Josh's remorse came two weeks later... it was the third letter Claudia had received since he had left... he was "filled with deep sadness,"... he was "offering prayers for her recovery"... and her "release from fear" and "praying (he) could forgive and be forgiven"... and there was a plea to attend Zach's graduation from St. Francis Prep the next week. She gave the letter to Kitty when she arrived at her session. Kitty read it several times and looked at Claudia.

"What do you think about this?"

"Frankly, I think he's sick... This is a familiar pattern of his... it's all my fault... he's praying for *my* recovery...for *my* release from fear... but nothing about *his* recovery...nor *his* aggression... nothing about getting help for his violent behavior. But, I am confused and vacillate between anger and forgiveness... then when he said, 'don't be hasty about anything – I am going to take care of you...I do care.'..." Tears filled Claudia's eyes and she choked back the sobs.

"Let it out Claudia...Tell me... what's the real reason you don't want to leave? Why are you so reluctant to let go?"

"I want to believe him because I want to be loved and cared for...I always want to believe him!" They sat for several minutes while Claudia regained control.

"I feel sorry for him, Kitty... He had such a difficult childhood... but mostly I am so humiliated that this is my second marriage... and it's disintegrating! What's the matter with *me*? Is this whole thing my fault? I was raised to believe that no matter what happens you stay together... and here I am getting a second divorce? Even though intellectually I know we have to separate because the abuse is intensifying, I keep thinking... What if it *really is me!*"

"Well, Claudia, maybe it is you... so does that mean he can abuse you physically and mentally? Suppose you do get bitchy or moody at times... most people do. Does that give him the privilege of calling you incredibly filthy names?... of kicking you?...spitting on you...hitting you? Can he really love you, Claudia... is this the kind of "love" you want? And what about Zach... what is he learning from this?"

There was a long pause before Claudia answered.

"I hear you, Kitty. The answer, of course, is that Josh and I cannot under any circumstances continue to live together. Love? At this point in my life I'm not sure if I am capable of love... except for my children. I don't know what love is right now. And, as for Zach, I came here today to talk about the children, and I've done a lot of writing to prepare for it... so, do you mind if I start way back... at the beginning?"

"It's your session, Claudia... say anything you want."

"O.K., I'll start with our happiness when I became pregnant with David. Before Gerald and I were married, I had a gynecological exam, and was told I'd never bear children... Another misdiagnosis!" She and Kitty laughed and Claudia recounted how David was so loved... the first boy and the special bond she felt as her firstborn. Matthew was born 18 months later... It had been a difficult pregnancy and birth...and Matthew had injuries at birth... a black eye and cuts on his face which had been quite swollen.

"Gerald was very upset during my pregnancy with Matt, and began to drink excessively. I was frightened because I could feel him slipping away from me. So, after the birth, since I was Catholic, I tried to get permission... a dispensation... to use birth control, and made the rounds of confessionals and making appointments with priests, hoping for their blessings."

"I thought Gerald was non-Catholic?"

"He was... is... but he hated using condoms..."

"So the sole responsibility for birth control was on your shoulders?"

"Yes...Well, after I was rejected and demeaned by all the priests, I wrote a letter to John Rock... you know, the doctor who developed the birth control pill? And, he actually responded to me... in a letter that was so spiritual and affirming, that it helped me make a positive decision to follow my "conscience."

"So Gerald was off the hook with condoms?"

"No... I had a lot of side effects from the pill that could have been potentially hazardous, and it forced Gerald to use protection. He became very vocal about how 'they'... the condoms were ruining his sex life..."

At this point, Claudia began to giggle... Kitty joined her and they relaxed for a few moments.

"Well, Zack was conceived in a moment of passion, but even though being pregnant again was unexpected, it was a joyful time...I had a new doctor that was terrific, and a new hospital...it was the easiest birth, and from the beginning, Zach was a calm, peaceful and loving child. I can't begin to tell you how wonderful it is to have a son like Zach, Kitty. He is incredibly funny, upbeat, kind and caring beyond belief! His love had been the only stable love in my life... except for my brother, Jamie's love when I was a child.   But sometimes I feel that I'm a burden to him... He seems to have an excessive sense of responsibility toward me, and I wonder if I am ruining his life... "

"There you go again, Claudia... You can't ruin a life with love...I've seen you and Zach together and am quite satisfied that you both have love and respect for each other and clearly understand the boundaries in your relationship. Zach does what he does because he wants to... you both have an understanding that families have to pull together when the occasion demands responsibility. You helped Zach grow into manhood... you were always there for your children, and Zach was wise enough to know that love helps one to heal... he contributed to your growth and self- esteem... parents need that as well as children."

"You always know the best thing to say, Kitty... thanks for that."

"So, Claudia what else do you have in your notes."

"Well, I've done a lot of writing about Matt, Kitty. I've been very concerned about him and have lots of questions that I hope you can help me with."

"Such as?"

"I've known for some time that Matt has a problem with alcohol... I am positive that he is an alcoholic. Then, recently, he announced to me that he is a homosexual, and that he is currently involved in a relationship with another alcoholic homosexual... a guy that is quite a bit older that he met in a bar...Matt is only 23 and this guy is in his 50's... but what I want to know is if homosexuality can be genetic?"

"I don't have a lot of experience with this issue, Claudia, but I do have a very good and close friend, a psychiatrist/neurologist who has specialized in this area for many years, and he tells me there is the usual controversy and diametrically opposing opinions that you might expect with the whole subject of homosexuality. Current thinking seems to be heading in the direction that sexual orientation is a physiological condition present at birth...meaning that a person is born this way. Whether or not genetics is involved has not been determined, but my friend does not think so... he cited some twin studies in which identical twins had differing sexual orientation, which makes him think that homosexuality is a learned behavior... a response to painful childhood experiences such as sexual abuse, chemical exposures or other environmental factors...some even believe it may be diet. The bottom line is that most likely all these things might be present. What's your concern about genetics?"

"Well, if you remember, I told you that when Gerald and I moved to southern New Jersey there was such a lack of anything intellectual or cultural in my life... so, I began going to a therapy group in New York City, and talked about Gerald... how he was becoming more emotionally remote and sexually unavailable. The consensus of the group was that he was having an affair...some thought with another man, some thought with a woman who was my friend...Helen."

"Why did some of them think that Gerald was gay?"

Claudia related the conversation she had with Sophie and related the concerns she shared about Gerald's time in college.

"What did you think?"

"Honestly, Kitty, I didn't have the foggiest notion of what 'gay' was or what homosexuals looked like. It was upsetting to me in group therapy because I was mocked...laughed at...for being so 'naive.' As a matter of fact, I remember one particularly horrible session when I was made to stand on a round table in the middle of the group therapy room, and they all yelled insults at me...one of the men actually hit me... all this so I would learn to respond defensively."

Once again, Kitty was incredulous to learn of this extremely unprofessional pattern of humiliation and abuse that Claudia had been exposed to... to think that a group member was permitted to strike another member... to expect her to tolerate cursing, and demeaning put-downs... it made her ashamed of segments of her profession. All she said was, "I'm so sorry that happened to you!"

"Well, the reason I brought this up today is that it got me thinking that if Gerald was a homosexual or maybe a bi-sexual... could be genetic... could Matt have inherited the disposition. And then I wondered about the alcoholism...Could you help me understand it better?"

"Once again, Claudia, there is a lot of controversy and wildly divergent opinions about alcoholism... addictions in general. Is it a disease or is it a choice? The disease model of addiction asserts that addiction is a disease of the brain that is caused by a combination of behavioral, environmental and biological factors and that when a person ingests a drug or alcohol, there are physiological changes in the brain... new neural connections are made which will set up a pattern of need... the person will need the substance... that is the drug or alcohol... to feel normal. Then there are others who dispute the disease model and contend that addiction is a choice...that saying it's a disease is an excuse that denies the concept of free will...that addiction happens because of poor coping skills... that there would be no physiological changes in the brain if a person did not choose to take a drug or alcohol. The big thing according to research with addictives is that genetic factors account for about 50% of the likelihood that an individual will develop an addiction."

"You know, Kitty, Matthew was injured at birth... I told you when they brought him to me his face was swollen, he had a black eye and cuts on his face. The doctor played it off, but Matt was so big... almost 10 pounds, and he had projectile vomiting every time I fed him...and then when he was 3 years old, he had bleeding from his penis. When I took him to my allergy doctor in San Francisco, he said that any idiot in his first year of medical school should have known Matt had severe food allergies and that his dyslexia, the hyperactivity and other school problems he had as a child, and the eventual hypoglycemia he suffered from could have been alleviated with the proper diagnosis. But I can't get him to even acknowledge any of this... I feel like a failure as a Mother, especially with Matt."

"Guilt is not indicated here, Claudia...Matthew is a grown man, now... he is responsible for his actions and behaviors, and he will have to live with his decisions like we all have had to do...I have no children, but know from my many clients who are Mothers how much you worry and how you want the best for your children. We've never talked much about your life after Gerald divorced you... would you like to share that now?"

"Yes...that's when my guilt first began... life was not easy and in spite of the fact that I loved my children I made some poor decisions. I felt very alone, Kitty... Gerald's lack of interest and involvement hurt very much. Sometimes, I think that the death of a spouse is easier to cope with than divorce...that way we could all grieve and eventually move on...but, for me, every 5 weeks a man called Dad would invade our lives, spoil the children with food and presents and a day and a half later they would be returned to a house they hated and would think of their Father as a hero and be sad for days afterward. There were so many demands... for so many years... All the medical problems, the colds, toothaches, bouts of stomach flu, eye exams, Zach's diabetes, the inexhaustible minor crises that always occur with children...All the school problems... especially with Matthew, and the resulting scrutiny of me because I was divorced and the 'school snoops' as we used to call them, coming to the home and insisting that we go to Family Therapy...then there were the soccer games, the track meets, and other school activities... the house and cooking chores I had to do, and the part time job I had... it was sometimes overwhelming. I wanted my children to have a sense of being loved and deeply cared about... I used to try to think of ways to make them feel special, like individuals with their own special abilities and talents. I think that I was trying to compensate for Gerald's absence. The children were angry about the divorce... especially about the fact that they were not told or consulted. And, Gerald and others were so damn judgmental toward me, that I became sort of the scapegoat."

"Did you ever tell your children how much you needed them? How much you needed their love and support?"

As Kitty asked this question Claudia sank back into the plump cushions of the sofa... she was like a wounded sparrow sitting there with head downcast, hands tightly clasped around her beautiful, flowered, linen handkerchief. It took her several minutes to answer...

"I didn't think I had the right to tell them that, Kitty... I was the parent... I thought I had to be the strong one... what right did I have to dump all my needs and problems on them, particularly after all that I had put them through..."

Tears welled in Claudia's eyes... and they began to spill over...

"What are you referring to Claudia... What had you put them through?"

"My suicide attempt... Oh my God, Kitty... whatever possessed me to do that! What was my thinking... it is so inconceivable to me now... how could I have been so thoughtless, so neglectful!"

The tears were now streaming... Claudia was sobbing, pushing out her words while gulping air... she grabbed a throw pillow from the sofa and covered her face but the sounds were still audible... they were woeful, painful... and the sobs were from the depths... Kitty sat next to her and held her... she said nothing... she knew this was the first time Claudia had ever vented this agonizing memory. With time, the tears subsided... Claudia put the pillow aside and wiped her face...

"There's more Kitty... what could Gerald have gone through? He's never talked about it but can you imagine coming home and finding your wife, the Mother of his children, almost dead? What could he have thought? And why did he come home early from work? My God, Kitty, it must have been horrific for him."

That day was a memorable breakthrough for Claudia... It was late afternoon, and Kitty was thankful she had no further appointments... She looked at her client and thought about the traditions in which Claudia was raised... submission to the husband... stringent religious rules and regulations on everything from birth control to divorce... careers as homemakers... and, in her case, perfectionistic indoctrination and performances as the only acceptable way to live. In her mind, Claudia thought of herself as a failure as a woman, a wife and as a Mother.

"Claudia, I want to say several things to you to take away with you. You must work on forgiving yourself... Don't make a liar out of God... he loves you so much and has forgiven you ... now it's time to change your thinking!... you are not a failure and you have to give up saying that and thinking that... You have done an excellent job and have overcome great odds. Your questions are 'why did you attempt suicide... what were you thinking... how could you have been so thoughtless?' Remember, Claudia that you obediently took the 22 different prescribed medications... the fault wasn't yours... it was the misdiagnosis and the indiscriminate disbursement of the medications that the doctors so freely dictated that you use... the truth is, Claudia, that you were not able to think... your brain was anesthetized...you were not able to make rational decisions... you were not able to decipher what doctors denied... all that you were able to discern was that you had failed... change your thinking! YOU did not fail... your support system, the doctors and medical community, failed you... move away from the inappropriate guilt..."

They talked for another hour... Kitty helped her to see that parents are grown up children, still needing love, caring and acceptance as they did when were young children, that she had missed all that support and love when she was a child but somehow managed to give her children all that love and compassion.

"You were not perfect, Claudia and that is very acceptable...Gerald was not perfect and your children are not perfect. I'm sorry they had to endure difficult times...an attempted suicide, a divorce and a difficult remarriage that was tragic... maybe their Mother did not emulate the scripted world of June Cleaver... but the reality of the situation, Claudia, is that bad things happen in life. You taught your children a valuable lesson... how to survive. They always had a nice home, warm clothes, good food and a lot of love... they haven't had to worry about how to get through college, or how to survive on the streets... they have had many blessings. There were two parents... but mommy was the convenient scapegoat! Blaming mommy was one of Freud's central themes, and ever since, it's been embraced by all segments of society, especially, I'm sorry to say, by mental health professionals. Mothers seemed to be blamed for not attaining the impossible goals that others set up for them...children and husbands and others can point their finger at Mom so they don't have to look at themselves... that's what people do when they choose not to grow. Another thing, Claudia, is that although you are not responsible for all the decisions that were made... you are responsible for how you handle the adversity as a result of those outcomes... of those decisions... You have had a great deal of guilt and shame in your life and in your prayer and meditation times, I want you to ask that this be removed from you. I want you to use the great gift of compassion that I have seen you give to others... on yourself...Work on being tender to you... Give up the sackcloth and ashes mentality and begin to nurture yourself...you need to honor God by loving yourself. And one last thing... our emotions are God-given... don't be ashamed of them or hold back expressing your love, or sadness, or joy... it is perfectly appropriate to express our emotions as long as we do not allow ourselves to be overwhelmed or defeated by them."

Claudia had listened carefully to all that Kitty said... she lifted her head and quietly said,

"I understand Kitty...I am going to continue to make these things a part of my life."

5

Josh left the Biltmore Sunday evening to move into Bill Murray's guest-house ... Bill was his corporate attorney... had been on his payroll for over ten years, and had shown proficiency in bailing Josh out of many tight spots. He had built this mini-estate in Alasek five years ago, after marrying his fourth wife... a rather vacant young thing with a gorgeous body engineered by the best plastic surgeons in Beverly Hills. Josh liked Alasek... it retained a rural charm and offered him some needed solitude. The 3800 square foot guesthouse was remote and self-contained, nestled in the middle of vintage orange and avocado groves. Josh had spent countless days and nights here in the years Bill had worked for him. The dwelling itself had been constructed with the intention of entertaining. The ground floor contained a spacious multi-purpose room... used for business meetings, office parties, and some bacchanalian "private" parties... a pool and spa area complete with two cabanas was accessible through the massive French doors.

Bill had graduated from St. Francis Prep and was a large contributor to the school. Every year, the senior class was invited to the guesthouse for a barbecue, to swim and to blow off steam... no school staff were allowed and Bill made sure that the kids had a good time. It was a night Josh always avoided... just like he avoided all of Zach's school functions... he was aware of his academic inadequacies and chose to circumvent anything that might cause him embarrassment.

The rest of the house was not glamorous or elegant, but was very attractive and extremely comfortable. On the second level, where he now sat, sprawled out on an oversized leather recliner, he was able to see the beginnings of a typical sunset. In a few moments, the mountains would be bathed in a brilliant shade of pink… a lovely phenomenon that occurred frequently in this small, agricultural valley. Walking to the wrap-around windows, drink in hand, he thought about Claudia, remembering their first meeting.

"I wonder why I was so attracted to her?" Josh pondered this, watching the sun begin its unfailing decent. Claudia was a different kind of woman from those he had known…she was such a little girl, naïve and trusting… at times it made him feel soft and tender, but then she'd get on her "high horse" and would piss him off. She was a little too regal and much too artsy-fartsy for him… not earthy enough… it made him feel like a peasant. She was so damned intellectual! So proud of all her degrees, always wanting to discuss things that only men should talk about… just like my Mother! Well, he'd show her… Claudia was not going to put the screws to him! He'd cut her off a little at a time until she'd beg him to come back… then he'd be in control and would call all the shots.

He needed time. Last year Bill had referred him to a high-powered divorce attorney in Los Angeles. The guy was adamant that Josh see a counselor to establish a pattern of marital conflict… to document Claudia's past problems. He had also suggested that Josh lay off the booze… totally abstain… and go to Alcoholics Anonymous. He was pissed off at this… but tonight, he wondered if it might be a good idea. Yesterday, he had called Claudia and had detected some subtle changes that alerted him… maybe she was seeing an attorney… well, they'd be surprised to learn he had taken as much equity out of the house as possible… he had done the same with his insurance policies and investments… it was all nicely tucked away in a Swiss bank account.

Josh moved to the bar and poured himself a bourbon... someone told him a long time ago that bourbon was the healthiest booze... "I wonder who that was?... maybe it was Lucas... God-damn you Lucas!" He threw the glass into the fireplace, feeling slightly insane... the whole room reminded him of Lucas...the fireplace... burning incessantly... the extra- large windows... "Lucas, you son of a bitch... you really screwed me! Why?... Why, Lucas?... were you just a rich bastard who thought I was a piece of shit?... I didn't need your fuckin' money, you bye blow... I needed your trust... your faith in me... Why the hell did you screw me, Lucas, you fuckin' bastard!"

■ ■ ■

It was late when Josh awoke the next morning... his head felt like it was in a vise, his legs were unsteady and he was nauseated. After some strong coffee, which increased his nausea, he called his administrative assistant for her to cancel his appointments and made some crucial decisions.

"I don't want to talk to anyone today, Nancy, do you understand?... no one!"

"What do you want me to tell everyone, Mr. Henderson?" Nancy had worked for Josh over thirteen years. Early in her career, she had made the decision to refer to any boss as "Mr." It set up boundaries and saved everyone a great deal of embarrassment... to say nothing of job security.

"Tell them... Tell them... I've had to leave town for an emergency meeting and I'll be back next week. Have Paul take care of anything that needs immediate attention."

Nancy was used to lying for Mr. Henderson. She never felt quite comfortable about it... but rationalized that it was really his lie... she was only following directions. Right or wrong, it served her conscience... she made a great deal of money, and even though Mr. Henderson was difficult to work with at times, she had learned to remain emotionally aloof... a strategy learned from the years spent with an alcoholic Father. If she were asked to characterize Mr. Henderson's personality in one word, she would say... moody. He was charming but sullen, kind but cruel, humble but controlling, and tranquil but angry. One day at work when things were slow, she had made a long list of his paradoxical traits. When she finished, she realized she didn't like him but kept this secret well hidden. For the most part, Josh was unaware of this plain and unattractive woman and rarely thought of her as a person, seeing their business relationship only in terms of what she could produce.

After talking with Nancy, Josh tried to find something to eat. There was bread in the fridge, and some unexpired eggs... he poured out the coffee and made some tea, toast and scrambled eggs. While he ate, he tried to listen to the radio, but some fuckin' liberal was expounding on the need for teachers to have more control over the children in the school system, and he pulled the plug from the outlet. While he took a hasty shower, he began to speculate on what it might be like to go to an AA meeting... maybe even therapy. He dried off, found a telephone book, and looked up some telephone numbers for AA. There was a meeting at the Episcopal Church at noon... Hell, why not go... it would look good. He donned designer slacks and shirt, and drove the short distance to the church.

When he entered the meeting room, he was caught off guard... there were women there which he didn't expect, and he recognized several men... it had not occurred to him that he would see anyone he knew and almost walked out before some guy was at his elbow, welcoming him and shaking his hand. They sat around a table discussing a topic called "the first step"... which had to do with admitting to yourself that you had a problem with alcohol. Hell, it wouldn't take a rocket scientist to know that he drank too much! Yeh! This would be a good place for him to learn to drink less... he'd have more control over things then.

After the meeting ended, some guy walked up to him and shot his hand out.

"Hello, my man, I'm Henry." Henry pulled a business card out of his pocket and told Josh that he was a pastor of some community church… that he did counseling… why didn't Josh give him a call.

"Why not now…" Josh looked for his name on the card… "Why not now, Henry… Let's sit down."

"Well…what was your name?"

"Josh." Josh had learned that you don't use last names.

"Well, Josh, I have a 3:00 o'clock appointment, but we could go to the office and chat for about a half hour, and make an appointment for tomorrow. C'mon… the office is this way."

Henry led him to a large office area at the back of the meeting room which Henry explained was set aside for AA members. They settled into uncomfortable chairs and Henry took the lead in conversation.

"Josh let's begin by me telling you something about me and how I work."

Henry Marquez began disclosing details of his life. He had been a gang member, had been indicted for petty theft several times, served time in juvenile court, had several failed marriages, discussed his affairs, his drug and alcohol addiction, and paused only when Josh interrupted.

"Henry, excuse me, I don't mean to be rude, but you're telling me all this garbage you've been through… how're you going to counsel me? My life is no picnic but it's better than yours!"

"Good question, Josh… I had an awakening… I joined AA and turned my life over to a higher power… then I felt a calling to become a minister of the word… we gather together on Sundays to share what our higher power is doing in our lives… we have pot lucks, softball games on Saturdays… we go on outings together… we are a family."

"O.K., Henry… let me think about it." Josh paused. He felt like he was suffocating. My God, it sounded so boorish, so inclusive and so exhausting! But Henry was busy getting his pen and memo book from his shirt pocket.

"Look Josh, I have a map here to show you where the church is… we meet at the abandoned packing house. The schedule is on the back… I have tomorrow open at 2:30 P.M.…. Why don't you come by then and I can show you around?"

Josh was not interested, but always charming, he acquiesced… he would cancel the appointment later.   Both men left feeling they had accomplished their goals.

That evening, Josh limited himself to two bourbons…. But he was bored… restless… he didn't know what to do with himself and decided to drive to the marina and work on his boat, but when he got there he just sat on deck and looked at the water.

"I have no friends… not real ones…"   He thought about Henry Marquez. Josh knew the guy was struggling financially. "He needs my money… hell, everyone needs money…" A plan was beginning to materialize in his head. "Why not play the game… I help him, he helps me… just like my attorney wants it. He gives me guidance, direction, and I give him an intriguing account of Claudia's carping, her crazed behaviors, the illogical and unreasonable financial requests." And so, an association was forged… based on Henry's lack of knowledge and expertise, which was exactly what Josh wanted… the perversion of truth would remain intact.

Josh left the marina but did not return to the guesthouse. Instead, he went to his office… lit the gas log in the fireplace, and after pouring himself a triple bourbon, retrieved a half-hidden photograph album from the top shelf of the massive bookcase.

There was only one, old, brownish photograph of his Mother… the only remembrance from his early life in England. His photo life began with his arrival in the United States… the house, the servants, Holly and Lucas, arms entwined… the images rekindled the struggles and the pleasures… but, once again, the stabbing pain of what he perceived was the ultimate rejection. When Lucas died, it was true that he left him the auto dealerships… and he could have had anything he wanted from the house. As it was, Josh took only this photo album that Holly had compiled, and the desk from the library where he sat at this moment.

"Why the secrecy, Lucas… was it a reproach?"

Josh was startled to see a picture of Frankie Fahey and his fat little cousin… he ripped it out of the book and tore it into little pieces… "That was the jam up!… I suppose I should've worn sackcloth and ashes for the rest of my life, eh, Lucas?… I suppose I wasn't worthy to be the true heir of the great Lucas Connolly… so who was the conniving fuck that hijacked my bloody legacy… and why don't I have a right to know who it was!"

The next morning, Nancy quietly tidied up the room as she had done on many occasions, and carefully reassembled the photograph album, making sure that Mr. Henderson would think she had not seen anything. Then she gently awoke Josh from his drunken stupor.

6

Norman Borg was born in Switzerland in 1934. It was a time of unrest in Europe...countries were jockeying for power and land after World War I... not very different from the struggles European countries had faced for many centuries... except now a madman was making plans to annihilate more than six million innocent Jews, and intended to become the ruler of the world... a plan that would result in World War II. Fortunately, the Congress of Vienna had guaranteed the neutrality of Switzerland as far back as 1815, and in both World War I and World War II, Switzerland was able to maintain its long tradition of freedom and independence. Because of their neutrality, Swiss banks had historically attracted depositors from many countries, with the assurance that their reputation for confidentiality and safety... probably the safest in the world... would be maintained. Norman's Father, Peter Borg, had been part of that banking system from the age of seventeen... he was dedicated to preserving the established procedures. The Borg's were a close-knit family. Maria Bellario Borg, wife and Mother, was a jovial woman... traditional... conservative... adored by her husband and three children... Norman... and two sisters ... Janine and Francesca.

Switzerland has, for the most part, been a prosperous country... the Borg's were not "rich" in the classical sense, but enjoyed an upper middle class standard of living that allowed them to take advantage of the many recreational activities that abounded in this culturally diverse and spectacularly beautiful European country.

Norman was raised in Chur, in the mountainous canton of Graubunden, known for its clean and invigorating air that fostered many health centers. Chur is the oldest town in Switzerland, and lies at the head of the Rhine Valley, surrounded by towering mountains. It was an important rail center and the largest mercantile center between Zurich and Milan. From early childhood, Norman was an extraordinary skier...through the years he attained great proficiency in the sport... both cross country and downhill... and had frequented the twenty top ski areas in Switzerland. Norman particularly liked the isolated terrain of his sparsely settled canton... whether skiing or hiking, he would wander for hours and not see anyone... not because he was antisocial, but the quiet, majestic beauty of these mountains was always a spiritually enriching experience for him, and sometimes, he would stay in the region for days before going down to the Val Bregaglia, one of the most beautiful valleys in the Alps. It was in the valley, at the museum in Stampa, that he first discovered the sculptures of Alberto Giacometti, who was famous for his gaunt, elongated human figures. Norman felt the non-idealized, sticklike figures expressed an anonymity and helplessness that generated a spiritual consciousness. It awakened a passion within him to pursue a career in sculpting... but, it would be years before that dream was realized... and would be fulfilled in an unforeseen and serendipitous manner.

Once a year, since he could remember, his family would drive the 80 miles from their home in Chur and join members of his Mother's family who would travel from Milan, for a family celebration in the town of Lugano, which was known as the cultural center of the Ticino. Built along the shores of Lake Lugano, this distinctly Italian-flavored Swiss lakeside resort town boasted of open, sunny, cobblestone piazzas, sidewalk cafes, Romanesque churches, museums and music that made each visit memorable. This area of Switzerland had a distinctly Mediterranean atmosphere and climate that produced lush, subtropical vegetation… palm trees, camellias, magnolias, olives, figs and grapes that generated rich, red merlots. Here, the families would relax, drink the rich, red wine from small bowls called boccalinos, eat ossobuco, fresh pasta, scampi with saffron risotto, saltimbocca, fresh fish and goose liver, and Norman would always indulge himself by having his favorite dessert, zabaglione.

When Norman was fourteen, his Father wanted to leave the banking business. He brought this to the family, and after much discussion, they decided to move to a small village near Lugano to partner in a hotel and winery business with Maria's brother, Antonio, and his family. It was an exciting venture for the family, and in the ensuing years, they worked hard and enjoyed the results of a loyal following of tourists they came to know as family. Norman was a vigorous helper during school recesses… he continued to pursue his skiing and by the age of seventeen was making plans to attend Lausanne University where he would pursue theology and art.

It was the winter of 1950-1951. Norman had enjoyed a festive Christmas with his combined families in Lugano… and they celebrated the New Year anticipating continued prosperity… the winery was successful as well as the hotel they now owned. On January 15, Norman left his family home for a short holiday of skiing before returning to school. His Uncle Antonio drove him to Bellinzona, where he boarded a train to Airolo… he would take a bus from Airolo… enjoy the dramatic Val Bedretto, savor the spectacular Gotthard Pass and go on to Andermatt. Ski conditions had been disappointing this winter… the snow was thinning and the resorts were feeling the tourist "pinch"… Because the skiing conditions were poor, he wanted to stay away from the "tourist traps" and the crowds he knew would be at St. Moritz, Zermatt or Davos. Andermatt had a decent cross-country piste… and with cross country, he would not be at the whim of slope conditions. Andermatt served as the Swiss Army's principal Alpine training center, and in Norman's younger days, he had

persuaded his Father to bring him there for a glimpse of the troops training for mountain warfare. It had fascinated him, and like many young
Swiss boys, he had dreamed of being part of these troops. So, his decision
was to go to the nearby Gemsstock summit and with the other langlaufers,
work off the holiday calories!

■ ■ ■

January 20th dawned gray and cloudy. Norman arose early anxious to
test the weather. It had been snowing for three days, and shortly before
dawn, he peered out the window and saw that the snow had stopped...
he was ready for the slopes. After washing at the small bedside sink, he
unpacked his rucksack to make sure he had not forgotten anything. He
tested his flashlight batteries, added more chocolate and assembled and
disassembled the shovel he carried with him at all times. Most people
didn't realize that there are hundreds of avalanches per week during ski
season in the Alps. He had encountered several during the years, and had
been fortunate to have received instruction in avalanche survival.

■ ■ ■

Lucas and Holly Connolly arrived in Switzerland on January 10th, three
months prior to Josh Henderson's arrival in the USA. Their plane was ten
minutes early and they were able to quickly disembark. Cointrin airport was
bustling and they were happy to spot their hired driver almost immediately.
It wasn't long before they checked into their hotel and fell into bed for a
short nap before bathing, dressing and enjoying a light evening meal at one
of their favorite café's in old town. After spending two days in Geneva taking care of banking and business matters, they were driven the forty miles
to the spectacular lakeside resort of Ouchy, where they checked into the
Beau Rivage Palace overlooking Lac Leman. Over a leisurely lunch, they
discussed their plan. They would spend a week apart... Lucas would drive to
Andermatt to see his old friend Neal Christen, and together they would do

some cross country skiing, while Holly would chum around with an artist friend and enjoy some favorite time at the day spas.

In the early morning of January 17th, Lucas and the young man he had hired as his driver began the three hour drive to Hospental... a modest village near Andermatt, where Neal maintained a small winter cottage for quick and easy access to the Swiss Army's Alpine barracks. As the small automobile progressed slowly on the snowy roads, Lucas reflected on his friendship with Neal. The two men had met many years earlier when Lucas had needed an expert witness in avalanche control. The men had bonded easily and through the years had seen each other as often as circumstances would allow. Neal's main residence was in Lucerne, but his active involvement with the alpine troops required his presence during the winter. Things were complicated for him this year. His wife had died the first week of December, and his communiqués had been filled with sadness and grief. Lucas was no stranger to grief... he and Holly had suffered the ultimate pain and learned, unwillingly, about the realities of life.

It had been a slow drive and Lucas was over two hours late arriving at Neal's. The two men embraced when they saw each other. Neal shed some tears, and led his friend to a warm cozy fire where a simple lunch of cheese, bread, sausage and a large pitcher of German beer had been prepared and set out. While they ate, they chatted freely but it was not until the dishes had been cleared, and Neal had lit his pipe, that he began to discuss his depression and apathy... his inability to sleep and his desire to withdraw and be alone. Lucas acknowledged the familiar feelings, sharing his experiences with Neal when his beloved daughter, Melinda, had died. During their discussion, Neal began to relax... it was good to talk to a supportive friend, and Lucas noticed that the sad, expressionless features were becoming more tranquil... peaceful.

An hour later, they were walking briskly to the army barracks, ready to do some skiing. During the silent walk, Lucas reflected on Melinda's horrific death. He had been a frequent visitor to his psychologist friend, Phil

Markowitz, for a long time after the incident. During those long months he knew what the author meant when he wrote…"a hero is one that knows how to hang on one minute longer." Holly had been stronger than he… she had comforted him and was generous with her love and understanding. Their marriage was strengthened, unlike a great many marriages that suffer with such a crisis.

By the time they walked the mile to the barracks, it again had begun to snow…

"Well, my friend, we'll get no skiing in this afternoon." Neal had stopped and turned to his friend to inform him of the decision. Neal was very conscious of avalanche conditions. He knew that there were multifarious and complicated factors involved… right now he would want to know if the existing snow base had stabilized enough to incorporate the new snowfall… that would have to be determined after the new snow stopped. Unfortunately, the men would not have a chance to test the conditions for three more days. Lucas had talked with Holly… she was having a "wonderful time" with her friend in Ouchy, and he decided to spend some extra time with Neal.

In the early hours of January 20th, the snow stopped. Once again, the men walked to the barracks and after some discussion, Lucas was granted the privilege of accompanying two of the alpine soldiers whose job it was to test the conditions of the langlauf. He was overjoyed… three days without vigorous exercise was adding to his feeling of bloat and blah! The "powderhounds" were anxious to get on the slopes this morning, so the three men moved off to prowl the area and carve a slidepath. Lucas was intent on getting some speed and soon found his-self alone, about two kilometers ahead of the 2-man team.

"My God… this is exhilarating!"… Lucas could feel all his cares falling from his mind and body.

He had no presentiment of the devastation that was to come.

■ ■ ■

Norman looked at the sky... he had become an expert at reading the clouds and knew that more snow was coming... and soon. The wind had increased... the temperature had increased, and the snow was beginning to feel heavy.

"Time to go home," he thought. He was uneasy. Norman knew that no avalanche erupts spontaneously... something must trigger it and he was edgy about the conditions he had noticed... apprehensive about the weight of the new snowfall reducing the stabilization of the base and of the increasing intensity of the wind. He was about an hour from the barracks when the snow began to fall... it was thick and intense. Then, without warning, he heard the menacing sound... whoosh! The whole mountain seemed to be "whooshing" down ... he was on the edge of what appeared to be a blanket of snow over 200 feet wide. He looked behind him in time to see the figure of another skier caught in the massive snow-slide... Norman had escaped... the other skier had not been so fortunate. Then, suddenly, the wooshing stopped. He knew he had to make a hasty search at the point where he had last seen the skier.

■ ■ ■

Lucas slammed his skis down hard, trying to ski out of the chaos. He was using a swimming stroke trying to swim out of the wild whirlpool. He was aware of being in the air, and when he landed, one of his ski poles was still attached to his hand. It was dark, silent... but he could breathe. He had his wits about him and remembered everything he'd been taught by Neal. He wasn't sure if he was face up or down... he tried spitting but the minute bit of liquid never really came out of his mouth.

"I'm face up... that's good... I can breathe so my mask must be closed... I have a bit of air..."

Lucas began to pray... he remembered the man who had kidnapped, savagely raped and murdered his precious daughter. They had found her brutalized body at the old abandoned mill in Glenwood. In this mo-ment he forgave the mad animal that had killed and tortured his precious daughter... and then he prayed for every person he had harmed, know-ingly or unknowingly. In doing this he had prepared to die.

■ ■ ■

Norman spotted a ski pole and assembling his shovel from his rucksack, began to dig. Time was of the essence...within four minutes, he found the skier, lying face up, spread eagle, his skis lying to the side of his body. Snow covered the mask, but Norman determined the skier was alive and began to gently extract him from his snowy bed. The blizzard had in-creased to the point where Norman had to yell into the skier's ear...

"Can you stand?"

The skier nodded... "I don't think anything is broken," he yelled back.

The skier was helped to his feet. He leaned on Norman for a few mo-ments and then opened his mask.

"I'm O.K. ... Help me reattach my skis and we can get going!"

This was done and soon the two men were on their way. Norman knew that the man had some injuries, but there was no time to strip off clothes to examine and bind the wounds. He led the way toward the bar-racks, stopping often to check the man for chattering teeth, blue lips and confusion. He fed the man chocolate to increase his strength and made him drink the hot coffee from his thermos. Without discussion the two skiers, in single file, slowly descended the mountain. Norman was a good leader... he knew what to do and how to go by the shortest route. Lucas was a good follower... Neal had trained him well.

Near the military barracks, Neal and his colleagues saw the two skiers and ran to meet them. They were quickly apprised of the situation... and while they were busy putting Lucas on a toboggan, Norman skied away confident in his ability, stamina and knowledge of trails to escape any further danger. He once heard that praise clouds the good deed. He was proud within himself for what he had done this day... at the same time, he was profoundly aware that there had been a strong spiritual force directing both skiers.

The wind-driven snow pounded on his goggles... visibility was zero. Then suddenly before him was the railroad station. There were a great many people... when they saw him, they came to his aid, gave him hot tea to drink, laced with some kind of whiskey. As he drank it, he was suddenly overcome with exhaustion and awoke many hours later to find himself in a train car, sleeping dormitory style. The train was not moving. When he got his bearings and walked outside, he learned the train tunnel was blocked. There was no communication available... but he was given a brief description of the deadly avalanches... all six of them... and of the incredibly rapid snowfall. Planes had already dropped supplies and Norman was given food and drink. He felt better and joined the many volunteers shoveling snow from the tunnel.

Norman didn't go back to the University... a week later he arrived back in the grateful arms of his family and was lovingly spoiled for the remainder of his stay. He pondered the swiftness of death and made a decision that week to live his life with meaning. He experienced many emotions... sadness for the many lives lost in the avalanches... love and respect for the infinite majesty of the mountains, and remorse for his need ... man's need... to test himself against their unyielding strength. He had broken the cardinal rule... "Never Go Alone!" He knew better... he had been educated... and had learned that many avalanches are caused by off-piste skiers. He had jeopardized not only himself but the many innocent people that could have been injured or killed if he had loosed an avalanche upon them.

Norman had been recognized at the barracks. Years later, he would emotionally revisit this day.

7

As the DC 10 circled the San Francisco airport, Claudia leaned her head against the window remembering a happier time ten years ago when she had been filled with love and excitement... and hours later when she walked into her house, she was acutely aware of the stillness... it was melancholic. The house seemed cavernous, the paintings and sculptures ghostly. Hoping to dispel the chill she felt, Claudia went from room to room, lighting lamps... turning on music... lighting the fireplace in her bedroom. She had never been fearful of outside physical harm in this isolated locale... what she lamented was the intimacy... the sharing. She and Josh had enjoyed times of laughter... of love and friendship... that special familiarity that exists between lovers. Yes, he had been abusive, but... the times he was joyful were difficult to forget. She remembered a day... perhaps a week after they moved into the house... when he had said, "I'm happier right now than I've ever been in my entire life." It had given her such hope... which, unfortunately, was shattered three weeks later. Yes, the intractability certainly existed in their relationship, but was not always present... and at times like this, it was difficult to know if she were doing the right thing. "God, how I miss the warmth and the tenderness that we used to have."

Claudia poured herself a glass of wine, stripped off her clothes, donned a silk robe, and fell on the bed with the huge pile of mail. There were five letters from Josh... she read them sequentially and with each one became increasingly upset. They were ambiguous and at times absurd... at times Josh saw himself as the victim..." You have killed my love for you" or "I have tried everything but nothing worked"... at times he was acrimonious... "You will have to learn how to communicate," "You need to make some concrete changes"... there was paranoia... "I think there's more to this...what's really going on? Are you trying to end things?"...There were small sentences about his love for her... "I'm only saying this because I love you" or "I'm telling you this so you can know I really care." Each letter contained some disastrous, financial news designed to tweak her anxiety and fear... and there were rambling directives about how she should live, spend the money, learn to live on less... but most interesting,... he was telling her he had received a "healing" and that she now needed to be "delivered from bondage, and then healed." Along with this directive, there was the name of a book she was to read, and then she was to come to his Pastor and go through "prayer counseling."

Claudia closed her eyes and leaned back against the pillows consumed with anxiety. Not only was he outlining terms of reconciliation, he was putting the responsibility of the estrangement on her. In that moment, Claudia was aware of what his psychologist had told her eight years ago... "he's not capable of any depth of insight or of remorse." She recognized, now, his inability for true insight... the melancholy that had assailed her previously was gone. Out loud she said, "who ever said I wanted you back, Josh... what- ever gave you the idea that you matter to me?"

The next day, Claudia explored the meaning of the letters as she sat with Kitty.

"What do you think this new healing bit is about, Kitty?"

"There are many church communities that have sprung up with prayer ministries... unfortunately, many of the leaders are poorly educated ...and more than that, they lack the needed and valuable insight when dealing with deep-seated psychosis or psychopathology. I'm not saying that they are insincere, but they do not have the experience or training to deal with psychopathology."

"But I believe in prayer… I believe that people can change when they are exposed to prayer, and unconditional love… and I admire those people who do turn their lives around… don't you? I mean, really Kitty, what about me?"

"I do believe those things, also, Claudia… for you and for all the others. What bothers me about this is that with someone like Josh, there's no depth, no real feelings of remorse, so that the 'healing' becomes superficial. Of course, there are exceptions to everything… but I guess one of my pet peeves is that there are too many people practicing psychotherapy who are not qualified… to me it's the same as a doctor practicing medicine without a license. The mind…the brain is a very complicated organ. It's valuable to share similar problems and challenges like AA does, but there is often more to it… people with serious maladjustments…. Sociopaths usually do not benefit from inexperienced therapists because the therapist is not sufficiently grounded in diagnostics… plus they usually reject the therapeutic process within a short time. The wonderful thing about continuing education is that the more you get the more you realize how much you do not know!"

"Well, I certainly agree with that! Now, back to the letters, Kitty… There's something else that bothers me about them. They're paradoxical. He talks about support he is going to give me and then takes it back… he refers to money, checkbooks and Visa cards he gave me that, in reality, are non-existent sources of financial help!"

"You need to speak to your attorney about that, Claudia, and I would suggest that you give him a jolt, and get that separation agreement completed. It's been too long."

"I have an appointment with him tomorrow. The house is for sale… I'm heartbroken about leaving it… but it's so expensive and so much work to maintain… Josh is supposed to meet with the real estate people this weekend. He has all the papers…"

"Is your attorney aware of all this?"

"I'm not sure. But I'll see what he comes up with tomorrow."

After Claudia left Kitty's office that day she spontaneously drove up to Alasek... sensing it was something she probably shouldn't do... but curious to see Josh's "new" church... hopefully to see his new pastor and to determine what his "new way of life" could possibly be. She found it rather easily... an old but newly painted packing house set back from the road in the midst of giant date palms, avocado and citrus trees. There was a large, Spanish style house on the grounds, which she surmised was the pastor's residence, complete with a playground and a swimming pool. Resentment nagged at her... she knew instinctively that Josh was most likely donating huge sums of money to this "ministry"... she had a negative view of people who donated money to so-called ministries while their family members were struggling financially... and she knew the gospel of giving that was being preached in so many bible churches was causing financial havoc in many families. She walked into the building... it was quite beautiful inside, with plush seats, lots of potted palm trees, and new carpeting. She remembered this old place... it had been an eyesore and deemed dangerous to the children in the area... but her guess was that it had been saved from the wrecking crews by Mr. Henry Marquez and his friends, and that there were no taxes or fees involved. Built onto the side of the apse, was an administrative area. She walked boldly into the secretary's office, and introduced herself giving a false name.

"I've heard so much about this place, I thought I'd come by and see it for myself"... she knew she was gushing, but the phoniness felt good.

"Well, it's certainly nice of you to drop by. Let me tell Pastor Henry you're here and I'm sure he'd love to give you a tour." The secretary disappeared behind a closed door, and soon, she heard the booming voice of "Pastor Henry" welcoming her. Claudia was dressed with great chic today, and she noticed his eyes appraising her.

"Come this way... is it Mrs?... or Miss?...Hartley?"

"Well, right now, it's Mrs., but you can just call me Margaret. I'll be Ms. In a few months."

They were walking through the apse that Claudia had just seen. Pastor Henry came close to her, took her hand and looked sympathetically into her eyes.

"I'm so sorry Margaret... divorce is such a terrible thing... I can help you, you know."

"Oh? how can you do that Pastor Henry?"

"I can help you understand that the man is head of the household, and that often, women do not respond correctly to their husband's headship. It causes problems..."

"My husband is very abusive, Pastor." Claudia had cut him off, curious to elicit his philosophy.

"Margaret, my dear, woman... abuse usually occurs when a man is totally frustrated. I can help you learn how to forgive your husband, and teach you new ways to respond to him so that he will be free to love you more. Women don't realize the things they say and do trigger negative responses from men. It's all tied to what I said before... headship... in every corporation, there has to be a President and CEO... that's the husband."

"And what can I be, Pastor Henry?"

"You're the Vice President in charge of the household. When major decisions have to be made, you can go to your CEO any time and he will prayerfully give you the right answer."

"Well, that certainly is enlightening, Pastor Henry... I can see already where I've been remiss... you see, I was taught that it's all about servant-hood... a man giving up his life for his wife, just as Christ gave up his life for his church... by the way, where did you graduate from seminary?"

Henry avoided her question, instead launching into an abbreviated version of the "vitae" he had given to Josh. He interjected his complete acceptance of God's will for his life, and the knowledge he had been "called" to counsel. They walked back to the office area... he gave her several brochures about the "church community" beseeching her to consider reading a particular book and to return for the prayer counseling. As she was leaving, he pressed her arms and would have hugged her... too warmly she conjectured... but she pulled away from him, smiled, and said goodbye.

Claudia was shaking as she started her car... she had been scared he would detect her identity... she knew it was foolish to put herself in this position, but felt vindicated, and with the pump of adrenalin, was experiencing some euphoria. She knew now what had attracted Josh. He needed to exonerate himself. What a perfect person he had chosen. "It's a match made in heaven," she thought roguishly.

8

Claudia plodded through the days... and the nights. She was faithful to her exercise, the prayer sessions, and now was preparing to move. As she packed box after box, the grief increased...she loved this house... many hours had gone into decorating and much creativity had been involved. Now, the house was beginning to look barren. She had packed up several boxes of household items for Josh and would leave most of the furniture for him ... it would improve the aesthetics until the house sold. Most of her beloved paintings, sculpture and personal effects would go with her.

Josh's barrage of letters continued with the predictable financial threats and the continuing insistence that she go to prayer counseling. "If you won't do it, I can only conclude you do not care what happens to us." And, "If you reject my request this is tantamount to refusing to reconcile." It confused her... she was unaware of any overture on her part to reconcile. The tone of all the letters was whiney, highly contradictory and the ramblings became more pronounced... his obsession with money was pathological, according to Kitty. Claudia made a chart based on his letters, documenting the contradictions, something her attorney had asked her to do.

In October, it was a relief when he went to Japan. Claudia used this time wisely. First, she wrote Josh a long letter addressing many issues...his many threats and intimidations... the physical, psychological and verbal abuse... and for the first time she named it correctly for him to read and digest. She addressed the issues of trust... the main ingredient necessary for any relationship, and how his many infidelities had destroyed any cohesiveness within the marriage, to say nothing of the health risks. She addressed his control issues, and made clear it was the *attitudes* and lack of insight he had that had destroyed the marriage. She also made clear she had no intention of following his directives to attend prayer counseling with Henry Marquez... she did not tell him of her visit. And finally, she addressed the issues of finances... the lack of honesty he displayed when he emptied their accounts, the secrecy and control he employed with her... the contradictions that were evident between his claim of Christian love, and the threats and intimidations as to how he would provide for her. She reminded him that based on statistics, it was estimated that after divorce, women who were fifty years or older, could expect a 72% decrease in income, while men after fifty, could expect an increase in income of at least 42%. She addressed the no-fault divorce laws as being a major component in the newly emerging poverty among older women. Claudia made copies of some of the statistics remembering that Josh frequently accused her of "inventing" things. She also reminded him that she had co-mingled her money.... both the cash gifts from her parents, including an inheritance from her deceased Mother and the child support from Gerald... in a spirit of trust. Of all the things she had learned from her attorney, this misfortune of "co-mingling" had upset her the most! The total sum of the money that had been gifted to her during her marriage to Josh had been significant... but the fact that she had not kept the money as a separate account, would now prove to be her downfall. Instead of an independent nest egg, she was left with nothing of her own with the exception of the meager amount she had squirreled `away from her household allowance. Josh had used all "her" money for paying the bills and, as she looked back, realized he had never divulged his income to her, and had cleverly manipulated the finances to his advantage.

The second thing she did was due to the generosity of Zach. He had saved some money and bought her an airline ticket to visit a monastery in New Mexico. When she arrived at the "Abby" she was impressed with the simple beauty of the buildings and the milieu. After she was welcomed and had settled into her private room, she met her "facilitator," an older, humorous, monk with a Ph.D. in psychology, who explained to her that she could stay for a week... he would be "on call" and would be available to see her at any time. At their first "session" which lasted for over 2 hours, she was impressed with his insight, compassion and knowledge. Claudia felt he was incredibly non-judgmental, an important detail since she had been treated with such condemnation by her parish priests in the last 15 years. The third night she was there she had an extraordinary encounter. It was 11:30 p.m... Claudia was unable to sleep so she tentatively wended her way to the deserted chapel. It smelled of the incense that she loved, the many candles were still flickering causing the lively shadows to dance and flutter. She lay on the floor, arms outstretched and called out to God... "Heal me, love me, forgive me, be with me, always..." The copious tears began to flow and within the next 2 hours, years of repressed hurts, fears and frustrations had flooded the soft carpet beneath her face. Then she felt hot, and experienced a surge of peace... of joy...of love... and knew at that moment that she would become a whole person. It seemed to her that all the hours she had spent with Kitty had now come to fruition, and from that night forward, Claudia was aware that she was the recipient of a new depth of wisdom and maturity... she discovered during the week at the Abby what unconditional love was and how it can repair and regenerate life... and with her facilitator, she also had an opportunity to work through the anger she had been wrestling with when her attorney had explained both the consequences of "co-mingling" and the discovery that there would be almost no money realized from the sale of the house, since Josh had taken most of the equity from it.

For some unknown reason, at the end of October, Josh agreed to continue her support at an increased rate...

She moved to her new apartment in the southwest community of Palm Vista on November 1st.

■ ■ ■

In retrospect, it was fortunate that Claudia did not anticipate the frustrations, the defeats and heartaches that became central to her life in the next fifteen years... but neither did she foresee the confidence, self- esteem and wisdom that would emerge as a result of the innumerable challenges she would face. She matured... and in addition to the new depth of wisdom she had gained at the Abby, she now had a pronounced sense of independence... in her sessions at the Abby, she had learned that there was no such thing as "safe love"...that love by its very nature is giving someone the power to hurt you, and it was important to stay vulnerable to forestall bitterness... this helped dispel the fear she had carried with her since childhood.

Claudia was fifty-two years old when she moved into her apartment in Palm Vista. It was a 2-story townhouse style with two bedrooms so that Zach would have his own room when visiting from college. In her customary manner, she scoured thrift stores and estate sales and decorated it to insure the utmost comfort and pleasing ambience, but it had been difficult to leave her Los Carmelo home... she was invested there ... she missed her friends, her activities, the familiarity of her milieu...the comfort, beauty and ease that she had been born to and had enjoyed a good part of her life. And... She missed Kitty, although she had been grateful for Kitty's promise to be available by phone if needed. Two things she did immediately were to join the local church and to get a subscription to the local newspaper. The two priests at the church welcomed her and displayed both compassion and humor.... they became her first friends, and others followed.

Unfortunately, she learned quickly that in the business world in the year of 1983, fifty-two-year-old women were considered expendable... obsolete... especially in her field of marketing and advertising. Society was youth oriented... employers used words like "bright," "energetic," "active"... it was the legally recommended way they used to exclude the Methuselian crowd.

Not having much to occupy her time added to the overwhelming loneliness. She missed Zach, who was away at college, and the one good friend she had in her new area informed her she was moving to Boston. In January, she felt her job search was futile, and began to explore the possibility of changing careers... returning to school... working toward another Master's degree in a field that was more inclusive of older women. For several weeks, she pondered over the idea of writing to her Father and asking him for a loan. She vacillated back and forth... one day it would be yes and the next day it would be no, never! Then, one day she summoned all her courage, and wrote the letter which included a pay-back schedule that included interest. James Fitzpatrick had never offered help to his daughter... he did, however, send her the yearly cash gift at Christmas... mailed to Claudia by her sister. When James received the letter he called Claudia... it was the first time they had direct communication in over twenty eight years. Claudia was shocked and nervous at first, but this changed to the old familiar shame and heartache when he expressed his deep displeasure at her plan, stating... "Go to the five and dime and get a job... stop feeling sorry for your- self... you brought this on your-self, you know... You used no sense... why would a man like Josh marry someone like you with three children."

Claudia then investigated nursing school. She was interviewed by the administrator who stated she made a practice of "forthrightness." She speculated that Claudia would not be able to find work after graduation. "Doctors like working with younger girls... hospitals usually do not hire inexperienced nurses in their fifties."

In February, a letter from Josh announced that commencing March 1ˢᵗ, he was no longer going to support her. Claudia recognized she was being terrorized... this man whom she adored at one time was betraying her. She called him, asked him to her apartment to talk. When he arrived, there was the old attraction... she asked him to please be fair with her. She talked about her experiences at the Abbey, and now wanted to create some kind of relationship where they could respect and care about each other. She was surprised when he began to cry...

"I just wanted to force you against a wall... Claudia, I know this was all my fault... If I had loved you the way you should be loved, none of this would have happened."

Josh knelt in front of her and took her hands. "Claudia, I know I've abused you physically and verbally... I know I've provoked the arguments. Please... please forgive me. I swear to you this will never happen again."

"Josh you've said many times it would not happen, and it does... what's different now?"

"I swear to you my anger is gone... I have no more bitterness... my heart has been softened... you are so precious to me, Claudia... I know you need my love... I promise you... I will love you into healing!"

"Josh, it could take a long time for me to trust you..."

"Claudia, I understand... but we will work everything out... every nitty gritty little detail"

She smiled, "it could take fifteen years."

Josh pulled her out of the chair... hugging her, caressing her hair, he told her, "I don't care if it takes the rest of our lives... we are going to get rid of all your hurts... we are going to talk it all out." He kissed her face and her hands... he held her close... "I am committed to you Claudia... I will care for you for the rest of our lives."

Josh led her upstairs but when they lay on the bed, he made no sexual overtures... "I just want you to know how I love you and want you to trust me again."

They held each other... Claudia cried... Josh comforted her and stroked her with the tenderness she had remembered on those many long, lonely nights.

Soon, Josh left, promising to call her soon. The next week was their anniversary. She received a card and a letter:

> My Dearest Claudia:
> This card is to celebrate the ushering in of our next ten years. I am truly sorry for having put you through so much in the past, and humbly ask your forgiveness.
> I am confident that we will be able to work through our difficulties, and I am committed to being your husband until death do us part.
> When you are ready, I would like to look at new wedding bands. It is my desire to repeat our wedding vows in conjunction with re-uniting permanently. Until then, and then thereafter, may you know love, peace and joy. I love you, Claudia."   J

Two weeks later, Josh repudiated his new-found love. Once again, he withdrew all the money from the bank account… sent her a letter with his plans of divorce… and told her, "The only reason I said I love you is because I am commanded to love you. But I don't."

Claudia vowed to never see Josh again, but for the next several years there were many menacing letters, designed to alarm, threaten and frighten her… until finally it was finished!

They say the dragon never sleeps,
He stalks his prey in silence cold,
And when he strikes, what evil fire within his bellow
One day, the snake in careless greed,
Dared seize a knight born of the sun
The bite burned deep, right to the soul
The snake held fast, damage done
But death could not win!
For tho the fire had pierced her through
Knight of the sun held strong and true

The fever broke, the serpent fled abandoning his prize
The knight rose up, these words she spoke:
You have broken my body, but not my spirit
I will not mourn, nor will I fear it;
BEWARE, dread beast, you have not won this battle!
My quest has just begun.

(anonymous)

BOOK IV

Part 1
"Letters"

...thank you Lord for being with me and directing my path...

May 15, 1979 - (A letter that Claudia wrote to Gerald after she had been diagnosed correctly by Dr. Maynard... her California Orthomolecular Physician. Her marriage to Josh was still fairly new)

Dear Gerald:

I just got back from seeing Dr. Maynard, my "doctor of last resort," and wanted to share some good and interesting information. During our once a month telephone conversations, our time is devoted to news about the children, but I wanted you to know that I have been seeing Dr. Maynard now for almost a year, and it has been what I would term, "Miraculous." Today, he took a great deal of time validating my instincts that the plethora of physical symptoms I experienced for so many years was a result of my faulty biochemistry and not the mental disorders that were erroneously attached to me. He even went so far as to suggest that the medications were the *cause* of many of my symptoms. I discussed the dreadful electroshock treatments with him... every so often, like a flash, a memory comes to me... it is disquieting! It seems I am, constantly, having to re-evaluate the many events and occurrences in my life and in the life we shared. He agreed that shock treatments were not indicated for me, and with his treatment, I have blossomed! No more depression, no more foggy head, no more of those crushing headaches or mood swings... and I have noticed an incredibly improved cognitive ability, a definite reduction in the Lupus symptoms and greatly improved physical strength. The ironic part of this whole thing is that the only other orthomolecular doctor that he knows of has an office within one mile of the clinic where I spent so many tortuous months.

When I look back on the gross mis-diagnoses, it makes me realize that medicine has a long way to go in recognizing the synergy between the body and mind. How many

others are suffering in hospitals and institutions with diagnosed mental disorders when they could be enjoying
freedom and good health instead of the drugged, senseless
creatures they are... like I used to be.

As long as I am writing a letter, I want to take this opportunity to thank you for what you did for me during the
years of my illness... We had both become victims of our
own ignorance... we believed the people we paid for information... they were the authority figures, whom we were
taught to respect and obey. We had no idea at that time
that what we ingest, what we breathe... that the biochemical
reactions that affect our brains can cause a person to experience depression, anxiety, suicidal thoughts, anger and
a plethora of other symptoms. Nor did we imagine that
I was a diabetic and we certainly never heard of lupus. I
wish you had not given up on me. You told me once a long
time ago, that the reason our marriage ended was because
you could not say "NO" to me, but I feel that the chasm
in our marriage began when I became aware of your affair
with Helen. It was a confusing time for me... I had gone
to group therapy and some of the members thought you
were a homosexual, based on what Sophie had told me that
when you were in college you dated a lesbian and had two
homosexuals for roommates. I loved you so much and felt
so rejected at that time... because I did not feel good about
myself, and because you noticeably withdrew from me. I
am raking up the past for a reason... it doesn't matter why
you divorced me, but what matters is that neither one of
us harbor any resentments ... life took us to places we were
unprepared for. I am sorry for my part in the dissolution
of our marriage, and I hope you are free from guilt or hurt.
It is difficult to say whether or not I'd have recovered without Dr. Maynard... but I do want you to know I am grateful

for the friendship of your Mother, whom I dearly loved, and for the friendship you extended to me. I feel rich in having had love from both of you.
Claudia

August 25, 1985 (A letter written over a year after Claudia left Carmelo)

Dear Kitty:

I know that I can call you, but writing letters is so much better for me... writing helps me organize my thoughts.

I wanted to let you know that, today, the status portion of my divorce from Josh is final. It was bifurcated due to Josh's rage over the money... his typical reaction! I will not know until November or December what the final financial arrangements will be but I can assume it will be a meager settlement.

So, today feels very sad to me. I sit here looking at my wedding ring, and reading the inscription inside... "Our love forever." What do I know about love? You once said that to you love means helping someone reach his highest potential. Inherent in this definition is the concept of exhaustive generosity, sacrifice and service.... having the attitude that you give more than you receive. When I look back on my marriage to Josh, there were none of these things present... I became so victimized by the abuse that I was unable to function or to grow... and Josh was so caught up in the abuse that he was unable to grow beyond his limitations. I think as individuals we have a responsibility, an obligation for constant growth, which is achieved when we renew and nourish our minds, update our values and opinions and expand our personalities. I remember when you told me that part of your job as a psychotherapist was to be a supportive and guiding force in helping me *understand* the problems and then for me to make *decisions* to benefit my future. You knew at that time that abuse completely robs a person of confidence, but I did not know that! I really had no idea whom I was at the end of my relationship with Josh... I was so used to denying my feelings, of trying to keep the peace... It was frightening to me that I might be that terrible person that Josh said I was, that Gerald didn't want anymore, and someone that my parents avoided most of my life.

We talked a good deal in our sessions about forgiveness.. Was it you who said to me that forgiveness is the most complete form of revenge? I so like that! Most important for me to have learned is that forgiveness does not mean forgetting and that it is a *process*... and most important, that forgiveness is really for me...*it takes the power away from my abuser*...

After my experience at the Abby, I finally grew up and came to realize that life will not only present good things, but might also present pain, harm, and maltreatment... we will always have occasion to practice forgiveness because I cannot control another's behavior, and neither understanding nor forgiveness alleviates the unwelcome grief or desolation, but they are both healthy pro-active stances. I want to thank you for the insights I gained, and for the transformation you helped me accomplish... I am truly grateful.

However, I was shocked (and still am) at the fear, discouragement and anxiety that I experienced during the whole separation and divorce process with Josh. When I went through my divorce with Gerald, I was so anesthetized at the time from all those horrible prescription drugs doled out by unthinking doctors, that I never felt the real depth of the process. Perhaps it was because I was younger and more hopeful...and was so busy with all the responsibility I had with the children so that I had little time to dwell on what was happening. Now, I am older and faced with the realities of surviving... I am aware of the resurgence of all the old shame and grief...all the negative memories of my childhood and reliving the many challenges I faced with both Gerald and Josh.

I've learned quite a bit about anger... namely, that if we keep expressing the same bitterness, that with time it grows like an unwelcome tumor and the bitterness can turn into rage. We need to analyze our anger, use it as a motivating force for change. So, I began to journal, and I'll share some insights that I gained.

The anger I felt centered on the lack of trustworthiness... integrity... and honorableness in those who said they loved me. Going back to my childhood family... with the exception of the reprehensible actions of my grandfather... and the inability of my parents to express love either physically or verbally... I was provided wonderful shelter, protection and a myriad of advantages... education, travel, most of the necessities of life... really a fine life. So, I chose to give up my anger toward that period of my life and to embrace the good things my parents provided for me, to recognize that what ever they did or did not do was a result of the beliefs and values of their generation... and inherent in their actions were all the good experiences and all the harsh experiences that they suffered...and they did not have the benefit of therapy!

Then there was the anger toward Gerald and Josh... two men who, in the presence of God and congregation, promised to love and care for me, *forsaking all others...* That was, and still is, more difficult to forgive, although the process is active. Perhaps my Father had insight onto Gerald's inadequacies and his ability to persevere, and perhaps if I had met you sooner, I'd have recognized Josh's pathology. There are lingering feelings of abandonment that lay just beneath the surface, but the lesson learned... not everyone will love me or even like me, but I can still love and be loving to others.

There was also anger toward my church and church members... and disbelief at the lack of compassion toward divorced women. Have you ever noticed that when a spouse dies, church people visit and bring casseroles and words of love and comfort. However, I have never had a visit or phone call from any member of my church including any member of the clergy. I still have a great deal of work to do in this area, but what I have done is to become extremely active within my church... joining a variety of ministries that help me to give and to receive blessings... and I was invited to attend a two-year course in lay ministry offered by the church hierarchy in my area.

The last anger issue ... the incredibly lax laws that presently allow a man to brutalize, terrorize, emotionally annihilate, and verbally degrade a person they "solemnly" promised to love, honor, cherish, protect... in the presence of God... until death. What goes on here? If a man hits another man in a bar, or if a man commits a hate crime, or if a terrorist is suspected of a crime... these persons are arrested, or jailed, or suffer some form of punishment. Why are the courts, the police, the medical community the clergy and the general public not crying out for justice against those men who abuse their wives... What can be done, Kitty? How can we begin to rectify these sexist injustices? The only lesson I have learned from this, is, unfortunately, that there really is no justice in life... but... every individual must plant a seed to help justice grow... we all need to speak out, to reject compliance to group think, to make value judgments for good.

Well, that's it for now... my love to you both and my prayers for your peace and contentment. And, as always, thank you for what you do and what you have done for me.
Claudia....

December 1, 1985

My dear Kitty...

I trust by now you have finished reading my letter of August 25th... it was a rather intense letter... this one will also be intense, but trust me... with a little time I will lighten up!

What a surprise! The financial part of the divorce has finally been signed. Josh wanted, actually demanded through his attorney, for my Father to take financial responsibility for me... The man is truly an original! Although he did forget to mention that he had benefited from the yearly cash gifts from my Father, also from the inheritance left to me by my Mother, and from all the child support money paid by Gerald ... all this cash co-mingled by me, in the spirit of trust, into our *joint* accounts... cash I never had access to because Josh was the financial head of our frugally-run, or should I say our penny-pinching, household! He commanded and he doled out ... the lesson learned and hopefully passed on to all young, unsuspecting brides, is this... do not co-mingle your assets... keep your own account separate from those of your husband. I realize this is controversial but I feel strongly about this... perhaps a different time or a different husband would change my mind.

So, the bottom line is this... I was awarded 5 years of "re-habilitative" alimony. Since I have been a young child, my goal in life was to be a wife and mother...the best wife and the best mother I could be, and in return, I would enjoy and appreciate a husband and marriage that would provide me love, loyalty and financial stability. When my Father disowned me, and reneged on the years of promises he had made that his children would be financially rewarded at the time of his death, I never thought about having to support myself. In my privileged milieu, few women think about being in the job market... and I foolishly ignored the fact that life is a series of positives and negatives and did not prepare myself for financial independence. So, here I am...fired from a job that I wanted and loved, and realizing that when I am 58 years old, I will have no income except for whatever I will be able to earn on my own. Pretty late in life to begin a new career.

It is traumatic for anyone to have to change careers at the age of 52, yet divorced homemakers are expected to do this without any regard for their personal feelings, desires, abilities or aptitudes. This is a time when most men are thinking of retiring but somehow judges continue to assume that a displaced, over fifty homemaker can enter the workforce and become a fiscal sensation...five years of "rehabilitative" alimony... the award does not take into account my age, the length of time I had been out of the job market, or the fact that while I am being "rehabilitated" I will be living on the welfare level and totally broke at the end of the award. The final insult is that I was forced to sign away any claim on future earnings, retirement/pension funds, medical benefits and insurance, and, of course, all the money Josh squirreled away in a foreign bank.

When the legislators enacted the no-fault divorce laws, there was an appalling lack of foresight as to how it would affect my age cohort, not only at the time of the enactment, but long range, how poverty would most likely be the end result for women in later years. I did some research and was not at all surprised to learn that divorced older women have the highest rate of poverty. I understand the theory behind "rehabilitative" alimony... an able-bodied woman, one who can earn a living, should not have the right to put a permanent lien on a divorced man's income… *if,* and this is a big component… after she receives education and training, it would ensure her a standard of living that would be equitable to what she had during her marriage… and given the age factor, it seems highly unlikely this would be the case.

Well, Kitty this documents one of the realities of starting over… And, I understand more than ever why many women do not leave an abusive marriage… I am one of the lucky ones… At least I have the education to compete with others, despite my age, for securing a job that will afford me a stable living… we'll see what the future holds.

My love to you both…

Claudia

December 25, 1986

Dear Kitty:

I was so very happy when I heard indirectly about Norman's inheritance and the wonderful way you both have chosen to use Lucas Henderson's money... from all that I have heard about this remarkable man, he would have been very pleased. I was aware that Norman was a great skier, but was unaware of the heroism he showed in saving Lucas Henderson's life so many years ago... it touched me very deeply.

After reading the series of articles in *Western Life Magazine,* I realize you kept silent about this and the subsequent inheritance for many years. It must have been somewhat strange for you to have me as a client, and to hear all about Josh... another piece in the puzzle. I often wish I had known Lucas and Holly... they sound like a special couple, and I wonder if they would have shared insights with me about Josh.

Last month I wrote to Josh's ex-wife, Monica, something I wanted to do years ago... I have always wondered why they divorced and wanted to let her know that I did not meet Josh until after their divorce was final... you know how strongly I feel about women making a play for another woman's husband. Today, I received a long, very enlightening response. Monica is still angry... she characterizes Josh as "sarcastic," "caustic," "critical" "plotting," and refers to him as a "cold, uncaring, supercilious bastard who is a pathological liar." Of course, her letter was full of recriminations toward me... he obviously lied to her about what I received financially, but I would expect that... he told me the same things about her. The cruel thing I learned from her was the disclosure that Josh was not divorced when he met me, nor was he separated. Monica was at their home in Palm Beach waiting for his return at Christmas... instead, she was served with divorce papers. How hurtful that must have been! I remember the time Josh went to see her after we were married and had a sexual liaison with her. He told me how "difficult" it had been for him... "I felt sorry for her... she was so pathetic..." Monica tells me in her letter that Josh "was glad to be back in [her] bed," and that they "had a good reunion." She shared with me that there were several subsequent sexual interventions... and while he was at her house, he was making telephone calls to another woman in New York with whom he was having a sexual liaison. I feel somewhat ashamed, but the letter cheered me. It was good to know that my own characterizations of Josh being a pathological liar, a womanizer and an abuser, were authenticated...but I did wonder why she was "glad to have him back in her bed" after her very negative characterizations of him! The interesting thing... she shared her childhood parental trauma that was similar to mine. I remember my irritation when you suggested at our first therapy session that men like Josh "target" certain types of women. Please feel validated.

I wanted to keep this letter positive, but I must say that this is the loneliest Christmas day I ever remember, but I know that this will pass... I will get through it! It has been a year since my divorce, and generally, I am doing better, but I suggested that Zach travel back East to be with his Father and siblings for Christmas. It is my part in trying to "set him free"... sometimes I do good and sometimes not so good. I did not want to be the fifth wheel in a family celebration so declined invitations to be with friends and their families and instead went to the food pantry and helped feed the 800 people who showed up ... so many homeless and so many elderly. I felt ashamed for feeling sorry for myself. When I looked into the faces of these people today, I saw a great deal of hopelessness and loneliness ...and the more I talk with women and men in my circumstances (divorced, widowed, alone and older) the more convinced I become that it is becoming epidemic in our society due to the disintegration of our extended families and the growth of technology that fosters isolation. Thomas Wolfe wrote, "Loneliness, far from being a rare and curious phenomenon, peculiar to myself and a few other solitary men, is the central and inevitable fact of human existence."

I've experienced loneliness on many levels... like the loneliness that comes from being in a bad marriage... or when I realized Gerald was having an affair... And with Josh, I remember lying on the floor, crying, begging him to stop the abuse and he would kick me or spit on me... I wanted to die at those times ... the physical pain was not as intense as the pain of the loneliness I felt. There is the loneliness that comes from being misunderstood... how often I have known this!.. and then there is the loneliness that comes from rejection... being too fat, or too thin, or disabled, too assertive, too old, when your best friend (or a husband) rejects you... or when people are too judgmental of you or make fun of you or gossip negatively about you... even being rejected for being too wise! But the end of this story is...I felt so much better when I was at the food pantry helping to feed all those other lonely people. And some were able to laugh or to tell a story. The lesson: You already know because you have done it for years... get out of yourself and give to someone else.

Again, congratulations on such a wonderful series of articles. Christmas Peace to you both, and a New Year filled with love.

Claudia

P.S. I have purposely not included any updates on my progress but will write a long letter when I can.

May, 1991 (5 years later)

Dear Kitty:

    I pray that this finds you and Norman in good health and as much in love as always. The last time we talked, I promised to write you with the details of my progress in life. If you remember back when I made the break, we were both confident that my advanced degree would secure me good employment, but that's not what happened. I discovered many layers of prejudice exist and I was either "underqualified" or "overqualified" ... an amusing paradox as to how I could be both. After a time of trying to find meaningful work and failing to do so, I took a job for a short time as a cook and housekeeper for a pastor friend who had lost his wife... it was a low point, but it was a safe and quiet atmosphere and the pastor(s) were very kind to me. At the same time, I realized that I must find a new profession... one that would accept a person for their knowledge and skill... where age would not be a deterrent.... and that meant returning to school. I searched around and found a great advanced program in psychology that accepted a good portion of my past academic work, and I clepped several subjects so that I could save money by not repeating classes I once had. Again, money was paramount and, at the age of 53, I worked two part-time jobs... one was working for the county elder program, and the other was a paid internship in a psychiatric facility... and then I went to school at night. Mercifully, Zach and his girlfriend moved in with me and helped in so many ways, shopping, cleaning, cooking, so that I could devote all my energies to academics. They were wonderful to me. I finished all my needed coursework in California, and then decided to finish off with another advanced degree and went to New York where I was admitted into

"Advanced Standing" and I could take advantage of the Aging Center. I went through a series of moves and crises, and loans and biting my fingernails, rented attic space in an old house in Westchester... my old stomping grounds... and worked my little brain to death for 10 months... sleeping on a mattress on the floor, and living with just a chair and my word processor. The loneliness was overwhelming, but I did it!

So, last week, I received my Doctorate degree at my graduation ceremony at Lincoln Center. Zach was with me and miraculously, David attended the ceremony and went with us for a drink afterwards. It was so wonderful to see him, and I was so proud that he came to share this happy time with me. Perhaps it was mere curiosity on his part, but I prefer to think that he was proud of me for what I have accomplished. You played a major role in all of this, Kitty.. but I can hear you saying, "No, Claudia, you did the work, and you made the good choices... you are the one that needs the accolades."

So, here I am at the age of 58, and I will now try to make my mark in life. I have already secured a job at a private psychiatric hospital for older adults, where I can earn a living while doing my two year internship... I've passed my initial boards, and have secured a mentor. I've also been able to rent a *tiny* apartment where I work... it is dirt cheap by New York standards, and I don't have to do any driving to work... just walk across the grounds. My intention is to specialize in brain disorders in the older adult... there is so little being done for them... and I have recognized that they are very over-medicated and their needs largely ignored. It seems to me that too many health care workers think that mental health problems are part of the aging process... but this is not true. Older adults suffer so many losses... not just death of loved ones, but the loss of control, loss of beauty and status, loss of mobility due to multiple health issues, loss of recognition... the list is so very long... and I cringe at the lack of respect given to this age cohort. When you think of the baby boomers who will begin to reach maturity by the year 2011 and that by 2020 older adults will be 22% of the population, it makes sense that there will be a great need for mental health professionals specializing in treating the burgeoning older population... especially in the mental health arena, as it is projected that this cohort will suffer a higher percentage of mental health issues than ever before seen in our society. Right now there is no comprehensive approach to this future problem... my hope is that in years to come, we can move from an administrative/business school approach to a professional approach in treating mental health issues.

Well, I certainly didn't intend to involve you in a seminar! I hope you can intuit that I am quite passionate about my new role in life, and that I will be able to help many people... like you helped me.
My love to you both,
Claudia.

December, 2009   (18 yrs. later)

Dear Kitty...

This is going to be a long letter, and I hope that you
and Norman will take a bottle of wine, some cucumber
sandwiches like I used to make, and hike into the hills behind the beautiful home I lived in, and read this together.
I wish I could be there with the two of you, but, being legally blind, I no longer drive, and my health has drastically
declined... this will be my heartfelt thank you letter, and
my good-by letter...

It's been a long journey... I don't even recognize that person you met almost thirty years ago... there have been so
many changes... in me and in my life. When I look back, I
wonder how I survived the very difficult years... there were
many lessons learned.

When I received my doctorate, I, again, thought I had
it made... but it takes time to become established, and although I made a good living and was able to maintain a
nice lifestyle, by the time the bills were paid, I was never
able to save enough money for retirement, and what I did
manage to save, I placed with great trust in the hands of
2 financial planners who managed to lose all that I had
invested. (I have learned through the years, that this is a
rather common occurrence among the senior population,
but there has not been the outcry against these "criminals"
and their financial abuse as there needs to be.)

As long as I have mentioned finances, I am going to
give you my final thoughts on this subject... perhaps you
can take some of my thoughts and pass them along!

When we read or hear of domestic abuse, it usually
centers on the physical and psychological scars, the costs
to communities, the loss of work, but rarely the financial

losses suffered by the victims... women who have remained trapped in the abusive relationships due to their partners who drain their joint accounts, or hide assets, or skim money off the top. We read a lot of statistics... how this crime affects the economy, medical institutions, corporations, and society as a whole... the billions of dollars it costs taxpayers. But, somehow, the victim gets lost in the statistics... and the message should be... **financial independence is the key to leaving an abusive relationship.** This is the answer to all those people who ask why women stay in abusive relationships. And the next sentence should be... "How can we make it possible for women to leave?" To this end, society and corporations, as well as individuals need to promote volunteer programs and financial and mentoring programs to assist women to leave... to provide legal help, to get job training and opportunities, to find good childcare, to find safe housing at reasonable prices, to establish credit, and, when necessary, to establish new identities.

I am quite sure that if presented properly, there could be many suitable volunteers within communities who would mentor these women, and that money could be found within community budgets to fund educational programs for clergy, law enforcement agencies, the legal population, and medical and mental health workers.

Back to me...not having a pension has been grim... this is a legal matter that needs attention at the time of divorce to assure that "the oldest old" will not have to endure end-of-life poverty. As a financially blessed child and young adult, I never realized how people are forced to live when they do not have money... even basic needs are often lacking. Pensions are becoming extinct, and, like me, the number of older adults that rely solely on their income from Social Security is increasing.

Among older women (80 y.o. +) surviving becomes critical... 23% live below the Supplemental Poverty Measure (SPM) which could be because women in many cases are severely penalized in divorce cases, and typically receive less money per year than men. I was also surprised and somewhat disillusioned to learn that approximately 33% of the people receiving Social Security benefits are NOT elderly... These are people, who for the most part, have not paid into the fund... those with physical and mental disorders, children, family members etc. I think that this is a mistake... these people need financial help but not out of the Social Security Fund... that should be strictly for those who have paid into it.

So, back to lessons... the first lesson is that hard work does not always pay off... No one worked harder or longer hours than I did, but I was not able to achieve financial independence. In my case, I started a career too late in life because in my generation the belief was a woman's place is in the home... we were not trained for employment. Also, keep in mind that most abusive husbands do not want their wives to work... it decreases their control...and if the wife does work, he often harasses her at her place of employment which often ends her career. The second lesson I would teach anyone who would listen is ... stay in school... get your degrees when you are young... then go and do what you want, but have a plan in place to be able to support yourself and to have a retirement account. Fortunately, my dear son, Zach, is generous and caring, and this year he bought a condo for me to live in ... how wonderful it would be if more adult children would be this generous with their parents. I am awed by his love... and each day I review my many blessings... I could have been bitter... but I did not choose that option... and for that I want to thank you.

I remember it clearly... one of the many, valuable lessons I learned from you... it was a day I was pouring out my sad story and was in the throes of being a victim. You stopped me and said in a kind and caring voice... "Claudia, today is the first day of the rest of your life... today you have a choice... do you want to remember and continually rehash all the hurtful, negative things that have happened to you, and keep all that bitterness inside you, or do you want to be free... do you want to change the way you *think*... do you want to let go of all the negative *feelings*, all the hurtful *feelings*..." and then you proceeded to teach me how the way I *think* determines how I *feel*... what a revelation to me! I always thought that the things that happened to me in my life caused my negative feelings, and now I was learning that it was the way I process what happens to me that determines how I feel... if I think correctly... then I will feel more peaceful. But, there was much more, such as the difference between *positive thinking* and *correct thinking*. Positive thinking is good, but it does not solve the problem... it's like putting a band aid on a deep wound, whereas correct thinking is accordant with the situation or events. You taught me that feelings are neither good nor bad in/of themselves but it is what we do with the feelings... how we process them that causes the problems ... that feelings produce what you termed "self- talk" and continually allowing negative feelings to flood our consciousness will certainly produce a miserable life! I spent a good amount of time learning about *"cognitive distortions"*... those nasty little thought patterns... the "brain maps" we develop as children and continue to follow as adults that keep us mercilessly entwined in negative thoughts, behaviors and physical symptoms. I had been so programmed through all of the years that I was in therapy to *express my feelings....* punch the pillows, scream and yell, let all the feelings out. Looking back on the some of those therapy groups I attended, (like Primal Scream) I realize that we can become addicted to anger... to the bitterness and negative emotions... and all the years I was taught to scream and yell... I never felt better... Instead, it increased the negative feelings, and increased the victim role. How many thousands of times had I been asked... "How did that make you feel" instead of "How did you think about that?" ... or "How did you react to that?" You taught me that feelings are important... they are a barometer, given to us by God that give us an awareness... a perception of occurrences in our lives... but feelings should never dominate our lives or obscure our appropriate cognitions. As I told you...therapy never made any sense to me... all the years of rehashing the same events... I never knew I had choices, that I, alone, could control my life... or learn how to think and react differently to the things that were happening to me. I also learned that I had to practice forgiveness ... not to forget... but through an act of my will to remove the power from the miscreants in my life... from all those who knowingly or unknowingly caused me harm... and to empower myself. It was a revelation to me... I didn't have to punch those damn pillows or scream anymore! I worked hard and long to learn to reprogram myself with your expert help. Thank you so much for this lesson. I think that learning this and coming to recognize the inevitability of the escalation of the abuse... were two of the most important motivating factors in my ability to leave Josh. When I think back to the first time the verbal abuse happened... three months after the children and I moved to California... and how stunned I was... and how I allowed myself to endure the abuse for 10 years... hoping it would disappear... believing Josh when he told me it would "never happen again." This is the lesson... it does not get

238 KATHERINE B. HEATON

better... it increases in intensity and becomes more danger-ous with time. The first time a woman accepts abuse, she leaves the door open for more...and she becomes weaker and more frightened.

I still have residual anger and react negatively when I hear people say, "Why didn't you leave?" Are they kid-ding? Where are women with children supposed to go? How are they supposed to support their children, let alone themselves? Where are they supposed to hide in order to escape the ire of the abuser? What has society or the courts or the lawmakers **really** done to help these wom-en and children? Domestic violence, or domestic abuse, is still not taken seriously by a large part of our society... if it were, we would be hearing questions like, "Did they ever prosecute the husband for battery or put him in jail?" "Why was he allowed to interact with the children?" "Has he been ordered to support her and the children?" "Has this woman, been given protection?" "Is someone men-toring her, so that the danger of her going back to the destructive milieu will be alleviated?" We need to correct our thinking.

So, Kitty, I now know I am one of the very blessed, but after this ordeal, I wondered, for several years, if I would ever again find happiness. And so I began a search for this elusive thing we call happiness... it was quite revealing. I started at the beginning... what is happiness? How do you get it? How do you keep it? I'm not going to regurgitate the wisdom I uncovered during my research about hap-piness... but for me, the lesson was that happiness is not something you search for... it's not an inalienable right ... but to me it is a sense of peace, of satisfaction, a feeling of contentment that you *choose* on a daily basis. It was Viktor Frankl's, insightful book, *Man's Search for Meaning*, that first helped me to realize that what I call happiness is my choice... and a powerful and long lasting lesson to me about happiness is that I can find joy and contentment in being present to others.... I finally chose the right career as you did.

Another component inherent in the pursuit of happiness and a return of joy, is the forgiveness process. Without forgiveness, I do not believe we can ever be free ... but I do remember the caveat's about forgiveness... one, that it is a process and it takes patience, two, it is an act of our will and three, it is not necessary or even sometimes not wise to "forget." But, we do need to move on, and to continually monitor our inner dialogue in order to proceed with the "process." We talked quite a bit about this in our sessions together, and what I learned from you about the whole subject of forgiveness has remained an extremely important lesson.... one that we frequently have the "opportunity" to practice in our lives.

I remember clearly the first time I heard myself laugh out loud... what a beautiful sound! In my work I have realized that, in addition to anger, we can become addicted to suffering... and to expect adversity. Guilt becomes our middle name ...and, as a child, I remember learning about the great suffering of the saints, and thinking that is what God wants of me... Thank goodness I have been able to update my belief system.

In the latter years of my life I became known for my venturous spirit. This was born out of my ability to realize that life is not a continuing day-time drama... and I found myself able to do new things... things that used to frighten me... to take a risk... and each time I did, my self- esteem and confidence increased. Not everything worked out that I tried... but I was able to go on to the next thing and land on my feet. Yes, there were times of adversity, times of tears and fears... but in the long run my life was enriched from the adventure.

The last word I have about happiness is that in every-thing I have read and gleaned... there is a spiritual compo-nent in happiness. This got lost when I was on so many prescription drugs. When I re-connected with my spiritu-ality... I call it my conversion experience... it was the begin-ning of true, long-lasting happiness which, to me, means a peaceful heart.... and please note I said "the beginning" because it took time and effort... it did not happen all at once, and I have had regressions, which last shorter and shorter periods of time with the advancement of age. This has given me a true, loving image of myself... The power of God and goodness within us gives meaning and purpose to all that we do. I do not believe that anyone can truly heal without this spiritual component.

When I talk about taking risks, and growing in self- esteem, there is an integral component necessary and that is the abil-ity to embrace **change.** This did not come easily to me in the beginning of my recovery. In the world I knew of country clubs, debutantes, private schools and knowing the "right" people, I had missed out on the greater education of diversity.... diversity in people, situations, cultures, ideas, be-liefs... and when eventually exposed to the multifarious con-cepts that make up our world, it was a time of great change for me. Someone once said that to change is to grow and to change often is to achieve perfection... probably not possible in one's lifetime, but change can be exciting... it can also be frightening because we relinquish the familiar. It takes courage to change... but to put an end to things is some-times the brave thing to do... even things that are pleasant to us... but especially things that are injurious to us. When I finally had the courage to walk away from Josh it was with trepidation... There I was, 52 years old...I had never had my own bank account, or charge card... I had no family support

and there were no agencies to fall back on like there is now...
It was the mid-1980's and employment for older women was
very limited... even with advanced degrees... and because of
the lack of any support, I had to become ultra- responsible.
I am proud of myself for what I was able to accomplish, for
all the decisions I had to make, and for all the mistakes I
had to overcome. I remember when I was able to buy my
first home *in my own name*... it was exhilarating... as was
marching up on that stage and accepting my Ph.D., and the
experience, knowledge and wisdom I gained with the passing years. There were many lessons learned...

And now, I am in the final phase of my life...the exact time
and day of my passing is a mystery, but I am told it will be
soon... within some months. For me, it is a time of enormous transition... but it is without fear. If you remember,
I experienced being clinically dead those many years ago
which was a deeply spiritual and a most beautiful event...
infinitely peaceful and euphoric.

My only regret will be leaving Zach, my loving son and
the greatest gift I have ever received. But I will be able to
nurture and protect him from my new home. I am grateful for my life, and for all the lessons learned, even the difficult ones because these were the ones that have prepared
me for my ongoing work in the afterlife. For now, I am
also grateful for my clear mind and ability for continued
learning. It is a fascinating time for medical research...
especially the research they are doing with the brain... I am
sure in years to come it will come to pass that there is no
such thing as "mental illness" as it is defined and understood today. More and more, research demonstrates that
what was once considered mental illness is, in reality, nothing more than brain mis-firings of the chemicals within
the brain necessary for optimum functioning.

Finding you was one of the best things that ever happened... you were my loving Mother, my trusted friend, and my wise sage, offering stability when there was none in my life, and always telling me the truth... which ultimately set me free. I am eternally grateful to you (and indirectly to Norman) for all that I learned from you... for your love, interest and unselfish dedication to your work. In some spiritual manner, I am sure that Uncle Lucas brought us together... and I pray that the work you and Norman perform will continue to enrich those lives that you touch.

With heartfelt love and gratitude... Until we meet again. Claudia

BOOK IV

Part 2
"Considerations"

Lord, help me this day to be present to all aspects of those you have sent to me for care and comfort. Let my words heal and console, educate and restore these children of yours to the life that you desire for them. In Jesus name, I pray for guidance.

PROLOGUE TO BOOK 4... PART 2.....
"A LITTLE HISTORY"

When I chose the title of this book, I questioned whether or not the word, *Miscreants,* was too harsh or judgmental to use in depicting the people in Claudia's life. But when I reviewed all the material in her chart, I determined that it was the perfect word for describing the dominant characters that negatively impacted her life.

For every client I have seen, there is a chart that contains what is termed a History and Physical [H & P] These are quite detailed and by law, for my particular profession, must contain specific and consistent elements, such as a Presenting Problem, Family History, Medical History, Financial History, Military History, Social History, etc., and, of course, a Diagnosis based on the Diagnostic and Statistical Manual [DSM]. This H & P is usually completed during the first to third sessions, although there can be exceptions to this practice. Claudia Fitzpatrick was an excellent historian, unafraid to reveal vital personal information which is so valuable when helping clients recover from their perceived stated problem.

Psychotherapy,* like every scientific approach to human behavior, has gone through a metamorphosis. Since ancient Egypt and throughout many centuries, the maltreatment of people exhibiting any form of mental dysfunction is well documented... they were usually victimized by persecution, many forms of tortuous treatments and abuse... the poor were crowded into small, dark cells with a mattress on the damp, dirty floor, often chained to walls, beaten like wild animals, sterilized, judged to be weak, immoral, and demon possessed. The rich were hidden away by their families in attics or inaccessible rooms, never to see the light of day. In the sixteenth century, the famous mathematician and "father of modern philosophy", Rene Decartes, aggravated a dire situation by dividing mind and body... the mind, was to be cared for by the clergy, and the body to be cared for by physicians. The first hospital to treat the mentally ill humanely was the Pennsylvania Hospital in Philadelphia founded by the Quakers in 1752. Treatment was rudimentary but the patients were kept in clean surroundings, fresh air and light, good nutrition and humane care. By the latter part of the 18th century, physicians began to claim that mental disorders were a medical problem, an illness, best dealt with by doctors, and psychiatry emerged as a specialized branch of medicine. Benjamin Rush, the first psychiatrist in the United States, opened the first psychiatric hospital in 1769 in Williamsburg, Virginia and it stood as the only institution of its kind for 50 years. This was the first "public" hospital for the mentally ill, and, by today's standards, would not have been considered humane... we are still struggling with that word and there are still psychiatric hospitals that exist today that need scrutiny and re-vamping... Mental Health facilities frequently attract workers who are, themselves, in need of counseling, and patients suffer from their negligence and misjudgments. Many in the world of healthcare still do not recognize that a difficult patient is often created by the miscreant behaviors of the staff...many with control issues.

Dorothea Dix emerged as a champion for the mentally ill and for 40 years during the decades of the 1840's and throughout the civil war years, established 30 hospitals for the mentally ill. Because of her leadership and persuasion, Congress passed legislation authorizing federal aid to the states for mental institutions. It was later vetoed by President Pierce in 1854. Doctors in the early 20th century were more interested in the *moral* causes of mental illness ... intemperance, jealously, marital problems, pride, daydreaming and excessive ambition were thought to be the real causes of mental illness. It was not until after World War II [1945] that the traumatic problems of the returning soldiers prompted the development of medications and the recognition that mental illness was a bona fide medical and social problem. During the Kennedy administration a new generation of psychotropic drugs became available and they were dispensed like candy with little attention to the short term side effects and insufficient research on the long term side effects such as impaired thinking and memory, depression, mood swings, hostile and erratic behaviors, just to name a few. Unfortunately, this is the period of time when Claudia's misdiagnoses began.

It was not until 1999 that there occurred the first White House Conference on Mental Health due, in large part, to the activism of Tipper Gore. Former Surgeon General, David Satcher, stated...

> *We recognize that the brain is the integrator of thought, emotion, behavior and health. Indeed, one of the foremost contributions of contemporary mental health research, is the extent to which it has mended the destructive split between "mental" and "physical" health. [Satcher 1999]*

I have included this very brief history of mental illness because it is important for you, the reader, to realize that the treatment of mental health issues was still in its infancy when Claudia was diagnosed in the 1960's, and as I move forward to the following issues for you to consider, it will help you to realize the context in which women found themselves. There are no statistics available that I could find, but it was brought to my attention that in past decades, when a husband wanted to be "set free", in order to avoid the cost of divorce, they would manipulate circumstances to have their wives institutionalized. A tearful discourse by the husband, that included all the indignities and mistreatments that *he* suffered, and a colorful description of her bizarre behaviors would usually suffice. In the intervening years, we have developed laws that help to prohibit this practice, but there still exists unethical practices and remnants of the "good old boys club" that unjustly punish women.

Before we begin the discussions on abuse, it is important to understand the variables of anger and to compare the differences between frustration, anger, aggression, rage and abuse. So, the first thing to do is to define each:

> FRUSTRATION: This is a feeling of irritation or annoyance usually when one cannot get his or her own way, or when one is unable to find a solution to a pressing problem or at other times when one is being opposed.
>
> ANGER: Anger is a universal emotion that can generate positive change or it can be a strong/powerful maladaptive emotion... meaning it can be unsuitable, counterproductive, damaging or harmful.
>
> RAGE: Violent, uncontrollable anger
>
> AGGRESSION: Refers to behaviors that can result in both physical and psychological harm to oneself or to others. It has many definitions but to simplify for our purposes here, the intent of this behavior is to control, to infringe on the rights of others, to bully, intimidate or domineer another. Aggression can be physical, verbal, relational, direct or indirect.

> VIOLENCE: This is an extreme form of aggression...
> usually referred to as a "subtype" of aggression. The out-
> come is usually harmful to oneself or others.
> ABUSE: Cruel and violent treatment of a person or ani-
> mal; to use (something) for a bad purpose. An action that
> intentionally harms or injures another person; inappropri-
> ate use of a substance such as alcohol or drugs.

Anger is one of the most common human emotions. It is said that anger
is a secondary emotion, a reaction to fear, frustration and hurt. There is
appropriate anger that can be a powerful motivating force for positive
activism and injustice... for people of faith you are aware that Jesus dem-
onstrated righteous anger on several occasion. And, there is inappropriate
anger that can be dangerous and injurious. Anger can ruin relationships,
destroy marriages, and turn affection into fear and revulsion. We will
call this type of anger self-centered, selfish anger or rage or aggression or
abuse... the type of anger that was present in Claudia's marriage to Josh.

It has been hypothesized that these extreme forms of anger are not innate instincts... they are learned behaviors... a person can become habitu-
ally aggressive because, for him, it is a successful, goal seeking behavior,
dominated by a need to manipulate others... to get his own way. Therapy
for this person does not always produce positive outcomes due to the fact
that the perpetrator is not there to be healed but to learn how better to
manipulate others.

There is a psychiatric diagnosis known as Intermittent Explosive
Disorder (I.E.D.), a behavioral disorder that falls into the category (DSM)
of Impulse Control Disorders, and is characterized by explosive outbursts
of anger and violence, often to the point of destructive rage, that occurs
in response to relatively minor or inconsequential events. To some mental
health professionals as well as others, this disorder is viewed as nothing
more than a manipulator's learned temper-tantrum, but to other providers, it is an illness to be treated with talk therapy and a number of medications, and still to others, it represents a serious brain disorder, a chemical
imbalance that requires testing and further diagnosis.

For many years, there has been a lack of agreement (and cooperation) among doctors/allergists as to whether or not brain allergies or ecological mental illness* can cause heightened mood swings or personality changes. In 1979, a San Francisco murder trial garnered great attention when the defense team for the perpetrator used the defense of depression caused by ingesting Twinkies and other sugar laden junk foods so that he was not able to think clearly... impaired judgment... and reporters jumped on this as the "Twinkie defense." This was the subject of a book and a movie, so I am not going to discuss the pros and cons of the defense except to say that we are responsible for our behaviors no matter what we ingest, but also that Claudia knew and I learned through the years that food and chemicals (especially medications) can create severe emotional behavioral and mental symptoms such as panic attacks, depression, hallucinations, psychotic episodes and episodic anger... also lesser symptoms such as "brain fog", confusion, concentration problems, and irritability. In spite of the skepticism and incredulousness that has existed in the media, in the orthodox medical profession and in society at large, medical literature has documented the abnormal reactions involved in brain allergies for many years... these abnormal reactions do exist and do manifest themselves in some persons.

It has been said that the longest journey begins with a single step. In the journey toward thoroughly understanding how brain chemistry affects anger and abuse, that first step is for the individual to have an intense desire to change and that s/he is willing to embrace educational therapy that will produce a new and better controlled outcome, and for those in the medical, religious and law enforcement segments of our society to become willing to scrutinize the ever developing body of knowledge involving brain allergies/ecological mental illness.

CONSIDERATION 1....
ABUSE IN ALL ITS FORMS...

After years of private practice, I am convinced that no one can truly appreciate or understand the impact of abuse on one's psyche...on their spirit... unless they have experienced it first- hand. Long term abuse, whether it is psychological, physical or verbal, can cause severe emotional trauma in the victim, including depression, anxiety, post-traumatic stress disorder, eating disorders, fatigue, and many other conditions that demand exploration of the abuse syndrome. During the many sessions I had with Claudia, it became evident that there were layers and layers of injury that had begun in early childhood, and that she had developed characteristics that were certain to attract those people that would ultimately hurt her... people who would denigrate her, those that were scurrilous and ruthless, some who were cruel and abusive and those that exploited her naiveté.

Every person is defined by those who love them and those who refuse to love them. If you believe that love demands sacrifice and helping one to reach their highest potential, it is clear that love was woefully absent in Claudia's childhood, with a Mother who demanded perfection and was so emotionally injured herself that she lacked the ability for true intimacy, and an emotionally remote Father who, in spite of being a charming public figure, frequently employed a method of communication with his daughter that included excessive bullying, and domination.

Claudia was systematically rejected, abandoned and emotionally neglected as a child Recent research, in the form of brain imaging, shows that rejection triggers the same circuits in the brain as physical pain... imaging also shows a change in brain chemistry that equals that of grief and loss.. the depression-despair response. Never, did any medical doctor or any therapist ever mention the word, "abuse" to Claudia. Understanding what has happened to us is critical to recovery.

Psychological and Verbal Abuse-(*Mental Abuse or Emotional Abuse*)

I consider verbal abuse (lewd, vulgar, profane, threatening, highly demeaning words) to be part of psychological abuse and will lump the two together under the title of "psychological abuse"...and, I have purposely placed these forms of abuse ahead of physical abuse to highlight their importance. As previously stated, all abuse is damaging to the victim, but I consider psychological/verbal abuse to be more insidious and detrimental to the victim because these forms of abuse are often undetectable to the onlooker, and far more difficult to explain by the victim whose confidence and self- esteem are usually completely eroded.

Psychological abuse is designed to degrade, control, intimidate demean and subjugate the victim. It involves a pattern of verbal humiliation, shaming, threatening and bullying behaviors, which involves calling of names, and giving one demeaning labels. Other elements of abuse: a highly controlling individual who might tyrannize their victim; trivialize a partner's needs, talents, opinions; diminish one's self worth, making subtle and cruel remarks; chronically using threats and manipulation; lying, mocking, subjugation and isolation... These are all behaviors and words antithetical to love, dignity, respect and mindfulness.

Psychological abuse involves a disregard for healthy communication, and instead the abuser will often yell, use sarcasm, or cutting and deprecating humor, which is often a style used by so-called comedians who, in truth, rarely have humorous routines... Claudia was familiar with this type of humor and communication often employed by her Father and sister.

The sad part of this type of abuse is that it can be very minimized by police, health workers, doctors and society as a whole.

Physical Abuse

Physical Abuse is the intentional physical harm to another person. No one has the right to assault another person with any part of their body... (This includes the mouth which often causes more harm than a physical blow.) The phrase, "physical abuse" has become synonymous with "spousal abuse" or "domestic violence"... and one of the first questions the police will ask a victim of abuse is, "did he hit you?" Physical abuse is devastating and dangerous, and cannot be tolerated, but at the same time, the horror of psychological abuse should not be diminished ...the unfortunate thing about physical abuse is that it can kill a person... the unfortunate thing about psychological abuse is that it can kill your spirit...and lasts a lifetime in the mind and heart of the victim.

According to the National Coalition Against Domestic Violence (NCADV), "an average of 20 people are physically abused by intimate partners *every minute*" and accounts for 15% of all violent crime. On a typical day, "more than 20 thousand phone calls are placed to domestic violence hotlines," and between the years "2003-2008, 142 women were murdered in their workplace by ...intimate partners." According to many, physical abuse has become an epidemic...it is the leading cause of injury to women ages 15-44 and there are few systems in place to control it.

Spousal Abuse (Domestic Violence)- Why don't women leave?

Spousal abuse is highly complicated and very individualized... it is very underreported (as little as 20% - 10% of all cases) and is also very misunderstood by those who are sworn to help victims... for instance, it is well documented that statistically, police have a very high rate of domestic violence within their own homes (approximately 40%) and that many clergy who have absolutely no training in this area, counsel women to go home, pray for their husbands and be submissive to him since he is the head of the household. It is for this reason that I did not always counsel a woman to call the police or to see their pastor.

When Claudia was married to Josh, spousal abuse was not discussed or even thought to exist to the extent that it is today. During the 1970's the women's movement helped to focus attention on this issue... and fought to have it considered a crime. However, respondents frequently ignore the problem, believing it is a "family matter" and take a mediation position instead of viewing it as a criminal offense, and if there are no apparent bruises they often lose interest. It is frustrating to enforcement agencies that when they go to the homes to intervene that the woman will not press charges. Why?

Many women do not press charges and many women will not leave the relationships that are so harmful to them for a variety of reasons:

- Generations of women were taught that no matter what happens you don't leave a marriage... marriage is forever...
- After years of being brainwashed that she is "stupid", or a "mental case", or that "no one would believe her," a woman will be afraid to report abuse, or to press charges, or to make the monumental decision to leave a relationship.
- Most abusers make it very clear that the woman will get no money and no support of any kind. How is a woman who has been out of the job market for years supposed to support herself and possibly children? If she is lucky and has a job, there will be constant threats that her children will be taken from her... that **no one will believe her** or be supportive of her. The big questions every victim struggles with: *Where can I go? How can I survive?*
- It is well known that when a woman leaves, she will possibly be hunted down, physically harmed or even murdered. Then there are often threats that the children will be harmed. Over 70% of domestic violence murders are committed **after** the woman leaves the relationship.
- Yes, there are shelters. Bless them, but living in one room with children, fearful that the abuser will track down the woman and children is terrifying.

- The abuser may be the kind that expresses sorrow after an explosive episode. Tears, promises that *it* will never happen again, murmurings of love and the sex that follows... Women will often tell you that she loves her partner... As Claudia said... "He is not a monster...he can be loving and gentle..."

Remember... underneath that manipulative intermittent miscreant is a charming, sometimes loving, a seemingly caring and tender individual.

What Can Be Done? How Can We Help?

1. Stop blaming the victim: If a woman says she is being abused, listen to her and if you are a mental health provider or in law enforcement, explore her definition of abuse; does she understand what "abuse" is? is it cultural? are there drugs involved especially with the perpetrator? Do not make a judgment based on your possible silent acceptance of certain behaviors that you, yourself, might be guilty of.
2. Increase and/or demand that there must be special training required for handling spousal abuse by police, clergy and medical providers.
3. Make it mandatory for perpetrators to be referred to mental health providers specializing in spousal abuse for counseling from the very first time that a call is received from the victim. It must be mandatory also for the victim to be referred to a separate group therapy or separate therapist.
4. If every church in America had a program to house a victim of abuse for a discrete period of time, and for that church to have trained volunteers to act as mentors to make victims aware of therapeutic support groups, resources for jobs, for food, for HUD housing, for clothing, and for miscellaneous needs, we could fulfill Hebrews 13:16: *Do not neglect to do good and to share what you have, for such sacrifices are pleasing to God.*
5. Prohibit *public* courtroom trials in cases involving spousal abuse and any form of sexual abuse, especially rape. The humiliation

experienced by women having to publicly describe the details of abuse is medieval. Until privacy and dignity are afforded these psychologically injured victims there will continue to be a terrible injustice and a grave underreporting of this crime.

When I first met Claudia, she gave the impression to all that her life was enviable... her stunning looks, her gorgeous and quite charming husband, her beautiful home with all the trappings of wealth... but no one could have guessed that Josh had perpetrated lewd and vile verbal tirades, or that he regularly threatened and demeaned her... or that he threw her on the floor and kicked her in places where bruises would not be noticeable ... that he was a chronic womanizer, a liar and a manipulator. Claudia had been groomed from childhood to accept these behaviors as a result of her failures ... she was sure it was her fault... she had been humiliated when her first marriage ended, and she was determined to make this one work.

Today, we emphasize the teaching of self-esteem to our children. However, we forget to teach children about the civilities of life... kindness to others, respect, courtesy and politeness...values that were prominent in past decades. The result is that we are raising a society of entitled, sociopathic people... the teachings are out of balance. Many times I have heard, "that's who I am, I'm not going to change for anyone!" This attitude will not foster a stable relationship. All of life is compromise... there are rules... if something is highly objectionable to one partner there must be an attempt or at least a discussion with a neutral party to correct the behavior.

Sexual Abuse

The sexual abuse in Claudia's life received no attention until we met. During my practice years, I had occasion to treat many women in their late adult years ... 60's. 70's, even 80's... that had experienced sexual abuse as children and were discussing it for the first time. The perpetrator in some cases threatened harm to the victim or the victim's family, and often they had to die before the victim felt safe enough to tell. In other cases, the subject of abuse was just not discussed... the perpetrator would instill in the victim that if she told, she would be humiliated because no one would believe her... that she would most likely be punished, and that he was her only friend. In Claudia's case, she never felt important enough to disclose this information to any of the psychotherapeutic doctors in her life. She was conflicted for many years about the incidents, and carried with her a sense of guilt... Part of the shame and guilt victims carry with them is the fact that often they feel responsible for the action of the perpetrator... as Claudia did. She shared with me that before her Father died, she had an occasion to visit him, and when they got into an argument, she told him about her Grandfather's abuse... his response was... "you're a god-dammed liar." This response solidified her feelings of guilt... after all, Claudia had been programmed from birth to think of herself as deficient, and the sexual abuse served to magnify the negative feelings she felt toward herself. As mentioned previously, we must prohibit public courtroom trials in cases of sexual abuse of any kind... childhood rape/molestation and adult rape. It only exacerbates the psychological damage these behaviors have effected, and reduces the possibility of women coming forward to report the criminal behaviors.

Little has been written or discussed regarding sexual abuse from medical doctors/therapists. It is a particularly heinous form of abuse, due to the total trust a patient wants to extend to their medical workers, especially a therapist. Sexual abuse is covered in the *code of ethics* that every discipline embraces, and today, legal action and discipline is usually taken when this crime is brought to the attention of the governing boards for each therapeutic discipline. However, back in the 1960's (and sometimes today), things were not as regulated, and patients were less likely to report sexual abuse for many reasons. Psychiatrists can say that a patient is paranoid... or they are delusional... or that they are schizophrenic... or that they are suicidal... and they can then arrange for hospitalization... or attach a myriad of other professional sounding diagnoses. It is difficult to bring this crime to a just conclusion, which should be loss of license and incarceration. The psychiatrist that was sexually aggressive to Claudia was well known, very well connected, and was widely acclaimed... having received many honors for his work. Had Claudia tried to bring charges against him she would have been decimated.

It is sometimes difficult to assess the real damage that sexual abuse causes within a person... male or female... especially if they have buried it and held it secret for many years. I can tell you some of the common traits and characteristics I have seen in my clients... all of whom were women. Extreme vulnerability... a chronic sadness often buried beneath a mask of extroversion, competence and sophistication... a pervasive feeling of shame and guilt, often acted out in flirtatious behaviors. I've also seen sexual abuse patients who have suffered with extreme shyness and lack of confidence... unable to make decisions, and afraid of confrontation and/or disagreements... consequently, they form unstable or unequal relationships because they have no "inner core"... no sense of self. These patients often suffer from depression and anxiety... and find it extremely difficult to move forward due to the lifelong *programming* of helplessness and victimization. To Claudia's credit, she overcame her deep rooted insecurities, began to view herself, and behave, as a strong, healthy, assertive woman... and she did all this with courage and with wisdom.

Financial Abuse

Financial abuse tends to insensate during a divorce, which I feel is an issue that is ignored by most professionals. Rarely do we hear of financial "abuse" when women are plunged into financial destitution during and after the divorce process... what we hear about are the sensational media portrayals of men being "fleeced" by their wives, and, although this does happen at times, it is largely a myth.

Of all the common negative issues that couples fight about in a marriage, money disputes are the best harbinger of divorce (sex, in-laws, and children are the other most common)... and it often becomes the controlling issue in divorce. Many research studies reveal that women are disproportionately penalized, financially, for the rest of their lives after a divorce. The following chart was prepared by The Social Security Administration's Office of Policy: Unpublished

Tabulation, March 2000:

Marital Status	Poverty Rate (%)
Divorced	20.4
Never Married	18.9
Widowed	15.9
Married	4.3

In Claudia's case, it is difficult to imagine that this once wealthy debutante would be destitute at the close of her life. How did this happen? Greed by family members and 2 financial planners....

When James Fitzpatrick died, his assets were handled by Connie's daughter, who had been appointed executrix. The contents of the will were not disclosed to Claudia who received a small "remembrance" which she entrusted to a financial adviser.... a man who promised her that the small sum of money would grow and be available for her "retirement." Claudia initially trusted this man who ultimately betrayed her and the small sum of money that she believed would increase became non-existent. Claudia worked hard until she was 75, worked long hours, and was flexible in locating jobs in different areas of the country that would enhance her career. However, because of her age, she was never compensated at the rate of younger workers, and when she was able to go into private practice, she became certified by Medicare/Medicaid... and accepted the very low rate of compensation that they paid. It satisfied her mission to help the older adult, but unfortunately did not help her near poverty standard of living. Having your own business is this country is difficult due to the increased taxes one has to pay when self- employed, and she soon realized that she was working to pay taxes. So, she took all she had worked so hard to save, went to a new financial planner, a charming, "dedicated" young man who promised her that he would treat her assets as carefully as he did his own Father's assets.... but again, Claudia was deceived, and, once again, her life savings were lost. Your first question might be... Why didn't she go to a lawyer? The answer is simple... lawyers cost money and women without money rarely have any appeal to lawyers. Furthermore, financial scams rarely grab media attention unless there are high profile persons involved and are quite difficult to prove in court. So, at her advanced age, Claudia was financially adrift... no provision had been made by her divorce attorney for any shared retirement from Gerald... or from Josh... both of whom were quite well off. And, because of her low paying jobs, her Social Security was miniscule.

No-fault divorce laws were signed into law in 1969 and although the law diminished the acrimony and abuses that were inherent in the longstanding divorce laws at that time, proponents did not take into account the unintended consequences of these laws. For women born in the decades prior to the 1950's, shock and resulting poverty became a reality when the rules of the game changed. Women did not enter the workforce with any regularity at that time... in 1950 only 20% -34% (depending on what statistic you read) of the workforce was comprised of women, and the gender pay gap was in the 50% to 60% range during the 1950's, 1960's. This, of course, would affect a woman's income not only at the time, but in later years due to lower retirement income, social security income and, in many cases, no retirement income at all.

Claudia believed the proud and obsessive childhood promises by her Father that his children would always be cared for financially. She believed her husband[s] when they promised to care for her financially... she believed the two financial planners when they promised to protect her hard earned assets... and she was betrayed by all of them. If a person "fleeces" an elderly person, or a child takes money that has not been authorized, a criminal court case would ensue. However, a husband, divorcing his wife, is allowed to reach a settlement that often leaves an ex-wife destitute, and people cheer at his good fortune.

Divorce and Divorce Abuse.

As previously mentioned, divorce was especially traumatic for Claudia given her religious beliefs and determination to succeed in whatever she did. For a great many people, divorce is the ultimate rejection... it robs a couple of the anticipated future... all the dreams, the plans, the fantasies... Claudia felt that Gerald was her best friend, and she had dreams of growing old together, of grandchildren and family reunions, of a big, close-knit family. These dreams were never to be fulfilled, but one cannot condemn Gerald for leaving the marriage. By his own admission he did not want any demands put on him... immature, yes, and some might say that he was weak... but he chose not to divulge his real reasons for leaving and unfortunately invented what became truth to him ... he became the victim. Perhaps a different man would have been more aggressively involved with his wife's treatment, questioned the doctors, listened more attentively to her symptoms and advocated for more than she was given. Being a highly intelligent man, perhaps he could have investigated the many alternative methods of treatment for Claudia, but instead he found other women to lean on and to grow old with... women who would sublimate their own needs. Through the years, Claudia was consistently blamed for everything that went wrong in the marriage and lies and half- truths were circulated through the active grapevine... among her family members and former friends. And Claudia embraced the blame. For years, there was (and still is) an anti-mommy culture in most segments of society that has been inherited from Freud's antagonism toward women... he viewed women as suffering from penis envy, and therefore, inferior to men, morally and intellectually. Blaming mommy for everything that goes wrong within a family or a member of a family, can be great sport... when mommy is the scapegoat, others can deflect responsibility from themselves.

CONSIDERATION 2....
MEDICAL MISDIAGNOSES

The fateful diagnosis of **clinical depression*** that Claudia received in the 1960's was crucial in determining the further negative outcomes in her life... and the years of mis/maltreatment that she endured because of the ongoing misdiagnosis. From the first family practice physician, and to all the doctors that followed, Claudia stated, and exhibited, clear, unambiguous signs and symptoms of hypoglycemia/hyperglycemia and food allergies, which mimic many neuropsychiatric conditions.

> *"My legs felt like rubber...I was shaking all over...I could not think clearly...My head felt like there were cobwebs inside...My stomach was shaking inside...My hands and feet were ice cold...I had a terrible headache...I was tearful..."* etc.

Unfortunately, most orthodox medical doctors did not and still do not very often participate in discussions of alternative modes of treatment. They do admit that the mind affects the body but are less likely to agree that the body affects the mind, therefore, when they observe a cluster of symptoms such as Claudia presented, they will attach a classic DSM* diagnosis to a patient without the benefit of a differential diagnosis.*

At the time of her marriage to Gerald, Claudia weighed 106 pounds... she had two babies in three years ... the first weighed nine and one half pounds, and the second weighed just under ten pounds, yet she was never tested or treated for gestational diabetes.... the glaring symptom of large babies was completely ignored... nor was there ever any follow up on the kidney stones she passed just before her first birth. Claudia's doctors never took her physical symptoms seriously. This sexist tendency is often reflected in the female diagnoses that have come attached to my patients through the years. The long standing DSM* diagnosis of "somatoform disorder"* is frequently attached to women ...which implies a mental illness focusing on medically unexplained physical symptoms.

It was not until Claudia moved to California to marry Josh, that she was introduced to orthomolecular medicine, or as it is known today, alternative medicine, or holistic medicine, or naturopathic medicine. She located a knowledgeable *medical doctor* in San Francisco, an orthomolecular* allergy specialist, that diagnosed and treated her appropriately. Primary, was the diagnosis of "labile diabetes"*("brittle diabetes").... meaning that Claudia suffered from a type of diabetes with wildly fluctuating blood glucose... from very low blood glucose [*hypo*glycemia]*.... encompassing all the symptoms that Claudia exhibited ... to high blood glucose [*hyper*glycemia]* that encompassed all the symptoms (and many more) that were completely ignored by every one of Claudia's previous doctors. This diagnosis was supported by a 6-hour glucose tolerance test, not the more familiar blood test. In addition to these symptoms were the added symptoms of food allergies (more correctly defined as maladaptive reactions to food or hypersensitivity to food and chemicals). The food allergies were classic! For years, she suffered from projectile vomiting bordering on anaphylactic shock when she ate such things as popcorn, beef, and shellfish, and had distinct mood swings when she ingested sugar, caffeine and alcohol. The orthomolecular doctor made the comment that "any first year medical student should have recognized the symptoms..." He put Claudia on a very regulated diet for the blood glucose problems, did extensive allergy testing and eliminated the toxic foods from her diet ... including caffeine, sugar, eggs, wheat, corn, beef, and many others. [A brief note: When Claudia was tested in a hospital lab for caffeine allergy, she passed out... indicating a severe caffeine allergy. Remember the 12 plus cups of coffee she drank for years? She learned we crave the foods we are allergic to.] Besides the food allergies, her doctor also determined the presence of hypo-adrenocorticism (adrenal under-functioning) which indicates the body does not handle stress well... stress in the form of **reactions to the wrong medications**, and to the wrong diet that produce a myriad of symptoms including excessive fatigue, headaches, mood swings, anxiety, mental fog, nausea, projectile vomiting, diarrhea, depression and suicidal tendencies that Claudia complained about for years. During the years that Claudia ingested the 22 different prescribed psychotropic drugs, her personality, her spirituality and her thought processes all changed under the influence of these drugs. "I felt totally battered... like people were all around me wearing boxing gloves... punching my head and body," was one of the statements she made during her initial assessment. It was known in the aging community that were my patients, that drug toxicity is not rare, but what is rare is for doctors to consider that drugs might be responsible for memory loss, disorientation, seizures, dizziness/falls, hallucinations and a myriad of bizarre behaviors. As a person ages, there can be a marked decrease in the ability metabolize drugs due to the decline of liver and kidney functions. It is the resulting accumulation that causes toxicity... and it is possible to take a medication for a long period of time before an adverse drug reaction occurs. Often a patient is given too many meds - such as the 22 different mood altering drugs *prescribed* by Claudia's doctors. Drugs can even cause paradoxical results, meaning that an opposite effect is obtained than the expected result.

In San Francisco, Claudia's treatment was individualized, for the first time. Recovery took longer to accomplish but from the time Claudia became acquainted and involved with the treatment, *she never needed another psychotropic drug, never experienced any further "clinical depression" and experienced mental fog and mood swings only when she ate foods to which she was allergic, or when her blood glucose was unstable and widely fluctuating. Her "adrenal fatigue" was treated for over a year with twice weekly intravenous feedings, (a European treatment successfully used by her physician) and her diabetes was controlled for a long time with diet, then with oral medications, but eventually she had to become insulin dependent.*

Medical misdiagnoses are not rare... both intentional and unintentional misses occur in approximately 12 million outpatient and clinical patients, and within the mental health field, there are an estimated 40% of mistakes made due to lack of professional training, poor judgment on the part of counselors, DSM confusion, and intentional and unintentional practices for insurance reimbursement.

CONSIDERATION 3: *SUICIDE*

Often said...suicide is a permanent solution to a temporary problem. There is a lack of a consistent operational definition to cover all situations when we are dealing with mental health issues...and suicide is, at best, a very complicated and sometimes mysterious and tragic mental health issue that lacks clear understanding. There are many professionals with intense opinions on the subject as well as large segments of society with extreme views... it is a polarizing issue.

First, and foremost, suicide is highly individualized and in most instances, is not some bizarre and incomprehensible selfish act of self-destruction. It is the **logic** of persons often experiencing hopelessness, who see death as the only alternative to the extreme physical or psychological pain they are experiencing. The reasons for suicide are as varied as those who choose this method of escape. I have heard many rationales from a variety of patients... unremitting physical or psychic pain... fear of being put into a nursing home... fear of dementia... an inability to cope with an agonizing and/or debilitating disease ... intense loneliness or social isolation...the breakup of a relationship... alcohol/drug use... severe financial problems... revenge... the list is quite long. An important factor in suicide that is most often overlooked is the prescribed and illegal medications/drugs a person is ingesting. Prescribed psychotropic drugs, pain medications such as oxycontin, fentanyl, and other opioids, street drugs such as cocaine, heroin, ecstasy, cannabis, et.al., and even over-the-counter drugs can **cause** suicidal fantasies... they can cause a person to experience a blunted sense of moral turpitude... they can alter a person's personality, and the resulting thought processes negatively influence the **logic** a person employs in making decisions. In this day of managed care, family practice doctors do not have the time, nor do they receive the education in medical school to correctly prescribe or monitor the psychotropic drugs they hand out or prescribe to their trusting patients, often indiscriminately. Big Pharma sends their drug reps to the offices of physicians promoting rewards for using their brand of pills... but neglect to tell the physicians that these same pills that they push as safe and non-addictive, can, in reality, be addictive and often the culprits for dangerous side effects, including suicide.

Given Claudia's intense spirituality, it is incomprehensible that she would choose suicide as a means of escape. She firmly believed in the teaching of her church that suicide is an attempt against the ownership of the Creator... and a serious offense (sin) against the charity (love) which man owes to himself. There are widely differing opinions regarding suicide... some scholars look at the issue as a matter of personal liberty, while others look at it as murder, and think it should be treated as such. When Claudia attempted to end her life, she lived in one of the six states that, at the time, considered suicide as a felony. She had no knowledge of this, which would have been an additional deterrent her. She loved her children too much to subject them to any kind of interrogation or to abandon them. This suggested to me that she had a profound drug induced personality change. During the 1960's, there were many bizarre psychotherapy groups, and Claudia was naively entangled in several of them. Prior to this time, in her world, "pot" was a container in which you cooked food... but at one of the groups she attended, "pot," or "cannabis", was dispensed freely by one of the group participants and Claudia noticed that she lost all her inhibitions when she smoked the "joint." Instead of being condemned by the doctor, this practice was condoned, and after the hateful quarrel with Gerald, when she arrived home that Monday night and Gerald ignored her, she smoked a joint, had a martini, and then ingested all her prescribed nighttime medications... and without any food went to bed, alone, for a restless sleep. Tuesday was a holiday for her and after Gerald silently left for work, she began ruminating... she adored her children and had a profound love for Gerald but knew he was having an affair... it was her fault... she was driving him away... but she was at a loss to know what to do to make things better or where to turn for help...their quarrel over the weekend had deeply wounded her... his reaction of harming her and rejecting her intensified her feelings of failure. In her dulled and drugged condition, she obsessed over her illusory perceptions of being inadequate as a woman, as a wife, as a mother... she was besieged with feelings of shame because she could not live up the perfectionist expectations that had been ingrained in her from childhood. When Gerald had come home that Monday night, Claudia wanted to run to him, to love him, to have him hold her and declare his love for her... but when he ignored her, she despaired... she had ruined it all. So, she got out of bed that fateful Tuesday morning hating the feeling she had every day... the foggy head, the headaches, the fatigue, and the psychic and physical pain. She remembered going to her medicine cabinet and counting the medications she was taking... 22 different bottles for all sorts of symptoms, plus the cannabis that would exacerbate her problems.

This was Claudia's narrative to me...

"I remember writing a note to Gerald... I was crying uncontrollably, remembering the intense friendship we once had, the wonderful moments we had shared... I felt empty, disconnected, ignorant, guilty, and humiliated all at the same time... I felt I was harming my children and I loved them so much I remember thinking they would be so much better off without me... I didn't want to hurt them anymore... it never occurred to me that I would be abandoning them... just that they would be... well, like I said... better off without me. At the same time, I remember feeling very frightened and calling out to God to take this fogginess out of my head... to help me think clearly..."

So, Claudia's flawed **logic**, was that she was doing her family a favor by killing herself. For years she had been unable to function correctly... she had caused everyone too much aggravation... "I've done nothing but complicate things," she thought...she was too confused to realize there was an alternative. She had yet to meet the one doctor that would recognize the symptoms of her illness, and help restore her to health. Fortunately, Gerald arrived home early that day... and he did the right things.

When Claudia regained consciousness on the eleventh day of her hospitalization, Gerald was called to come and see her. He held her hand and she spoke to him saying, "Gerald, I didn't make it... I couldn't even do this right!" Unfortunately, Gerald had already decided he was finished...he had chosen to renege on his vows ... "in sickness and in health" ...and instead of walking with her, decided to run. Was he frightened? Was he feeling guilty? No one will ever know because he and Claudia never discussed it.

Some relevant thoughts I want to leave with the reader is that there is usually anger, grief, shock, feelings of rejection and/or self-blame that family members experience from the suicidal actions of their loved ones. These are the normal feelings present in the face of all losses but suicide has always had a societal taboo probably due to the religious prohibitions through the years. However, I challenge everyone to refrain from judgment... do not blame the victim and do not blame yourself. Life and death issues are personal and complex. Reportedly, substance abuse is involved in half of all suicides and the unfortunate explosion of addiction to heroin, alcohol, and painkillers, must be questioned. Is some of this being driven by the indiscriminate and casual distribution of these drugs by physicians, and by the proliferation of advertising by pharmaceutical companies?

CONSIDERATION 4...
A DISCUSSION: DEPRESSION FACTS AND CLAUDIA'S WORLD OF THE 1960'S

Clinical depression or, as it is known in the industry, Major Depressive Disorder... or Unipolar Depression... is a serious medical illness that reportedly affects approximately 22% of the population every year and causes significant stress and/or impairment in social, occupational or other areas of functioning and is classified, according to the DSM, as a Mood Disorder... and characterized by a *sad mood, extreme loss of interest in usual life pursuits (Anhedonia), hopelessness,* and *extreme loss of self- esteem...* symptoms that last for a period of at least two weeks. The stated statistic is very approximate... there are many unreported cases of depression, especially among the male population, and there are many misdiagnoses of depression due to the misuse of the word and due to the lack of differentiation among diagnosticians. One reason for misdiagnosis could be due to the inadequate and understated depression scales that are used in diagnostics. Many people are unable to connect with or understand the signs and symptoms of depression... for instance... older adults frequently experience or report higher rates of anxiety and irritability rather than a "sad mood," or the depressive symptoms are obscured by somatic complaints. Commonly, the depression co-exists with other medical conditions such as diabetes, stroke, surgeries, and substance abuse. Men, in particular,

experience feelings of anger, suffer anti-social symptoms, decreased sexual drive, alcoholism and feelings of intense failure.

Depression is comprised of a cluster of symptoms that are many and
varied, and differ in individuals. What also differs is the definition between "sadness" and "depression." *Sadness* occurs as a *temporary* grief
reaction to inevitable life events such as death of a spouse or child, or
the numerous losses and challenges experienced by what professionals
call "transitional life experiences," which are episodes in life that require
time to process in order to achieve emotional healing. *Depression*, on
the other hand, is an illness that involves chemical changes in the brain,
and is always distinguished by the presence of cognitive distortions* and
loss of self- esteem. It usually demands temporary treatment with medications together with psychotherapy... cognitive behavioral therapy being
the treatment of choice.

There are several different classifications of depression... Major Depressive
Disorder, Bi-Polar Disorder I, and II... Dysthymic Disorder... Cyclothymic
Disorder... Mood Disorder Due to a General Medical Condition...
Substance Induced Mood Disorder... As you can see, for the layperson,
this can become very confusing... it is also confusing to many professionals,
and many times there is disagreement among therapists treating the same
patient. In recent years, Bipolar Depression has received much attention.
It is difficult to diagnose... it is often misdiagnosed as Major Depressive
Disorder (Unipolar Depression), is associated with a high rate of suicide,
and is usually classified as treatment resistant when medications used specifically for Major Depressive Disorder are erroneously prescribed, and
only serve to intensify the symptoms of the Bipolar depression.

It must be noted that if the prescribed medication does not alleviate
the depression, and several medications have been tried without success,
then there must be a further attempt at assessment and differential diagnoses* to determine the cause of the depression, including assessment
for ecological, food and medication allergies... endocrine disorders*... substance abuse... and other general medical conditions. We often see celebrities talking with media people, stating that a relative committed suicide

because of depression... this is only half true... so many suicides, particularly among younger people, are the result of drug addiction.... the *cause* is *not* depression ... the *cause* is substance abuse... the depression is the *result* of the ingestion of the drugs. I think this is an extremely important distinction... we must shift our thinking in these circumstances to think of suicide often as the result of drugs**... legal and non-legal.** The acceptance of drugs in our society is astounding and extremely worrisome... I have seen first- hand the indiscriminant prescribing of drugs. Because they are prescription drugs does not make them any less lethal than street drugs... and when I see the profound personality changes that some people experience when taking drugs I wonder what will become of our society if this is allowed to continue. I have also read about the skewed data of drug testing, and witnessed, first hand, the danger of drug trials. When money (greed) is the motivating factor for approval of prescription drugs (**billions** of dollars are made by the pharmaceutical companies) **people** become less important, and thousands of people die each year worldwide because of the side effects of experimental and approved drugs, including children and babies.

Many times, when patients come to me and tell me they are depressed, I often know that depression is not their problem but that their *thinking* is the problem. Negative, inaccurate or incorrect thoughts which incorporate our values and beliefs, produce depression... these negative and incorrect thinking patterns are called "cognitive distortions"* and develop over a long period of time... they are habitual and ingrained ways we think about or process events in our life that maintain our negative emotions. These distorted habitual patterns of thought that we develop cloud our perception of truth... and because they are so ingrained, they become automatic... so that when an event happens in our life we automatically react with a negative emotion.

What Causes Depression:

As mentioned previously, depression is a complex illness with no single cause at this time in history. The most common causes are thought to be:

- **Genetic** Among researchers, there has always been a strong genetic component attached to depression. "Genetic" means something we inherit from our parents, and, although there does not seem to be a direct genetic cause to depression, there appears to be a "vulnerability" toward depression. Many believe that this vulnerability is a learned behavior rather than a genetic cause. For instance, cognitive distortions* can be learned and reactions to life situations can be learned (did Father handle negative events by drinking too much? Did Mother handle negative events by going to bed and crying?)

- **Biochemical** This usually involves the alteration of neurotransmitters,* especially serotonin, dopamine and epinephrine. Neurotransmitters are little "chemical messengers" in our brain that transmit impulses or messages between nerve cells, and can affect our feelings of happiness and pleasure.

- **Hormonal** This involves endocrine disturbances*...i.e., the overproduction of stress hormones, and cortisol.* There is extensive research being done on the biological causes of depression. (See Glossary, Appendix A for more information)

- **SAD** Known as Seasonal Affective Disorder, this is a type of depression that occurs at the same time each year, usually beginning in the Fall into the winter, although it can occur in the Summer into the Winter especially in very hot, humid climates.

- **Substance Abuse-Pharmacology & Medical** - Depression can be linked to side effects of medications i.e., cardiac and antihypertensive medications, sedatives and hypnotics, steroids and hormones, psychotropic medications, analgesics, and anti-inflammatory medications. It can co-exist with other illnesses, i.e., neurological, endocrine, systemic disorders, inflammatory disorders, postpartum disorders, vitamin deficiencies, etc., and is particularly linked to substance-induced disorders.*

- **Transitional Factors** - Changes in life circumstances i.e., death of loved ones, divorce, moving, other losses such as loss of a pet, of driving privileges, of health, etc. Transitional factors are particularly relevant in depression affecting older adults and is classified as "Adjustment Disorder"* in DSM.

- **Limbic System*** Research has focused extensively on the biological causes of depression, and in particular, on disturbances within the limbic system. (See Glossary, Appendix A for more information)

In Claudia's world of the 1960's and 1970's, mental health theories were still largely based on Freud's research, and modalities for treatment included insulin shock therapy*, electroconvulsive therapy* and lobotomies.* There sprung up several new group modalities, such as "primal scream" therapy and a form of "reality therapy" in which a patient would punch pillows that represented a parent, and was taught to scream, "I hate you! You have ruined me!" ... or other negative, hateful messages. Known as "dumping," this catharsis of negative feelings was thought to release the repressed anger, and give credence to the idea that the patient was not responsible for their feelings or behaviors, and that with time, and the release of the anger, healing would occur. There are still remnants of these therapies practiced by mental health professionals unaware of updated research that indicates these modalities only lead to increased anger and irresponsibility for changing one's own behaviors.

At that time, very little research was being done on the brain itself... especially on brain chemistry and interaction/side effects from foods and pharmaceuticals. Drug companies were not required to report side effects from medications to the public until well into the 1980's.

So, Claudia, in her innocence, trusting her doctors without question as she had been taught to do, accepted her diagnosis despite her protestations, and acquiesced to the ECT... 22 treatments in all, until she looked, and felt, like a "zombie". No one really knows why ECT eliminates depression in some people... it is still used as a treatment although infrequently and is highly controversial. In Claudia's case, it was detrimental... she never did regain all her memory... it did nothing but exacerbate her many and varied physical symptoms, and certainly gave her no power or control over her life... as a matter of fact, at no time did any doctor suggest to her that she could give up being a victim, change how she thought, eliminate her medications, or have choices and control of her life.

Had Claudia been my client from the beginning, the treatment plan would have focused on the ingrained irrational beliefs that had been such a large part of her life. My assessment would NOT have included Clinical Depression/Major Depressive Episode, because I viewed her as a highly intelligent, highly functioning human being, wanting to make changes in her life...Any "depression" she experienced was but a reaction to several serious life events... therefore, "Adjustment Disorder" would have been a more appropriate diagnosis. She did not view herself as a victim... but she had been programmed by her doctors to think of herself as a victim. I would have refocused her back to the time she was in college when she said... "I began to realize how much fun and distinctively different life could be when I made the decisions for my life."

I would have immediately referred her to one of my naturopathic physician friends for assessment, and Cognitive Behavioral Therapy* would have been the therapy of choice for Claudia. She had become lost in the lovelessness... in the negativity... in the loneliness... in the overwhelming responsibilities of her life. It was obvious that screaming was not going to help, or that punching pillows was not going to help, that ECT was not helpful and certainly the plethora of pills prescribed for her did not help.

As a tribute to her tenaciousness, many things did help Claudia. Among these things were two important events: 1.) that momentous night at the Abby when Claudia had a conversion experience...she not only regained her spiritual life, but found a friend who loved her for life; 2.) the day Claudia realized she had not only the will but also the power to choose how she wanted to live her life. That was the day she read Viktor Frankl's book, "Man's Search for Meaning"... and his words became her mantra... *"...everything can be taken from a man but one thing: the last of the human freedoms - to choose one's attitude in any given set of circumstances, to choose one's own way."*

Claudia Fitzpatrick (Parker)(Henderson) went to her eternal reward on May 5, 2010... it was the anniversary date of her marriage to Gerald...Zach was with her...Zach, faithful and kind and caring until the end held her hand and honored her wishes for a quiet, dignified death at home.

- **A.P.A. =AMERICAN PSYCHOLOGICAL ASSOCIATION (also American Psychiatric Assn.)** This is the largest scientific and professional organization of psychologists in the United States. Founded in 1892, it is a membership organization that serves as a system of checks and balances, licensing, ethics, the issuing of policy statements and publishing educational books and journals.
- **ADJUSTMENT DISORDER** Characterized by stress related responses to distressing events in a person's life that may be traumatic or non-traumatic.
- **AXIS (as used in the DSM)** In diagnosing mental disorders according to the DSM, there are 5 parts to the diagnosis. Each part is call an *Axis*, and calls for different types of information on each axis. The 5 Axis: 1. Clinical Syndromes II. Personality & Mental Retardation III. Medical Condition IV. Psychosocial & Environmental Problems V. Global Assessment of Functioning.
- **BI-POLAR DISORDER** This condition is characterized by extreme changes in mood (depression & mania), energy and sleep. All people experience ups and downs, but for a person experiencing Bipolar disorder, there is greater intensity and frequency. The DSM notes 4 different types of Bipolar disorder: Bipolar I, II, cyclothymic & NOS. Genetics, diet, stress, & trauma can all play a part.
- **BRAIN ALLERGIES OR ECOLOGICAL ALLERGIES** Ecological allergies or brain allergies are general terms used to describe any abnormal reaction to a food or chemical or other irritant or substance within our environment that creates psychological, emotional or neurological symptoms, i.e., depression, anxiety, irritability, memory loss, inability to concentrate or process thoughts, brain fog, asthma, eczema, and many other symptoms.

Common offending substances can include: foods, chemicals such as perfume, cosmetics, cleaning fluids, pesticides, newsprint, treated fabrics, and many other substances.

- **BRITTLE DIABETES** A type of diabetes characterized by dramatic, recurrent swings in blood glucose. It can be present in poorly controlled Diabetes I or II. It can be caused by gastrointestinal absorption problems, adrenal insufficiency, thyroid problems, drug interactions, and hormonal malfunction especially in the presence of stress. Depression and mood swings are common/frequent side effects.

- **COGNITIVE BEHAVIORAL THERAPY** This is a solution-focused intervention used by psychotherapists to correct negative or distorted thinking patterns and long-held irrational belief systems. It is an educational method of therapy that is based on the idea that the way we process or think about the things that happen to us will determine our behaviors and feelings. It essentially gives the client/patient the benefit and the power to be in charge of the outcomes of situations.

- **COGNITIVE DISTORTIONS** are habitual, exaggerated and irrational patterns of (faulty) thinking and long-held beliefs that lead to problematic emotional states, particularly depression and anxiety. For more information read "Feeling Good" by Dr. David Burns.

- **CORTISOL -ENDOCRINE DISORDERS** Cortisol is one of the most important hormones in the body, manufactured by the adrenal cortex. Called the stress hormone, it is essential to the maintenance of homeostasis (the tendency of an organism to maintain balance/equilibrium) and to the regulation of blood glucose levels, blood pressure, anti-inflammatory action, immune responses, et. al.

- **DIFFERENTIAL DIAGNOSIS** the process of distinguishing the probability of a disease which may mimic the signs and symptoms of another disease.

- **DSM -** The Diagnostic and Statistical Manual of mental disorders, now in its 5th Edition, is published and periodically updated by the American Psychiatric Association. It offers professionals, within the mental health field, common language and, according to the publishers, serves as a universal authority for psychiatric diagnoses. First published in 1952 it is translated into 20 languages, and is regarded as necessary for insurance reimbursement... but continues to be controversial regarding the content and use by various mental health providers.
- **ELECTROCONVULSIVE THERAPY** This procedure involves passing an electric current through the brain to trigger a brief seizure. Electrodes are attached to the head that, when stimulated by a small electric current, produces the brief seizure. It is hoped that the outcome will alleviate the depression the patient suffers from. There is usually a loss of memory post procedure. It is not known how or why this procedure helps some individuals. It is very controversial.
- **HALLUCINATIONS** A visual, auditory, gustatory (taste), olfactory (smell), tactile (touch) or somatic (feeling within the body) perception of an external object(s) that is/are not there.
- **HYPERGLYCEMIA** Commonly known as *high* blood glucose (sugar). The most common cause of chronic hyperglycemia is diabetes mellitus, usually caused by insufficient pancreatic insulin production or the failure of the body's internal control mechanisms to maintain an optimal level of glucose, or by resistance to insulin at the cellular level, which, in turn, prevents the body from converting glucose into glycogen (a starchy-like substance stored in the liver) which in turn makes it almost impossible to remove excess glucose from the blood. Some varied symptoms: Excessive thirst, excessive urination, frequent and pronounced hunger, blurred vision, fatigue, cardiac arrhythmia, poor wound healing, dry & itchy skin, dry mouth, tingling in feet or heels, male impotence, frequent infections such as UTI's, depression and other psychiatric disorders.

- **HYPOGLYCEMIA** Commonly known as **low** blood glucose (sugar). Normal blood glucose is usually acceptable between 70-130 (some doctors have different criteria). This is a serious disease that results when the pancreas produces too much insulin or when the mechanisms that regulate our blood glucose fail to operate optimally. There are many causes, including: pancreatic tumor, exhausted adrenal and/or pancreatic function which can be induced by poor diet, overuse of alcohol, medications/illicit drugs or genetic abnormalities. The symptoms are many and varied, such as: headaches, inner trembling, weakness (rubbery legs), excessive fatigue, tachycardia, leg cramps or jerking, compulsive craving for sweets of salt, lack of appetite, or abnormally high/low weight, fainting, blurred vision, crawling sensations on skin, waking after a few hours of sleep, mental confusion, forgetfulness, cold extremities, difficulty concentrating, dizziness and/or staggering when walking, indigestion, changes in mood (usually irritability), anxiety, panic attacks, nervousness, depression, crying without cause, emotional outbursts, unsocial or anti-social behaviors.

- **IED = INTERMITTENT EXPLOSIVE DISORDER** Characterized by a periodic failure to control verbal aggression and/or physical violence that is grossly out of proportion to the precipitating stressor. The outbursts are usually impulsive and can be difficult to predict; however, there is some research that they occur within calculable time frames. There are often feelings of regret and embarrassment following the explosion. This is a chronic disorder that continues for years. Prior DSM's statement that this is a rare disorder, more recent research now states it is quite common, that it appears to be familial, and can co-exist with other mental disorders. The controversy is whether this is a bona fide mental disorder or a misclassification of a mental illness and is nothing more than untamed temper tantrums.

- **INSULIN SHOCK THERAPY** Usually performed on patients diagnosed with schizophrenia, this treatment consisted of a patient being injected with large doses of insulin to produce coma and often seizures would occur. The daily treatments would be given anywhere from 2 months to 2 years with the hope that patients would eventually be "healed." ("...jolted out of their mental illness." Fennel 1996). Used extensively in the 1940's and 1950's, there were no established protocols for its use and was largely discontinued as inhumane in the late 1970's.

- **LOBOTOMY** An umbrella term for a series of different neurosurgical procedures in which brain tissue was purposely damaged to treat mental illness. An incision was made into the prefrontal lobe of the brain to sever the connection to the rest of the brain, thereby hoping to stabilize an individual's personality and emotions such as suicidal ideation, depression, schizophrenia, etc. This was most widely performed between 1949-1956. Highly controversial.

- **LIMBIC SYSTEM**
  In my opinion, the research involved in the limbic system is most valuable and insightful. The brain is the command center of the human body, it controls the basic functions of our bodies, and regulates our moods. Buried deep within the brain are several structures, known as a group, as the Limbic System... and the three significant structures within this system involved in depression are the hippocampus, the amygdala, and the thalamus. For instance, research shows that the hippocampus is smaller in depressed persons and that stress can suppress the production of new nerve cells in the hippocampus. Research, although incomplete, has suggested that nerve cell connections and new growth have a major impact on depression.

- **MANIA** is typically characterized by an unusually intense of high energy. Other signs and symptoms can include grandiosity, irritability, little need for sleep, racing thoughts, distractibility, agitation, continual talking, risky behaviors such as hyper-sexuality, criminal behaviors, psychosis and fugues (impulsive trips from one's usual milieu coupled with a loss of awareness of self).

- **MOOD DISORDERS** "Mood" as defined by mental health professionals refers to a persistent emotional state of an individual and how the individual perceives the world. Characterized by a significant change or disturbance in a person's emotional state.

- **NEUROTRANSMITTERS** These are powerful chemicals in the brain that relay information between nerve cells (neurons) and, therefore, involved in how nerve cells communicate with one another. According to research, there are approximately 10 to 100 billion nerve cells within our brain, and they are organized to control specific activities. Again, research has reported there are approximately 30 transmitters that have been identified, and there are associations to depression with three primary ones: serotonin, dopamine, and norepinephrine...all three involved in the regulation of emotion.

- **ORTHOMOLECULAR MEDICINE** This is a form of alternative medicine that maintains health through nutritional supplementation. It literally means "right molecule" which was coined by 2-time Nobel Prize winner and molecular biologist Linus Pauling, Ph.D. An orthomolecular doctor, through testing, will correct imbalances and deficiencies in an individual's unique biochemistry.

- **PASSIVE-AGGRESSIVENESS** A type of personality or behavior characterized by the indirect expression of hostility, i.e., a person displays compliant behavior that masks deeply felt aggressiveness/anger through alternate behaviors such as procrastination, manipulation, sarcasm, backbiting, pouting/sulking, avoiding confrontations and instead using gossip, using the silent treatment, sabotaging, keeping score, ... has an attitude of *I'm OK... You're not OK but I will let you think you are.*

- **PERSONALITY DISORDERS** A controversial theory contained in the DSM describing deeply ingrained and maladaptive patterns of behavior that cause significant distress or functional impairment.

- **PSYCHOSIS** There are various meanings of this word...in its traditional or narrowest sense it is used to denote delusions and/or prominent hallucinations without insight as to the pathological nature. Psychosis was often linked to Schizophrenia, with accompanying visual or auditory hallucinations, but we now know that hallucinations can be present in many and varied instances, including alcohol and cocaine withdrawal, use of LSD, dementia, certain medications such as codeine or amphetamines and certain psychotropic medications, in sleep deprivation, some grief reactions, depression, anxiety disorders and rare visual disorders.

- **PSYCHOTHERAPY** This is a collaborative relationship between a trusted mental health provider and a person seeking professional mental health help... a psychotherapist provides "informed and intentional application of clinical methods and interpersonal stances derived from established psychological principles for the purpose of assisting clients to modify their behaviors, cognitions, emotions and/or the personal characteristics that the participants deem desirable." (J. Norcross, 1990 APA) Because there are many and varied modalities of care and education, it is important to investigate a provider's methods and therapeutic approach so that the therapeutic alliance which will be established will be in line with the patient's values.

- **PTSD = POST TRAUMATIC STRESS DISORDER** This condition is characterized by anxiety, re-occurring intrusive thoughts (flashbacks), nightmares, and fear. It occurs in response to a traumatic or terrifying event, i.e., any event that threatens a person's life such as warfare, or any event that is terrifying such as sexual abuse. It is called by other names: shellshock, battle fatigue when it concerns men fighting a war.

- **SCHIZOPHRENIA** A brain disorder characterized by disturbances in the limbic system that produces abnormal patterns of thought and behavior. Present are two of the following: delusions, disorganized speech, hallucinations, grossly disorganized or catatonic behaviors. There are 5 subtypes of schizophrenia, and in the 1960's, Paranoid Schizophrenia was widely used by Psychiatrists as a diagnosis for insurance reimbursement. Fortunately, this practice has greatly diminished.

- **SUBSTANCE INDUCED DISORDERS** Refers to the immediate effects of substance use (intoxication) such as drugs and/or alcohol.
- **SUBSTANCE USE DISORDERS** Refers to the long-term effects/consequences of chronic and frequent use of alcohol and/or drugs.
- **SOMATOFORM DISORDER** In the current issue of DSM (5) this is now called "Somatic Symptom Disorder" but still retains the original definition denoting a person with physical complaints for which no medical explanation is found. There are other components for this disorder (such as pain disorder, body dysmorphic disorder, hypochondriasis, etc.) which the reader can look up. My only reason for including it in the glossary is to register my disagreement with the premise of this disorder. Doctors commonly dismiss the signs and symptoms of food allergies (and other illnesses) which can cause muscle pain, digestive pain and dysfunction, vomiting, diarrhea, headaches, fatigue, obesity, and a myriad of other symptoms. Because they do not understand, or even accept the concept of, food allergies these symptoms are erroneously diagnosed as SSD, which was part of Claudia's misdiagnoses.

ABOUT THE AUTHOR

K. B. Heaton, is a licensed psychotherapist, and a Medicare/Medicaid certified provider, dedicated to helping older adults work through their often misdiagnosed and overlooked depression and anxiety.

K.B. earned a BSW from a Southern California University, two Master's degrees and a Ph.D. degree from Universities in New York and California. She has worked as an Administrator and Clinician in corporate and private practice for over 25 years, was involved in the clinical direction and in establishing in-patient and out-patient psychiatric/mental health care facilities. She was an Associate Professor at a prominent Southwestern University, where she taught Aging Social Policy, and authored a text book of the same name.

For many years, K.B. was awarded grants for community seminars and lectured on a wide range of subjects, including all forms of abuse, alcoholism, anxiety, divorce recovery and the resulting financial inequities, depression, suicide and older adult transitional challenges. She is a deeply committed cognitive-behavioral therapist who incorporates a spiritual component into the therapeutic process when appropriate.

www.ingramcontent.com/pod-product-compliance
Lightning Source LLC
Chambersburg PA
CBHW061516020726
47502CB00006B/2104